G000244299

ED TREWAVAS was born and raised in Bristol. Following a torrid education, he's held jobs including van driver, technical author, office mule and sports journalist. He has worked in South Bristol in a social work capacity for the last thirteen years, has two teenage daughters and a doomed love for Bristol Rovers. When city life gets too much, he takes sanctuary in the wilds of west Cornwall. *Shawnie* is his first novel.

Shawnie

Ed Trewavas

Tindal
Street
Press

First published in March 2006
Reprinted in July 2006 by
Tindal Street Press Ltd
217 The Custard Factory, Gibb Street, Birmingham, B9 4AA
www.tindalstreet.co.uk

A CIP catalogue reference for this book is available
from the British Library

ISBN: 0 9547913 8 X
EAN: 978 0 9547913 8 4

Typeset by Country Setting, Kingsdown, Kent

Printed and bound in Great Britain by Clays Ltd, St Ives plc

Contents

SHAWNIE

just what men dooz

The curtains were closed but a bit of sun crept through where the ook was broke and lit up the crumbs of pizza crust caught in the airs around er belly button. Our Ma was asleep when I come ome from school. Often is. This time she was flat on er back on the settee; one leg on, one leg dangling over the side with er foot on an empty glass. The bottle wouldn't be far off. Er tracksuit was riding up er body and stretched over the rolls of fat. She never ad no bra on so you could see everything. No knickers an' all, shouldn't wonder. I ates that. She ad, like, smears down er including fag ash and pizza – she adn't changed since last night then. Or the night before. Or the night before. I ates that an' all and I'm always clean, in me body like. I tells er to wash and that but she's like, 'Wossa point Shawn? You only gets dirtay gehn.' I've started washing me own clothes but then I gotta do our Jason's and our Ma's and Steve's an' all.

The empty bottle was down the side of the settee with er fag packet which was over alf full. Well it was until I took four out and slipped them into me school bag. It ain't like she gonna notice is it and I reckons I earns em. I picked up the bottle and the ashtray and got rid of them both in the kitchen.

'Right Mahl, I'm ome,' I shouted as I come back in. I bent down so's we were face to face and shook er by the shoulder.

'Ello, knock knock, es thurl anyboday thurr?' Our Ma just wobbled about a bit and er eyes stayed closed.

I eard music and voices upstairs so I reckoned our Jason was ome with is mates. Must ave been bunking off school again. Jason's me brother and e's fifteen and e's lush. Some of is mates ain't so lush mind, but our Jason's brilliant. E looks out for me and e even elps me with schoolwork, though e never goes a school, cos e's really clever look and I ain't. I goes a Florrie Nightingale which everyone round Knowle West knows is the divvies' school. They says I got 'moderate learning difficulties' and 'emotional and behavioural difficulties' which means I'm thick and naughty. At least that's what the teachers says. The kids round ere says all sorts, well, they calls me all sorts and our Jason beats em up and that when e catches em. They says I'm a fat slag and I smells and that and some really dirty stuff that ain't true. And I ain't a slag. Our Jase just smacks em one and everyone's scared of im but I ain't cos e's always nice a me. E just gives I a cuddle and e's like, 'D'worray Shawn, I'll look after yowe,' and e do. No one else ever talks to me really. Some people shouts, like teachers and our Ma . . .

We often aves a cuddle cos our Ma don't do that so much no more and our Dad's been in nick for ever and it's the best place for im cos e's orrible. E used a beat our Ma up all the time. Every day. E'd do it in front of us an' everything and she'd be crying and dribbling and begging im a stop and e'd just laugh. Then e'd say, 'Get up they sturrs kehds; me an' yer Ma's gotta sort summat out,' and sometimes we'd listen up the top of the stairs and e wouldn't be itting er and kicking er no more but she've still kept on crying. Our Jason would put is arm around me and say, 'S'alright Shawn,' but it weren't cos we both knew what e was doing. Then e'd come out grinning and say, 'Sortehd, way unnerstands aitch uvvurr now,' but we never come straight down cos our Ma would still be crying and weeping and that and you could see summat bad ad appened and we didn't want a see er that way or ave to pretend everything was alright. We just stayed in Jason's bedroom most of the time and played games and played music and our Jase would give I a cuddle.

Before our Dad got put inside e used a beat our Jason up an' all. Like to see im try now. Our Jason's getting big and e's a good fighter – vicious like. Our Dad never beat me up but e used a smack my ass. Pull me pants down and smack my ass even when I adn't ardly done nothing. Our Ma would try an' stop im and that's when she got the worst beatings. Our Dad used a say it was my fault. Suppose it was. If our Ma would ave let im smack my ass mind, it would of been alright but she used a go nuts and call im – well, really bad stuff and then she'd get a kicking. And the rest.

Sometimes e phones us up from nick. Can you believe that? Can you believe they lets im do that? Our Ma won't talk to im. She just says, 'I ain't lestnehn a ehs fehlf,' and goes up the club or up the Venture, look. I'm like, 'Alright Dad? Ow you doehn?' and that and I tries a talk to im, I wants a talk to im but e just asks me really private stuff like about boyfriends and whether I've started me monthlies and that. Well I ave but I don't see what it's got a do with e. Then e says, 'Tell yer Mahl I'm gonna . . .' and it's just a load of dirty stuff then but I can't say nothing cos I'm crying so much and our Jason just snatches the phone and swears right back at im and slams the phone down. I was glad when we got cut off. Then Steve come into some money and got us connected again, worst luck.

Our Ma's ad loads of fellas since, mind, and they all smacks er about. She says it's just what men dooz. She've got Steve now. E almost lives up ours. E's a Cockney and our Ma says e's a bit of a Jack the lad with it but e's alright.

I ain't gonna tell you what our Jason says. Steve come down a Bristol for work and never went back. Our Jase won't talk to im. E just takes the piss every time Jase opens is mouth: 'Oooh arrr, zoider boy' – stuff like that. I reckons *e* talks funny.

Steve smacks our Ma about a bit but not like our Dad or some of the others. It's only when e've ad a few. Our Ma says she asks for it really.

'Right Shawn.' That was Jason, e smelt of cider like our Ma. Is mates, Scott and Scott, anged about behind im. Scott One nodded and Scott Two dogged me up like a lot of fellas dooz these days.

'Shawn, our Mahl ain't waken up en a urray. Tidy the place up a bet and do us some tay for bout sehx, yeahl? I'm off out.'

'Whurr to?'

'To get my faverert ses a birfday prezzay,' and e flashed me that smile. You wanna see it – e'd charm the pants offa you an' all. I thought e'd forgotten like everyone else. Except Our Nan, mind: she sent us a fiver and a card and our Ma never saw it. I've got it idden now cos if she knew, that'd be eight cans of White Lightning fore you could blink.

Five pound – that'll be a jumbo Monster Munch, some Somerfield banana milkshakes, some chocolate, some nail varnish, a pork pie and some pick 'n' mix up Broad Walk. Thirteen today. Appy birthday Shawnie.

LISA

you don't laugh, you cries

I must ave dropped off on the settee cos one minute I was watching an Aussie soap on the telly and aving a nice vodka and Coke, next thing I knows is me tracksuit's up me arse and our Shawnie's in the kitchen doing chips. And smoking. 'Shawnay, you ben penchen me fags again?' I shouted. I looked in my packet but it seemed about right.

'Oh ello, yer wev us. No, I nevurl, I brought em.'

'Where jew get the fucken monay to?'

'Stop swearehn, eh's disgustehn.'

'I'll do what I bloody wants en me own ouse.' Especially when I feels this rough, I thought. Must be coming down with summat but me tits was urting summat wicked an' all for some reason. I mean it weren't me monthly or nothing.

'What time's eht, Shawn?'

'Time for you a change yer clothes an' ave a wash. Jew know what that room smells like?'

'Woss the fucken time, Shawn?'

'Jus gone fucken sehx, Ma.'

Cheeky bloody cow. 'Don't yowe talk a may like that, girl,' I said. Our Shawn never swears.

'You dooz eht,' she said, which was a fair point but I ain't being bloody cheeked by no twelve-year-old.

'Yer twelve yurrs ode,' I said, and she never said nothing but she laughed and it was a funny laugh, like it wasn't funny at all, if you know what I means.

'Whurr's our Jase to, Shawn?'

'E's back any meneht, Ma.'

I was glad e adn't come back before Shawnie. I mean I loves im an' that but e can be a swine; when it's just the two of us up ouse e can be a swine. E shouts and swears at me and, no word of a lie, e slaps me about summat wicked. E've always done it, even when e was a babby, three years old look. Never cared much when e was a babby: I just laughed and said, 'C'mon beg boy, you can do betturl un thaht. Ave anuvvurr go.' Didn't urt then look, did it, but now . . . E've watched Shawnie's Dad, ain't e? And the others. It's what men dooz innit? I ain't never known a fella what didn't smack me around. First our Dad and me brothers an' all; Chris (that's our Jason's Dad); Tony (that's our Shawnie's), oh e was evil. Even blokes I've known since. Steve's the best of them really, e ardly dooz it at all; just the odd slap when I asks for it. It's just what men dooz innit, but Jason's been learned by some good uns, mind. Once e've reached nine or ten e's stronger than I, ain't e? There weren't nothing I could do about it. When it's been bad, I've ad to lock meself in the bathroom for when e comes ome from school. E don't ardly go no more. I've ad the, whatsit, Educational Welfare Officer, round loads. Hugo. Tosser. Don't make no difference do it? Our Jason dooz what e wants and there's bugger all I can do. Hugo says I might ave to go to court but I reckons that's just mouth. Ain't like it's my fault, is it?

Steve's a laugh. E come down from London. E've got is own business, mind: builder, look. E got a contract over St Phillips and never went back cos e met me, look. I must ave summat, still. Me tits elps. We aves a laugh me and Steve. E gets is mates, the lads from the site look, e gets is mates round and they always brings a bottle or three. They knows I likes me vodka and Coke. Things can get pretty wild but Steve don't mind. E encourages it. I thinks it turns im on. Plenty a share around, that's me. Well, we all gotta be good at summat, aven't we? Talking of vodka and Coke, I'd lost me bottle. 'Shawnay, whurr's me fucken vodka to?'

'You drunk eht, the bottle's en the behn.'

'I nevurr fucken feneshed eht.'

'Eh's in the behn, go an' ave a look.'

'Shawn, you nevurr feneshed eht ded jew?'

'You knows I don't, Ma.'

It's true, she don't. Says she don't wanna be like er Ma. Must a been me, suppose. I just aves a laugh, that's all. You got to, ain't you? You don't laugh, you cries. I dooz a lot of both these days.

'Blumen Jason said e'd be back. Jew want an egg wev yer cheps, Ma?'

'Just salt an' vinegerl an' ketchup, love. Oh an' get us that can look, en the frehdge.'

Me clothes were all over the place and I tried a sort them out without standing up, while I was waiting. Shawnie give us the chips and a fork and said, 'No can, Ma.'

'Thurr ehs, I left e thurr thes mornehn.'

'Ain't thurr, Ma.'

I should of known better than a leave it in the fridge. 'Oo've ad eht?'

'You ave, Ma.'

'I bloody ain't, eh's that thievehn toe-rag bruvvurl a yers.' Talk a the devil, in e comes, Lord bleedin Muck, through the front door.

'Right Shawn?' e barks.

'Whurr's me fucken can to thehn?' I said, which I realize ain't the friendliest greeting, like, but I was riled, what with me vodka *and* me cider. I stood up staring at im and sorting out me unmentionables at the same time and e walks up with one 'and behind is back and this orrible smile on is face, dead sarcastic like, and I thought e was going a nut me or smack me one or summat but e just leans over and kisses me on the cheek and says, all posh like, 'Hello Mummy. Hard day?' I don't know where e got this 'Mummy' lark I swear. E ain't never called me Mummy in is life. E walked into the kitchen and I could see why is 'and was behind is back now cos e was oldin one a they slabs of fags, you knows, with ten packs in it?

'Appay birfday, Shawnay,' e said and e give er the slab. 'Sorry I nevurr wrapped eht or nuffehn,' and our Shawnie said, 'Awww Jase,' and flung er arms around is neck and Jason gives er a big ug and gives me that orrible smile again over er shoulder. I turned away and looked at the telly and I wanted a drink so much and there was tears in me eyes and all I could think was, shit shit shit.

JASON

a little bit of senseless violence goes a long way

What a day. Our Ma was unconscious in the front room, just for a change, bits of spotty flab anging out of er clothes, smelling like God knows what, so I says a Steve I was off a school. In fact I never cos I never bothers wasting me breath on the Cockney twat, but e asked and I nodded like and went out the door with me bag after giving our Shawnie a kiss.

She's a gem, our Shawn, top kid, and I loves er. In fact, she's the only fucking person I do love – no lie. Don't get me wrong, she ain't Brain of Britain or nothing. Pretty fucking long way from it truth be known but she's loving and she've got a eart of gold.

I looks after er, look, cos she's slow and the other kids picks on er. Well, not twice they don't. You messes with our Shawnie, you messes with me and you messes with me you're fucking dead, man. I bet you ain't gotta clue ow to fight. You gotta damage the other cunt. You ain't gonna do that then don't bother fighting, just run away, just fucking leg it. You gotta get in first and urt them, really fucking urt them in the first two seconds. Don't go piling in mind, arms and legs flapping all over the shop, cos anyone who knows what e's doing's gonna take you out. You gotta stay calm, like you're watching yourself in a film, move in fast, with bad intention and do some damage. Like Vinnie Jones in *Lock Stock*. Urt em straight off: kick em in the knee or the bollocks, nut em. Don't fuck around ere, you gotta smash is kneecap, break is nose, crush is bollocks. Urt the cunt.

Then, when you got im down, then you do some proper damage: crush, cut, crack, split, dislocate, gouge. Use a weapon if you can. Break a bone, snap a finger, stick your thumb in is eye socket and rip is fucking eyelid. Always, always give em summat a remember you by. Make certain they ain't gonna come back at you and when you done that, when they're unconscious or screaming or begging . . . give em a bit more. A little bit of senseless violence goes a long way cos they won't never come back for more and once they thinks you're a nutter and everyone else thinks you're a nutter, knows you're a nutter, they leaves you alone and they dooz what you says. People round ere won't even look at me no more – they looks down before they catches my eye. And you never, ever backs down. Not if the other bastard's bigger, not if e's murdering you. Shawnie's Dad's an evil cunt. I swear e's the most evilest man I ever met, but I'm grateful to e, I'm fucking grateful cos e taught me summat. You never, *ever* backs down.

I'd always got into a lot of fights, kiddies' fights look, where no one really gets urt, but one day – I must ave been about eight or nine – I got done over. I got me first proper kicking. From another kid anyway. There was two of em: Keiran McColl was one of em and is mate and they was older and bigger and they gave me a right fucking going over and I gets back ome and I was battered and bleeding and I tells our Ma and Tony (that's Shawnie's Dad) what ad appened and our Ma actually puts er drink down and says, 'Aww lovurr,' and give us a cuddle and starts wiping the blood away and that but Tony just walks straight out of the room. When e come back, e was olding a big spanner look, in one 'and, and e grabbed me by the air with the other and e dragged me out of our Ma's arms and through the all and out the front door and into the street. Then e put is face against mine so we was nose a nose look and e said, 'Yer goehn out thurr now an' yer gonna find the cunt what done thes an' yer gonna change es fucken face frevurl an' ef you can't do that, don't even fenk bout comehn ome cos I'm gonna keck yer ass from yurr a Bemensturr, no lie – I'll change *yer* fucken face, aright?' Well, it was very fucking far from alright but I knew who I was more scared of.

I found Keiran round the back of Filwood where e always ung out. E was smoking with is mates and they all laughed when they saw me. I ain't never been so scared in all me life but I knew what I ad a do so I walked up to im fast like, iding the spanner behind me, and e was still grinning when I kicked im in the nuts and brought the spanner down on is shaved ead with all me puny might. Is ead split open and started spurting blood and e went down like e'd been fucking shot. I got another couple of blows in and smashed some teeth before is mates got me. They give us another kicking of course, but it wasn't bad cos they was shitting themselves about Keiran who was spurting blood all over the shop and not moving, look.

So, Keiran gets a ride in an ambulance and a lovely new smile. I gets some new bruises and a shitload of *respect*. You gotta get respect: in your own patch, you gotta get respect.

I still knows im, Keiran an' that. E's alright. Still goes round the back of Filwood but e dooz browns there now. Still got the scar. And the smile.

When I got ome, I showed Tony the blood on the spanner and told im what ad appened and our Ma just sits in er chair and drinks and don't say nothing, and Tony puts is 'and on me shoulder and says e's proud of me. That's the only nice thing e've ever said a me and I'm glad e's banged up an' all but I always thanks im for what e learned me.

Shawnie's safe cos she's got me and that's ow it's gonna stay and I just opes they teachers up Florrie learns er summat pretty fucking soon cos she gonna need it cos she ain't going far on er looks that's for certain.

I used a go and smash windows up Florence Nightingale. One time me mate Chris fell down through the skylight when we was robbing it and mashed is face up good and proper on a sink there but I don't do that shit no more and I don't let no one else since our Shawnie started there cos er education's important. We dooz the nursery school next door when we're bored but, tell the truth, I reckons I'm growing out of that now. I means, it's kids' stuff. Shitting on your own doorstep an' that.

I give Shawnie a kiss and walked out the door with me school bag but there's no way I was going a school. I picked up the Scotts from the bus stop over Leinster and we eaded off up Broad Walk a do a bit of shopping. We smoked the last of Scott Two's fags. Scott Two's a wanker – dooz browns and that, but that's a 'andy wanker to know cos it means that e's desperate and you can always get im to do the really stupid stuff. And e just about lives with Jez and Marge and whatever druggies they got round over Padstow Road, so it's a 'andy place to crash or ang out when you needs it. Er name's Vicky really but everyone calls er Marge cos she spreads so easy. Wouldn't touch it with a pointy stick meself: might catch summat.

'Eh's a funnay feng, lads,' I said, patting me pockets, 'I seems to ave left me Murcan Express card at ome,' and we was all laughing as we went through the automatic doors over Broad Walk when, fuck me, this fucking security guard in a at latches onto us straight off and starts walking alongside. 'Alright pal?' I says to e. 'You got a problehm?' And e don't say nothing but another twat in a at starts walking with us the other side and e mutters summat into is walkie talkie.

'Ey, shit for brains, we ain't fucken done nuffehn,' I shouts at im which, for that day anyhow, was true, although, I admits, there ave been a few incidents in the past.

There's another of they cunts coming towards us so I says, 'Fuck thehs,' and turns round with the Scotts, the twats in ats following and they only stops when we gets outside the sliding doors.

'I thenk we might ave to take our custom elsewhurr, gentlemehn,' I said and we dived down the steps and eaded into the driveway that leads round the back of the shops. Always worth checking out the backs of shops. I've ad some of my best times round the backs of shops: first fag, first dirty mag, first shag, first skag . . . A lot of good times a be ad round the backs of shops.

Today being no exception. They were only unloading fags from the back of a van. Marlboros an' all. They were in bundles of four slabs with ten packs to each slab. That's four times ten times twenty, that's eight undred fags a bundle. Who needs school? Eight undred fags a bundle, piled igh on the ground in front of us and just one fat batty boy wheeling them in. Well, some things you just don't ave to plan, do you?

'Two each,' I said as I dived in and grabbed them and Scott One did the same and Scott Two only got one cos e's a prat but it did mean that e could leg it faster than us back onto the street. Fatboy Fat shouted, 'Oi, drop em,' which, on reflection, didn't seem like a great move so we never. I looked back and e'd run about four steps after us before fucking near collapsing in exhaustion, so I figured e wouldn't be winning Olympic gold or employee of the year somehow and I figured we were pretty safe but we kept on running cos when the adrenaline's going through you like that, you just can't stop. Scott Two ran down the path to Redcatch Park, which was a sound move, and we followed im right behind the bushes where we fell onto the dirty dry leaves in a eap saying things like, 'Fucken weck-ehd, man' and 'Seprert' and 'Dog's' and 'See that fucken fat boy' and laughing like lunatics.

Scott One's got alf a brain and e stopped all that by saying, 'So ow the fuck do we get em back? Thurr's gonna be coppurrs out looken alreaday, enneht?' which was a good point and one I adn't thought of. We needed carrier bags a ide the fags in and turns out that weren't a problem cos there was a shit-load right under our noses. Only thing was, each one ad a fucking dog turd in it. I've set fire to so many of they bins but luckily I'd never got to this un. We tipped the turds out as best we could and bagged up the fags. The coppers would be looking for three lads eading back to the estate so we split up and planned three different back-street routes to Scott One's Ma's ouse which, as it appens, was in Ruthven Road, just around the corner from Broadbury Road police station. She wouldn't mind; in fact, she'd probably elp us shift them cos she was always selling dodgy fags and booze. Scott Two went up past Knowle Park Infants, then across Newquay Road and down Ilminster; Scott One risked Broad Walk for a bit, then along Minehead and Salcombe; I went over the other side of the park, then along Redcatch, past the Friendship and through the back lanes to Wedmore Vale.

As I was walking back, first past the posh ouses, then the council uns, I was thinking ow much I would pocket at £1.50 a pack. That'd be a undred and twenty quid each for me and Scott One and sixty quid for Scott Two. Might even get two quid each for them, that'd be a undred and sixty. Undred and sixty quid. Now what did I fancy? Browns? Es? Blow? Maybe even a nice bit of coke. Ahh, decisions, decisions.

We stashed the fags over Scott One's Ma's ouse, sold er some and went and got some cans up the offy over Filwood to celebrate.

‘Less drenk em up mine,’ I said. ‘Our Mahl’ll problay be too out of eht a notehce,’ which turned out a be a good guess cos when we got there, at about two, the fat slapper was totally fucking comatose, completely out of it on the floor of the front room.

‘Fucken state a she,’ I said. She ad various stains down er clothes. She’d put er make-up on in that special way of ers: you paints your face orange like that David Dickinson wanker, and you smears mascara and eye liner round your eyes, panda-style. She’d slipped off the settee and that ad pulled er top up a show er big white belly. She’d knocked er vodka and Coke over and was fucking lying in it. The vodka bottle was over a quarter full but not for long Mummy, oh no. She smelt like a Fishponds Road tart after a eavy night.

‘Shhh,’ I said before taking the rest of er vodka into the kitchen and tipping it into a alf bottle of that fizzy piss that passes for Coke up Aldi.

‘Get that up the sturrs wev they cans,’ I said to Scott Two, who did. I put the empty bottle down the side of the settee and e come straight down again. She could keep er fags. That’s one thing we weren’t short of.

‘She fucken dead or summat?’ said Scott One. It didn’t look good but I’d seen it all before. I poked er ass with me toe – nothing. I kicked the same bit and watched the fat wobbling under er tracksuit but she still never done nothing. Scott Two played a drum roll on er bare belly with is ’ands and er ead flopped over and she said ‘Fckckckh’ or words to that effect and stayed unconscious.

‘Gev us a ’and getten er back on the settee,’ I said and the Scotts took a leg each and giggled. I took er under the arms, which ain’t me favourite place in the world look, and we auled er round and up.

She’s a fucking dead weight and it nearly done us in getting er up there. The Scotts dragged er down so as er ead wasn't anging off of the end and, oh yes, ere we goes, er top gets yanked up and er tits comes rolling out. She's a fat slag these days, our Ma, but I seen pictures of er when she was young and skinny and that and even then er tits was big. These days they're bleeding monsters. She wants a go into the porn business.

'Fuck may, look at they. Thurr fucken uge,' says Scott One.

'Enneht. Fucken massehv, man.' It was Scott Two's turn a state the bleeding obvious.

Now, I've seen they tits more often than I wants and frankly, I'd be appy never a see em again but the Scotts was transfixed. Scott Two gave er right tit a sort of shove with the flat of is 'and and then shot me a glance as the flesh rolled back down er body. E wanted a see if I was gonna ave a go at im for touching me Ma up but I couldn't give a shit. You gets yourself in that state and you takes the consequences. I didn't need a watch it, mind.

'Do whatevurr the fuck you wants,' I said. 'Ain't like she gonna notehce, ehs eht? I got a vodkal an' Coke callen may upsturrs.' So I left them to it. Last thing I saw, they ad old of one nipple each and they was seeing who could swing their tit round in the biggest circle.

Our Ma. My mother. Mummy. I sat in me room and swigged vodka and Coke from the bottle while listening a good sounds cos I couldn't cope with listening a they subhumans working over our Ma. The last thing I eard before putting the music on was, 'Ah shet man, state a they fucken kneckurrs.' I put the music on, loud, and I concentrated on drinking. If they wanted a miss out, that was up to them. They must be fucking desperate if that's ow they gets their kicks. Not being a total fucking loser, I got better ways of getting me pork.

I figured I'd see ow much of a dent I could make in the vodka and the Lynx Super before the Scotts finished and

Shawnie come ome from school, which would be about an hour. Shawnie, shit. It was only er fucking birthday, wasn't it? I'm always one step ahead and I can think me way through any problem and I drained a can of Lynx, lit up a Marlboro and smiled to meself. Shawnie wouldn't mind aving fags for er birthday would she? Course she wouldn't. I loves that kid – she deserves better than aving a slapper like that for a Ma. And a ooligan for a brother. And a psychopath for a Dad. And that wanker Steve.

I wondered what sweaty fumblings was going on downstairs. Don't bear fucking thinking about. I wasn't aving our Shawnie seeing it, mind. She's only a kid and she's innocent, look. She ain't like me. I'm a fucking ruffian, street kid; I knows that. She don't drink, don't swear, don't do drugs, ain't never ad a boyfriend. I knows that's gonna appen and that but e better do the right thing and fucking treat er right cos if e dooz the dirty or takes the piss e's a fucking dead man. I ain't aving no fucking orny wide boy like me aving is evil way. I'm a fucking slag, me. If it's got a ole and grass on the pitch, I'll ave it. Well, when you're off your face it don't make no difference do it?

That Lynx slipped down a treat. There was five cans left so I id two of them in me sock drawer next to the cans of White Lightning I pinches off of our Ma when she's plastered and I left three out and I shouted to the Scotts from the top of the stairs cos I really didn't want a see what they were doing.

'Lesten up, you fucken animals, whatevurr seck shite yer doehn, fucken stop eht and get er decent fore our Shawn gets ome. Few can get yer asses up erel en two menehts I might let yuhl ave a can.'

They got upstairs in two minutes, looking greasy and excited. I lit up a Marlboro, chucked them a can of Lynx each and cracked another one open for myself.

'Don't tell may cos I don't wannal ear eht.'

Scott Two said, 'Whurrs the fucken rest of et to?'

'You two were bizzay downsturrs,' I said. 'I enertained meself up ere.'

'Yer a fucken monsturr, man.'

'Enneht,' goes Scott One.

'Thas a bet fucken rech comen from yowe,' I said and they grinned like kids.

Just as we finished up our cans, I eard Shawnie come in the front door.

'Less make a move,' I said. 'Our Mahl ad better be decent, mind.'

'Chell,' says Scott One. 'She's just aven a lettle kep look, on the settee.'

When we got downstairs, our Ma looked alright. That's if you like your women unconscious, which, generally speaking, I do.

Our Shawnie was tidying up some of the squalor. I give er a kiss and told er I was off a get er present. She was so excited, er little face lit up. Actually it ain't a little face at all. It's a fucking fat un, just like the rest of er, but it still lit up anyhow.

We eaded off over a Scott One's place, where we stashed the fags.

By the time I got back, our Ma was back in the land of the living and being er usual charming self but it was alright cos she'd forgot our Shawnie's birthday and I never. Appy birthday, Shawnie.

STEVE

Mr Lovey Fucking Dovey

I fucking hate Bristol: it's all that's shit about London and none of the good stuff. North of the river, it's all the wannabe posh locals and overflow from the Smoke who can't afford the lifestyle there. East, it's just a bunch of coons and Pakis knifing each other and sticking crack up their arses, or whatever the hell they do with it. West don't really exist. South of the river's where I've landed up: Knowle West. South, it's the big white trash estates full of yokels, cider-heads, junkies, dole-scammers, slappers and failed wide boys all interbreeding and nicking their cruddy possessions off of each other in some giant, dismal rota. Or 'rotal' as they'd say round here. If they knew what it meant. This is an estate of twenty-five thousand people and one pub. They close down all the schools because they're shit. Ten seconds' thought tells you that the schools are shit cos they're full of shit kids cos the place is a shit-hole. Don't help nothing, does it? Just moves the problem. There ain't no shops or amenities or playgrounds or fucking nothing. Council don't do fuck all for white trash. Any spare readies they got gets blown on asylum seekers and lesbians. The only places that can make a go of it round these parts are offies, bookies and solicitors. Plenty of custom for them even if they do get turned over every other week.

It's an estate full of dullards but there is one thing they are seriously talented at round here: getting off their faces.

Heroin's the drug of choice in Knowle West, that's if you can call it a choice. Every scabby youth in a hoody or a baseball cap's doing it, only they call it 'browns' and they're so fucking naive, half of them don't know it's heroin. They hit sixteen with a £200 a day habit; a life expectancy, in days, the size of their IQ and the duty officer at Broadbury Road the only cunt they can trust. Some of them are starting to use crack an' all cos the coppers got sick of the silvery spoons in St Pauls shooting each other so they clamped down and said, 'Look, we're beating street crime.' Silly bastards: they just fucking move it, don't they?

And if they ain't junkies, they're drunks: booze fiends, zoider-eads, thirsty dogs the lot of em. I like a few sherbets but this place is fucking *preserved* in alcohol.

How sad is this? This happened recently. Local junky, for whatever reason, couldn't get his fix, so he's drinking himself into the land of the fairies with three litres of White Lightning when his mate tells him that alcohol gets you pisseder for cheaper if you inject it. This is true and it works nicely with vodka. (Word has it, the yuppies in the City snort it cos they ain't got time to go boozing. Goes straight in through the nasal membranes apparently.) Anyway, this shit-for-brains fills his hypo up with cider and injects it straight into a vein in his groin. Nearly dies of a fucking haemorrhage when the bubbles reach his brain. The headline in the local paper read: THE BRISTOL BENDS.

There's five thousand little red-brick houses in Knowle West and you can be lost for a lifetime walking these streets. Most of the cunts are. No shit mind, the council give em decent gaffs here: couple of bedrooms and little garden round the back. A cut above the high-rise shit-pit I was dragged up in, but what do they do? They trash em, they let em fall apart, they burn em and flood em. Sometimes they even keep fucking horses in the garden. Straight up. Number of times I seen some poor, clapped-out old nag, hide shrink-wrapping his sorry bones, chewing on the privet. Poor bastards can't hardly turn around, let alone fucking graze. I saw three in one garden the size of a snotrag. My mate Lee says he seen one in his mad brother-in-law's kitchen. They normally get saved, just before they turn up their hooves, by the local horse rescue centre in Whitchurch, what probably does a roaring trade in glue and dog food, truth be known.

Bloke I know, Gary, installs cable telly and went round some old geezer's round here. The door opens and there's the most God-awful smell. There's no wallpaper, no carpet, no lino, no nothing. Every floor is slate. This old nutter's sharing his council house with a flock of about fifty chickens. Straight up. Gary's fixing the cable up, getting feathers in his eyes, shit all over his kecks and his arse used for pecking practice.

So, this is where me life's taken me. Not just to a city of nearly half a million that can't even produce one half-decent football team, but right into the fetid armpit of that city (Hartcliffe being the other), with a bunch of smack- and cider-crazed hillbillies.

There's a sign on the Wells Road, Whitchurch yeah, at the southern edge of town, says: 'WELCOME TO BRISTOL, CITY AND COUNTY'. Only kids have changed it ain't they, so now it reads: 'WELCOME TO BRISTOL, CUNT'. Says it all really.

Probably Jason and his mates.

So, let me tell you about the good burghers what gimme shelter (but fuck-all satisfaction): Shawnie, she's a kind of quarter-ton McStupid burger with fat, dresses in all the latest Primark stretch nylon fashions, doesn't know that she's hit puberty and smells like a fucking fishmonger's on a hot day. Cooks me tea every night only so that she can eat half of it first and worships the ground that little shit-head 'arrr Jase' slithers on, 'shit-head' being a less than affectionate term for a Bristol City fan round these parts as well as someone whose head's made of shit. If I could flush that evil piece of crap down the khazi I would; do the world a favour, no mistake.

Ahh Jason, the lovely Jason. Is there anything worse than a teenage boy? Having electrodes attached to your genitals, obviously, but sharing a house with Jason runs it a close fucking second. He's the nasty bit of provincial white trash caricature they always use in them government anti-car-crime adverts, closely followed on screen by a hyena. Give me the hyena any day. You've seen him. You've locked your car door when you're stuck at the lights and him and his mates walk by; you've crossed the road when you've seen him coming; you've avoided eye contact and prayed that it's not your turn today.

Jason likes to play the hard man but he ain't pulling one on me. Jason likes to play the gangster but he don't understand, he's only playing. Jason likes all sorts of scum-sucking shit like knocking his mum around. Where I come from, your mum's a sacred cow, you don't say a word against her and you don't lay a finger on her and no one else does neither. Me and my mum never had nothing when I was growing up: she'd go without so's I could have food and new shoes – always a size too big, mind, had to make em last – and I never heard a word of complaint. Don't never hear sod all else from Lisa. Self-pity goes a treat with alcohol, don't it? My old Ma loved her half of lager but only if someone else was buying: she'd never put herself before me when I was a kiddie. She smoked, mind, boy did she smoke. Filled her lungs every waking minute and that's what done for her in the end: throat cancer and it spread all over. That's why I'm the only bastard in Knowle West what doesn't. I can picture her, sat at the kitchen table with a fag in her hand and that pinched look on her face. She'd stare out the window and forget to knock the ash off of the end so it always fell on the table. Doctors had her on them anti-depressants, year after year. Didn't do no good: they just made her even more vacant, but fuck it, she still put her little boy first.

Now, put her next to Lisa. Lisa, mon amour. Shall I compare thee to a summer's day? Well no, cos you'd come a pretty fucking piss-poor second, frankly darling, being as how you only got two redeeming features and they're hanging lower by the day. She's a classy bird is our Lisa. She got this lovely way of putting her slap on: she paints an orange stripe down the middle of her face, stopping where she can't see it in the mirror no more. This kind of papers over the Brillo-pad skin for about five minutes until last night's vodka and cider (sorry, 'vodkal an' zoidurr') starts sweating through. She goes heavy on the eyes, in a kind of early eighties way, which looks the fucking business once all the blood, sweat and tears have been flowing. Time was . . . time was. How many fucking disaster stories start with 'time was'? Time was, me and Lisa had a good thing going: good laugh, good sex, good everything. Time was, I could look at her without wanting to puke. Without wanting to smack her one. I don't know what the fuck happens. You spend time with a girl, you get that feeling in your belly, you look into her eyes, you tell her you love her and everything; some blokes even believe it. Jesus, I done all that shit; I was Mr Lovey Fucking Dovey. I bought her flowers, I put meself out for a loser, made meself look stupid and I ain't doing that again.

Me and Lisa spent a day right, a good day, in the Happy Landings on the Wells Road, a right rough house. We was drinking and laughing and snogging, watching England beat some no-hope East European team on the pull-down screen they got in there. She was clean in them days and I was touching her up and she was loving it: 'Wait till I get you home, doll,' I said after full time and the analysis and she was all, 'Wait tell I gets *you* ome, bad boy,' and it was nice and I was thinking I could cope with a bit of this life and then she goes to the Ladies and she's gone for ages and I go after her, as far as the door anyway, and there ain't no sign so I go for a Jimmy in the Gents while I was there, like. There was all this grunting and moaning and what have you coming from the cubicle so I thought, ay ay, zipped up and hung about really quiet like to see who come out and I guess it's a mark of what a dopey fucking state of mind 'being in love' puts you in cos it never even fucking occurred to me, never even fucking occurred to me that the second face I would see come out of there would be Lisa's. The first belonged to a drunken tosser called Deano. The third to his mate Dave. I stared at the blokes while Lisa looked down at the ground. 'Time for a sharp exit,' goes Deano, and Dave sniggered as the toilet door closed behind them. The next mistake I made was showing that I cared and I'll never make that mistake again. We spent the rest of the evening back at Lisa's, thrashing it out. Recriminations, crying, shouting, promises, apologies: 'I was drunk Steve, et was a one-off, et won't nevurr appen again.' When I say the rest of the evening, I mean until about nine o'clock cos that's as long as she remained conscious. I come back from the toilet and there she was, on the sofa in an unconscious heap. Slag heap. Never even give her the slap she deserved.

And that was it. Put myself out on a fucking limb and that's what I get for it. I let meself get taken for a mug, behaved like a fucking kid. Lisa loves one thing and it ain't me.

My old Ma loved one thing as well and that *was* me. Not that she could ever show it, like, but I knew. She spent her last three weeks in hospital, looking worse than I knew a human being could look. I spent every day by her side, just a kid. Watching her tube changes; her coughing up phlegm and blood; her convulsions; her pissing and shitting herself; her skin changing colour; the flesh falling off of her; the coldness in her eyes turning to bitterness and spite, then vacancy. My old Ma never had much of a spark but I watched her turn into a black hole, sucking all the light and warmth into it. And I done it alone, not one cunt there to share the load and not a fucking word of thanks, so don't talk to me about love.

I come back from the site and Lisa's in a hell of a state. It's like those nights when, no matter how much you get down your neck, it ain't enough. Don't matter how grotesque your binge is, it just don't do it. Imagine one a them nights, twenty-four hours a day, seven days a week, fifty-two weeks a year. You still haven't got close. This slapper *needs*, she craves, she covets, she yearns, she hankers. She drinks till she can't see. She drinks till she can't think. She drinks till she can't drink no more and she pukes and passes out, then she wakes up and drinks some more. And if she can't get the drink? She'll do whatever. She'll fuck anyone, suck em, take em up the arse. Whatever. Don't give a shit. More desperate than any junky. Trouble is, the more used and battered and drunken and sunken and downright bleeding fat she gets, the less willing the discerning Bristol punter is to part with his hard-earned for the dubious privilege of slipping her a length.

That's where I come in. The way I looked at it, Lisa had a problem getting enough jars in. I had a little problem with me cashflow. A lot of the blokes on the site – well, Brad Pitt they ain't and the ladies don't exactly queue up. Put all them things together and what have you got? One pissed and happy Lisa. One productive workforce, no longer bent double with sexual frustration, and me with a nice little wedge in me back pocket. *Workers' Playtime*. Sweet. Made me reluctant, mind, to have me regular poke with her ladyship, knowing where she's been an' all but fuck it, they could fucking have her and she wasn't fussed, long as she got her Red Square, and I was alright cos when you can flash the cash, the next bit of skirt's never that far away.

Truth was, I was fucking boracic. Knowle West suited me very nicely, thank you. A roof over me head and a resident cash-cow. Pig. Whatever. Shame about the piglets. Shame it all blew up. This is how it started.

Lisa's pissed, obviously, and still reeking from the night before, which was a bit of a heavy one, but she was distraught because she'd forgotten Shawnie's birthday. Shawnie was alright cos she'd had a stack of fags off of the lovely Jason and he was looking smug, just for a change. I said, 'Tha's a bit fuckin generous Jayson. Ow much that coscha?' He didn't say nothing cos he knows I'll take the piss.

Shawnie said, 'Leave off ehm. Least e've got us summat. E's the only buggurr what ave, sorray.'

Lisa kept staring at the telly with a face like a slapped arse.

'Come on, doll,' I said, 'less go up the pub.'

She'd obviously run out of alcohol and it was gonna be a long and ugly evening staying in. Well, she didn't need asking twice, and we was walking through the doors of the Venture Inn (can you believe that name?) five minutes later.

'Less ave a quiet night tonight, doll. Take it easy aftah last night.' The way she was smelling, I didn't want to lose any custom.

'Jus get us a vodkal an' Coke, for fuck's sake, double mind,' she said, tenderly, then, 'Right Kev lovurr?' when she spotted some loser she'd had. I'm amazed she can remember.

The Venture's a charming spot: you don't find a lot of fellas with a complete face in there. They got a collection of broken pool cues behind the bar. It's a pub for boozing and dealing dodgy gear and boozing and dealing illegal substances and boozing and falling over and boozing and fighting and then boozing some more. And then boozing some more.

We drank and didn't say much all night. I got her singles and told her they was doubles and she just necked em and demanded more but she couldn't really even be arsed to get plastered and slag around. I lost interest in the maudlin shit about Shawnie she was coming out with and started paying more attention to what was happening at the bar.

They got this Irish fella serving, Paddy, Ulsterman. Now, round Knowle West, you're treated with twenty years of profound suspicion if you got an accent that places you coming from a mile up the road in Hartcliffe or Bedminster. The likes of me and Paddy ain't got no chance. Paddy fancied himself as a hard bastard: he talked about being in the UDA once and I reckon that was bullshit but he really was a hard bastard, no mistake. Once. Drunk bastard now.

This local yokel, Dean, had been winding him up about something or other all night when suddenly Paddy rips his shirt off, displaying a bleeding acre of flab which he wobbles in a less than threatening manner, and he shouts, 'C'mahn beg man,' and a bunch of locals start shouting, 'C'mon Dean, ave the Padday,' and chanting, 'No surrendurr, no surrendurr, no surrendurr to the IRA,' without a trace of irony. This Paddy's swaying all over the fucking shop and I really don't know how he's staying upright and he half slurs and half bellows, 'Ale fate ye, Purnell, and Ale fate yer focken famleh.' At which fighting talk I was nearly pissing meself. Then he takes a fucking great swing at Purnell, misses by about a foot and a half and manages to actually fall over the bar, smack into Purnell's legs, knock him over on top of himself and the two of em flails around on the floor until the lads stop laughing long enough to pull em apart. Not a blow landed and no damage done but some top swearing still going on. Paddy uses his shirt to wipe some blood off his tit, which must have got cut from broken glass on the floor, puts his shirt on and gets back behind the bar. At least he had something to lean on. Purnell got taken off by his mates who were all, like, 'C'mon Dean, e ain't wurf eht' and all that flannel.

Lisa didn't hardly seem to notice. She was all, 'I've let our Shawn down' and 'She ates me, she ates er own Ma cos I'm a pafetec ode slappurr.'

I said to her, 'Don't be so ahd on yasself, gel: you ain't that old,' but she was in no mood for a laugh. Twenty-nine going on forty-nine, that's Lisa. I'm eleven years older than her and she makes me feel like a nipper. They don't have young birds round here. They go from teenage tart-hood to middle-aged slapperdom with no in-between.

I got her back home and took her straight up to the bedroom cos I didn't want to listen to that shit no more. I copped a little feel while I helped her out of her clothes and she was snoring five seconds after her head hit the pillow. That'll be all we hear from her until morning then, I thought as I found some interesting bits to wank meself off against. Well, it passes the time and she ain't never gonna know.

Wanting to hurt other cunts what's giving you grief goes without saying, but sometimes I feel like I just wanna fuck someone over good and proper, stomp on their face, just for the fucking sake of it. I was lying there in bed, stinking of smoke and booze and spunk, thinking nasty shit like that.

Thinking of Jason.

After an ugly fantasy or two, I scratched me arse and started planning Friday night. Three or four lads coming round. Regulars, they knew what to expect. I'd have to get her to have a shower first, mind.

I got up for a Jimmy. The landing light was on and as I walked across I could hear noises coming from Jason's room, although it was dark in there. The door was open a couple of inches so I peered in. It took a few seconds for me eyes to adjust to the light, or rather, to the dark, but when they did . . . well, I've seen some sick things in my time, I've done some sick things in my time, but when I finally made sense of what I saw in there, I could not fucking believe it.

SHAWNIE

the price of a cuddle

It was really nice. Our Ma and Steve went out. Me and Jason stayed in and cuddled up in front of the telly and smoked a *load* of fags. Jason ad a few cans an' all but I never cos I've decided I ain't gonna drink cos I seen what our Ma gets like. And a load of other people an' all but she's the worst. Soon as she starts on the vodka or the cider, well, she don't give a monkey's about me no more which ain't fair and I don't wanna be like that. I mean, I loves er and that but when she's pissed up she can be a right slut, if you'll pardon me language. You should ear *ers*; effing and blinding like no one's business. I thinks it sounds dirty.

Jason let me watch *Lion King*. I knows it's for kiddies and that but it's me favourite. Miss Teplakova asked me what me favourite film was once at Circle Time and I never normally said nothing but it's meant a be alright to say anything you fancies at Circle Time look, and no one's gonna judge you or nothing so I come up with *The Lion King* but everyone just laughed and took the mick and that and Miss Teplakova couldn't stop them. That was a year ago and that was the last time I spoke up in class, look. It's a brilliant film, mind. I likes the scary bits with Ska and the yenas: I puts me arms round Jason and e gives I a squeeze. And I always cries when Simba's dad dies. Wish mine would. I don't suppose you gets erds of deers or whatever stampeding through nick but I can dream. E normally phones on me birthday but e never for this un. Thank God. E probably forgot like everyone else. Except our Jason. And our Nan.

We turned the telly off at eleven and went upstairs. I changed into me Krazy Kat T-shirt which is uge and baggy and I always sleeps in. I was cleaning me teeth when Jason said, 'We'll ave a proper cuddle look, when they goes a bed, Shawn. Birfday cuddle, enneht?'

I layed in me bed, waiting for the front door and the stomping around. When our Ma and Steve come ome, I could ear that they adn't bought no one back with them this time, thank goodness. They gets so noisy. They didn't bother with cleaning their teeth or nothing, which I *always* dooz, and they were in bed in ten minutes flat. I could ear our Ma snoring.

I tiptoed over a Jason's room, being careful a miss they noisy floorboards on the landing and I didn't quite shut the door cos I didn't want it making a noise.

I'm like, 'Birfday cuddle, Jase?' and e pulled back is duvet and said, 'C'mon beauteful,' and I climbed in and give im a ug and e said, 'Yer the most beautefullest girl en the world, Shawn. Me faverert firtayn-yur-ode.'

E's so lush. Gives I presents, says lovely things, looks after I, gives I a cuddle. I'd do anything for Jase. And I do. I gotta tell you about summat now. I knows it's naughty an' that but sometimes I dooz stuff with our Jase. Stuff that you ain't gotta do. I touches im an' that, is willy look. I knows it's naughty but I can't understand why, I really can't, and we've been doing it for years and the world's still turning. We've always been close, look: never needed no friends and that, least I never. We used a share a bedroom when we was little. We'd lie there, just babbies look, and we could ear our Ma and our Dad fighting and stuff, and I'd always climb in with our Jason. We'd just ave a cuddle and that until we fell asleep. When our Ma found us in the morning, she thought it was really sweet.

One time, when I was four or summat, our Jase said, 'Look Shawn,' and is willy was sticking out of is pyjama bottoms, all ard like. I seen that before.

'You can touch eht,' e said and I did and it was a laugh cos you could make it boing from side a side or up and down. I'd touched willies before anyway. I likes sliding the skin up and down like the plastic wrapper on a Pepperami. Our Jase likes it an' all. It was just a bit of fun. Boys are lucky cos they always got summat a play with. Jason calls it a 'ard-on' or a 'bonurr' when it goes like that. Well, e kept getting ard-ons didn't e and e've always let us play with em and I don't see any signs of it stopping now, oh no. It's what lads dooz innit?

We kept on climbing into bed together for a cuddle. I used a make im get ard-ons so's I could play with them. It was a laugh and it kept im appy. Can't see no arm in that.

When I was about nine, the council give us our three-bedroom place over Lurgan Walk. It seemed like a palace and I even got me own room but we kept on aving cuddles when our Ma and Dad ad fighted which was always. Then our Dad got put inside for what appened a that old lady over Whitchurch: aggravating burglary. More than bloody aggravating what e done a she, pardon me French. E said e never but I knows im and what e done a our Ma. And me. Once e was inside mind, everything got even worse and our Ma tipped whatever money we ad down er neck and she was out more than in and when she *was* in she was asleep or pissed up so there wasn't no one else a get a cuddle from except our Jase. And I knew the price of a cuddle.

Jason always liked it best, still does, when I pushed the skin up and down over the bumpy bit at the end of is willy and one night, after e'd started getting airy down there, I was doing that and I felt it getting arder and arder and e squirted all over my 'and and is belly and e breathed all funny like our Dad used to when I was on is lap. Well, this was a new one on our Jason and e thought there must be summat wrong. E made me do it again to see if the same thing would appen and it did again and again but you did it often enough e stopped squirting but e still made the funny noises and that. I told im our Dad dooz it but e's a grown up. We was only kids. We didn't know it was naughty.

We done sex ed at school now and everything we dooz is normal so I don't know why it's naughty look, but I knows it *is* naughty cos our Ma walked in one morning and found me wanking im off (that's what Jason calls it) and she nearly ad a ead fit even though we was only little and it was before e could squirt or nothing. If grown ups dooz it why can't kids, answer me that.

She sat me down for a 'lettle chat' in the kitchen, later on.

'Shawnay,' she said. 'You ain't gotta do that a yer bruvvurr. Touchen em look, down thurr. Eh's dirtay Shawn, eh's what grown ups dooz.'

'Feh's dirtay, ow comes grown ups dooz eht, then?' I asked.

'Shawn, yer too lettle, lovurr. Jus wait tell you gets oldurr,' our Ma said.

'Ow old were you, Ma, when you first done eht?'

'Too fucken young an' don't you be getten persnal.'

'Stop swearen Mahl, eh's dirtay,' I said.

'I'll stop swearen look, few stops doehn that a our Jase,' our Ma said and we both agreed. And we both lied.

We were careful after that, mind, and we didn't get caught again; well, me and Jason never but our Ma kept swearing, look. It's a laugh and I loves it and it makes our Jason so appy and it makes im so nice a me. I ain't stopping. Can't see no arm at all.

Jason likes me a use me mouth these days and I ain't so sure about that. E calls it a blow-job but I don't know why cos you don't blow, you sucks and uses your tongue an' that. If e aves a wash and I knows e's clean look, I don't mind. It's like sucking a lolly. But if e aven't washed imself lately then I ain't aving it. E'll ave to make do with me 'and. I don't like it when e squirts in me mouth neither. I can tell when e's gonna squirt mind, so I always finishes im off with me 'and, look.

E never touches me. Says it wouldn't be right an' that, touching up is little sister. Suits me. Our Dad used a touch I, down there look, when I was little, before e got put inside. Our Ma ardly ever left us alone anyway. I thinks she just made im do all is dirty stuff a she instead.

I could feel our Jase ad a boner already, alf a one anyway, and e turned onto is back which meant I gotta give im a blow-job. If e turns on is side with is back a me, then it's a 'and-job, which I likes best, but tonight it was mouth e was after and e'd been so sweet, what with me present and all that, I just pulled the duvet back and slid down the bed and gave is alf-ard willy a little kiss on the end which made it jump up a little, then come down again. I gave it another kiss, this time longer and me lips went all round the bumpy bit at the end and it seemed a get twice as arder and grow in me mouth, look. It's so lush when it's just me and our Jase it almost makes me wanna cry. It's like aving a ug or a really lush chat when it's just the two of you. It's like . . . I don't know, it's like the only time I feels close to anyone. It's like love. I started moving me mouth up and down is willy but not too fast and not sucking too ard cos I wanted a make this last a long time and I wanted Jason a touch me, nothing dirty look, and it worked cos e got a old of me ead and put is fingers through me air. I loves that, it's lush when you feels this close. E started breathing eavy and e put is 'ands on me shoulders which I loves an' all so I slowed right down to make it last.

'Fuck may, yer good at thes, Shawn,' e said.

I said, 'Stop swearehn, eh's disgustehn,' at least I tried, but I ad a bit of a mouthful at the time so I don't know if e eard.

E was breathing really eavy and I was gonna let im squirt in a bit so I started gently pulling is nuts and sucking the bumpy bit at the end a bit arder when I eard a noise and before I knew what was appening, Steve's voice shouted, 'FUCKIN SLAAHG,' and e threw me off a Jason and into the wall at the side of is bed, which really urt and winded me look.

There was Jason, with is willy still sticking up and e was looking scared, which I'd never seen before, and there was Steve looking mad and scary like Freddy Kruger or summat. Steve grabbed old of our Jason's willy and shouted, 'You sick fackah, you don't know the fackin meaning of faamly,' and e twisted it round and I eard a cracking sound which I didn't like. Jason said summat like, 'Get the fuck offa may you fucken purrv,' trying a sound tough like, but really e sounded like e was nine years old again. Steve smiled and slapped im across the face really, really ard and Jason's ead bounced off the wall. Then e moved is 'and from Jason's willy to is nuts and put is other 'and around Jason's throat and said, 'You got summink ta siy, big boy?'

E started twisting Jason's nuts around and I knows that really urts boys and our Jase couldn't do nothing and I couldn't do nothing but I could ear crying sounds coming out me mouth. Steve was really angry and really, really scary but e was, like, grinning an' all. Our Jason was up against the bedroom wall now and e didn't ave an ard-on no more. Steve ad a good grip on is nuts and is face was two inches from Jason's and e said, 'You evil little cunt. I knew you was a nasty bit a work but I nevah knew jest ahh fackin evil you was.'

Our Jase takes a swing which was stupid cos e never landed proper and e just gets is nuts twisted arder and e cried out. Steve took Jason's nose in is mouth. E bit im, not ard like, and said, 'I can do whatevah I fackin want wiv you, my sahn,' and with that, e nuts im one, while is ead's against the wall so is nose sort of explodes and there's blood coming all down is chin and is chest. E can be so tight, Steve.

'Tomorrah,' e said, 'you're gonna tell yer old Ma that you got in a fight. Couple o' cunts from Artcliffe done you ovah.'

Jason was coughing and snorting cos I reckons is nose was broke and e was plastered in blood and Steve gives im a kiss on the forehead and says, 'Night night, little boy,' and e went out of the room.

I was like, 'Sorry Jase, sorry Jase,' and I started wiping the blood off with is T-shirt, which was 'andy and Jason said, 'Fuck off,' and e sounded like e was crying and e pushed me and I said, 'Jase . . .' and e shouted, 'Fuck off,' and e sounded dead young like, and e just pulled the duvet over imself.

I knew e was crying and I was crying an' all but I turned away and when I walked back to me room, I saw Steve in the bedroom doorway, just wearing is underpants and e was staring at me. I put me ead down and thought about the extra large bag of prawn cocktail Skips under me bed.

Our Ma was asleep.

JASON

damage

Shawnie come in for a cuddle after our Ma and Steve ad got back from the pub and clattered around a bit and gone a bed. 'Birfday cuddle, Jase?' she said and of course I said yes. She ain't never got fuck all from er Mum and Dad and she's pretty much stuck with me. And that wanker Steve. She been coming into my room for fucking ever now and girls needs ugs, dun em? I just dooz what I can, always ave.

Our Shawnie come in and got into me bed and she put er fat arms around me and we eld each other close. She's special; I loves that little girl and wouldn't never do nothing a urt er.

We must ave fallen asleep cos the next thing I knows, our Shawnie's screaming and that Cockney cunt Steve's got old of me nuts for fuck's sake. E must ave been well bladdered but this was bang out of order so I lamped im one and shouted, 'You fucken purrv, you gets yer kecks touchen fellas up do yowe?' and e'd ave fallen if e adn't got a good old of me bits, look. It felt like e was starting a do some damage an' all, the sick cunt, and it meant I couldn't do fuck all. Talk about an unfair advantage. I was thinking that Shawnie didn't oughta be seeing this when the cunt nuts me one and breaks me fucking nose but I got some body shots in and a kick to the bollocks and e backed off and give us some verbals and fucked off out. I told Shawnie I was alright and that she gotta go a bed. I cleaned up me face as best I could and thought about what

I was gonna do to im. I was plotting murder, man, and no mistake. I was plotting evil stuff. I could ear our Shawnie crying and I couldn't sleep. Couldn't get that Cockney cunt out of my ead. Couldn't shift what I was gonna do to im.

I got this mate right: Black Phil. E goes up Artcliffe look, which is meant a be my school since they shut Merrywood down but fuck that; I ain't wasting me days in a shit-ole with soap-dodgers for company. Black Phil's rough, you know? I mean you gotta be fucking rough a be a nigger up Artcliffe. Lot a racist cunts there. Phil talks Bristol when it suits and Jamaican when it suits. Ya man. Is family ome, in Jamaica look, got flattened by a urricane and e talked to is nan on the phone and come off and said, 'De ole plece mash up, man,' and that's what I'm thinking about Steve except I'm thinking of jumping on the cunt's ead, then I says a Black Phil, 'De ole fece mash up, man,' and e'd see the humour there. E don't go for that PC shite. Don't get me wrong, I ain't no fucking racist: I just calls a spade a fucking shovel, a fucking black bastard shovel at that.

I've mashed up more than my fair share of faces; no one on this estate says boo to me cos they knows what'll appen. You gets a rep, after a bit you ain't gotta dish it out. Steve. E's getting what's coming. End of story.

Next day I spun our Ma a cock and bull story about being jumped by some crew from Artcliffe. What can you do? She's all, 'Awwww Jase, lovurr,' and 'Jason, you gotta let the docturl ave a look, a meneht,' and I'm like, 'S'awright, Ma, stop fussehn, s'nuffehn,' and she's like, 'Jase, yer me beauteful boy – don't let they wankurrs take eht way from yowe,' and I thinks fuck that. I gets me pork regular; I knows what the girls is after and it ain't a pretty face. A few twists and turns to the nose just adds to the effect. Makes me look more of a fucking ead case an' all. Now all I needs is a decent scar.

LISA

I loves you Shawnay

Best night's sleep in ages I ad and I got up in time to see Shawnie and Jason off a school, but the state of e! E said e got beat up by a bunch of nutters from Artcliffe and e left one of em with a different face even though e was outnumbered. No reason, e said. E didn't seem fussed but I reckons is nose was broke.

'Jason lovurr,' I said, 'let the docturl ave a look. Jus go up the Walk-ehn,' but e just touched it with is finger and said, 'S'alright Mahl, eh's nuffehn,' and e wouldn't talk about it no more.

Our Shawn was really upset, mind, but Jason just give er the big brown eyes and said, 'Ain't I ansome nuff fer you no morl? I'll jus walk ten steps behind yer, few likes,' and Shawnie laughed and said, 'Shut up, Jase,' and smacked im on the arm and e pulled er around and eld er close from behind for a cuddle until they noticed Steve looking at them queer like, and they stopped.

Steve give us a lift up Broad Walk on is way a work, e went in late look. Thursday's Bingo morning up Broad Walk look, and it's loads better than the new one over Engrove and I always goes. Never bloody wins, mind, but I got close last week, I got so close. Just needed thirteen, I did. Well that's unlucky innit? No fucking chance there then. Some lippy fucking cow I seen over Filwood got five undred quid. Jumped all over the shop she did, whooping like a Yank.

I got myself a few cans over Somerfield's and ad to go on Shanks's all the way back ome so that I'd ave enough for some chips from the chippy over Leinster.

It was alf one when I got ome and I was parched so I cracked open a can of White Lightning and I tell you what the ole lot went straight down so I cracked open another to ave with me chips and put the rest in the fridge. I put salt and vinegar and tomato ketchup over me chips and they was lush. Over two hours to meself now. I lit a fag and curled up in front of *Neighbours* with me can.

Our Jason was first back. E looked shite cos the bruise was developing, look. E come in with one of the Scotts and another lad in a baseball cap who muttered, 'Alright Mess-ehs . . .' and e trailed off cos e never knew me surname.

'Call me Lisal, alright lovurr?' I said.

'Alright Messes Lisa,' e said and e went red and our Jason was all, 'C'mon you fucken tossurr, less wait upsturrs.' E never said nothing a me.

I cracked open a can, only me fourth, which meant I ad four left. I was going to tell that thieving toe-rag son of mine that I'd counted them an' all. Once Shawnie got back – e wouldn't it me then.

Shawnie come in with a, 'Right Mahl, ow manay you ad today?'

'Can't I ave a quiet drenk en me own ouse?' I said.

'Least yer stell wev us, spose,' she said. She looked at me tits, surprised like. 'And you got a brahl on.'

'Ooh Shawn, I ain't goehn wevout they fra beht. My tets urts summat weckehd. I don't know woss goehn on, I swear.'

'Ma, you ain't pregnant are yowe? We done that en school. That can make yer boobays urt, look.'

'No danger of that Shawn, no danger of that.' I wasn't, I can tell.

'Woss up then?'

‘Shawn,’ I said, ‘fiy knew I’d do summat about eht, wunn I?’

‘Go see a docturr, Ma,’ said Shawnie.

‘Wossa point, Shawn? E’d just say what e always bloody says, stop drinken so much and get some fucken exercise, like tha’s gonnal elp me tehts anay. They don’t know what thurr bloody doehn ovurr the Walk-ehn.’

‘What jew want fer tay, Ma?’ said Shawnie.

‘Just say woss thurr, Shawn. I ain’t ad time a shop.’

‘Shawnay,’ shouted Jason from upstairs, ‘come up yer a meneht, Shawn,’ and she lumbered up. That girl’s getting fatter I swear. I took a long swig and settled down for the second alf of *Countdown*. I likes *Countdown*: I can’t do the numbers, like, but I dooz alright with the letters. Other day I got ‘wallet’.

I must ave closed me eyes for a minute cos I missed the conundrum, not that I ever bloody gets that anyway, and *A Place in the Sun* was on. The Algarve today: very nice too. I was bursting for a piss so I went up to the bathroom but I ad to wait for Jason and is mates to go past on the stairs. The red-faced lad was still red faced and e said, ‘Bye Messehs. Fanks fer aven may,’ and the Scott giggled and our Jason said, ‘Shut up Carl, wankurr.’

‘Bye love,’ I said. Nice for one of Jason’s mates to show some bleeding manners for a change but Jason was right, e *was* a bit of a wanker.

Shawnie was in the bathroom washing er ’ands. I went in and pulled me tracksuit bottoms down and sat on the toilet. What is it Jason says? Faster than a fat bitch what sat down too fast; summat like that.

‘Shet, tha’s better,’ I said as me bladder emptied.

‘MA,’ shouted Shawnie, ‘they aven’t gone yet,’ and she kicked the bathroom door shut. I eard the front door straight after.

‘Yer terreble, Ma,’ said Shawnie. ‘What ef they seen?’

'Jus doehn what comes nachrul, Shawn. Way all dooz eht.'
'Not all of us dooz et en publec, Ma,' Shawnie said.
'I ain't got no secrehts, love.'
'I know, Ma,' she said.
Steve wasn't coming ome till late – said e was going for a session after work – and I wasn't expecting to see Jason again: e often stayed at friends and that suited me just fine, truth be known. Shawnie cooked us some nice chicken nuggets and chips and we ad loads cos the boys wasn't there.
For the evening, Shawnie ad a king-sized bag of prawn cocktail Skips and two boxes of Celebrations she said she got for alf price up Broad Walk. And a load of fags. I knew I ad some vodka left over for when I finished me cans cos I'd id it under the stairs. Fags and booze and comfort food. And no men. A perfect end to a lovely day.
Shawnie and me ad a bit of a natter and watched telly. I can remember *Buffy the Vampire Slayer*, and then some other stuff. We finished the Skips first, then we ad a box of Celebrations but I reckons Shawnie must ave ad most of they cos I never. I thinks I must ave shut me eyes for a bit after *Buffy*. Shawnie ad started the second box and *Caribbean Uncovered* was on (what a bunch of posh slappers!) when I ad an idea.
'Shawn, jew member ow much you loved that Chocolate Nesquek, double strength look, when you was a babbay?'
'Aw Ma, that uz luush,' she nearly moaned.
'Thurr's some en the cupboard, Shawn,' I said – I'd saw it when I was iding me vodka from our Jason. Shawnie got er fat arse off of the settee faster than I'd seen it move for a long time. I got mine off pretty sharpish an' all. I ad a new cocktail to create: vodka and double Nesquik.
'Make et reallay strong, Shawn, an' we'll eat em up en the microwave. Just alf a mug fer may, lovurr,' I said.
Shawnie took the steaming mugs out of the microwave and I got the Man U one and I topped it up with vodka.

'Less ave em upsturrs weth they Celebrations,' I said. We went up and I changed into me Smiley Face T-shirt and Shawnie got into er Krazy Kat one and we jumped into me and Steve's bed. I tell you what, if you ain't never ad ot vodka and double Chocolate Nesquik, you ain't never lived. If that don't get you a sleep nothing will.

Our Shawnie's a greedy mare: she was aving four Celebrations for every one of mine.

'Ma,' she said, looking sheepish, 'jew know our Jason's leven ovurr Scott One's Ma's? Well, e ain't lehven thurr but e's like, stayen thurr nights, look?'

I looked at er and breathed eavy like and didn't say nothing for a bit.

'E never fucken tells I nuffehn, Shawn,' I replied, 'not a fucken decky bird.' She never even told me off for swearing cos I ad tears in me eyes by then and I said, 'Our Jason ates is own Mahl an' I don't blame ehm neevurr. Look at the fucken state a may,' and I drained me mug and it was double lush cos of all the chocolate vodka sludge at the bottom.

'Et ain't you Mahl, ehs jus e can't, like, get on wev yer fellas sometimes,' said Shawnie, least I thinks she said that but it was ard to tell cos she just put two mini Snickers into er mouth at the same time.

I looked er in the eye and said, 'Then I won't ave no more fellas, Shawn. I'll detch em. I'll detch Steve; e's just like all the rest. They only ever urts you, look. Yer too young, Shawn. Don't ave nuffen a do wev em, Shawn, cos they only ever fucken urts yowe. When I was yer age I was fucken pregnant wev our Jason.' I was crying fucking buckets now and blurting this out between the sobs. 'I loves our Jason an' that but I uz too young, Shawn, too young. I nevurl ad no choice Shawn, but you do,' and Shawnie was whispering, really loud like, 'Shut up, Ma, shut eht,' when Steve walked in the door. I could tell e'd ad a few and I could tell e'd never eard nothing neither cos e smiled and said, 'Ay ay, woss all this en, gels' night in?' and before I knew what was what, e'd stripped down to is undies and jumped in. E smelled of pub and sweat. When we started up, e used a make an effort. With is appearance, look. E'd do is air and wash and smell of cologne. I liked that. We used a lay in bed and it was dark but I could still tell it was im cos I could smell is cologne. We'd talk for hours: e'd talk about London and all is mates up there; e'd talk about is business and what e was gonna do for me and Shawnie and all the money we was gonna get soon; e'd talk about ow Jason was gonna mess all that up and what a scumbag e is and ow I gotta kick im out; e'd tell me about is family and is Ma and that. She's dead now and I knows e misses er summat cruel; e'd say lovely stuff to me, you know, pillow talk, e'd say all these lush things before and after we done it and it wasn't shagging, it was making love. Steve's a lovely bloke really but e's full of bad stuff; anger and that and e takes it out on me and our Jason. I reckons e's scared really. Like all fellas. They gotta put up a front, ain't em? If anything knocks that front down . . . they've ad it, ain't em? I woke up on the settee once and there was this David Attenborough thing on about young stags in Scotland challenging the old ones to see who's in charge and who gets to do the shagging. They were all rucking and fighting and what ave you. That's Steve and our Jase that is. Steve don't smell good no more.

Our Shawnie was stuck in the middle. I put me arms around er as far as I could and reached for Steve. Steve done the same so Shawnie was sandwiched and we were all cuddling and I said, 'I loves you Shawnay, I loves you Steve.'

'I know, doll,' said Steve.

'Shut up, Ma,' said Shawnie.

Shawnie was gone when I woke up.

JASON

no one gets the bus back from an arm robbray

I ad a chat with Scott One about kipping round is for a while and that was cool. It was just e and is Ma (Sharon) and Aimee, is little sister, so I could ave the settee, look. Tell you what, is Ma's a bit tasty an' all, if you goes for the older woman, which I certainly could do. Knows a thing or two, dun em? Tricks like. She's dead 'andy too, for shifting iffy gear. She'd moved they fags in fucking no time and we got a pound a pack back. She could move booze, car stereos, wheels and other car parts an' all. Tidy tits and tight clothes; top bitch.

Look, I knows our Ma's a fucking slag but I tell you, I was fucking naive. I didn't know the alf of it. Black Phil's dad, Norris right, works casual for Steve. On the site, look; still signs on and that. Anyway, Norris don't know I got a connection with Steve and e tells Phil that Steve's old girl's a right goer, dooz anything for a bottle: 'and, oral, full, back door. You name it. Long as you gives Steve a sweetener, look. Black Phil looked at me close like, when e told me all this. Not crowing or nothing, just looking closely to see my reaction, and I just turned round and said, 'Fucken ell, Phel, I'm just glad she's getting summat for eht. I just thought she was fucken cheap. I mean, I knows she's fucked alf a Souf Brestol,' and that Steve, that

Lahhndan cunt gets money for fuck all. Made me think, mind. Steve's a cunt but e ain't stupid.

Black Phil's a good man for doing a job with: we done loads. E scares the general public cos e's big and black and e don't panic imself.

There's this Paki shop over the other side of the Wells Road – Knowle posh bit. We've turned it over before but they don't fucking learn. Just the one Paki in there most times and we'd been planning a do it again for ages.

We'd nicked an Astra (piece of piss, Astras) and we'd left it just round the corner. Me and Scott One waited outside the shop by the open door. Black Phil goes in first, doing the scary Jamaican bit. E goes over a the cans and this Paki's watching and getting lairy like, and Phil goes, in is best Yardie accent, 'Nah fackin Rade Stripe,' and the Paki walks towards im saying, 'It's just . . .' and Phil kicks at the cider bottles on the floor which scatters and the Paki says, 'You must not do that, you must leave now,' and that's where me and Scott comes in and I closes the door behind me and shouts, 'PAKAY.' E knows is name cos e turns round and Black Phil smacks im from behind and we all piles in and gives im some on the floor but there's no time for anything too devastating cos we needs a get out quick. I made sure I smashed is eye socket cos that really fucks up your face for fucking ever. I eard the crack and the crunch as I drove me eel down onto is face, twice. Scott One whacked the till till it opened but there weren't no tens or twenties. Paki cunt must ave stashed em someplace else but there was no time a look and no point asking im now cos all e was doing was spilling body fluids onto the floor and dreaming of Calcutta. Should ave checked it out first. Live and learn – like the Paki done. Scott grabbed all the fives and started scrabbling at the pound coins and stuffing them into is pockets. I got two carrier bags and give one a Phil and we filled the fuckers up with fags: B&H,

Marlboro, they Marlboro Lights what Shawnie likes, Silk Cut, Lambert and fucking Butler, you name it.

Scott One's started at the silver and I shouts, 'Fucken leave eht,' but e's scraping em up and dropping more than e's getting.

'Right, c'mon, go, go, less fucken go, NOW,' and Scott One snatches at some coppers and I yanks im by the arm and Black Phil's trying a put spirit bottles in is carrier which is fucking full of fags and e's smashed one already. I shouted again, 'Fucken leg et, NOW,' and as I done it the shop door opens and this flabby posh tart struggles through with a littl'un in a buggy – one of they three wheelers – and we freezes and she's so fucking preoccupied with the rat she don't fucking notice what's appening for fucking ever. Then she sees the Paki on the floor, out of it with is face all fucked up. She looks up and our eyes meets and she finally twigs just what a grim fucking predicament she's in. There's a moment of silence. I don't know what the fuck went through my ead but I knew we couldn't afford to urt a posh tart with a kiddie and I knew I didn't want er getting a good look at me neither so I puts me 'ands together in front of me face like I was olding a gun. I even fucking pointed me index finger and middle finger at er kid and I shouted, 'On the fucken floor or the babbay gets eht. DO ET NOW.' She dived on top of er littl'un with er back to me and said, 'I didn't see anything and I won't say anything. Just don't hurt my child.' We fucking burst past er out the door and made ourselves stop running and walk round the corner.

'Take et steady boys,' I goes. 'Wurr just good cetezuns strollen down the road wevout a curl en the world,' and we walked at fifty miles an hour back to the Astra, snorting and sniggering and swaggering and feeling like the masters of the fucking universe. Scott One and Black Phil got in the front and I got in the back and as soon as the doors shut we just fucking exploded with laughter. We was fucking crying, man.

'We gotta stop,' I said, 'we gotta stop,' and we all pulled exaggerated serious faces with pursed lips, until I caught Phil's eye and we erupted again. Scott sprayed a load of snot out of is nose and that just made us worse. This was getting fucking ridiculous. Phil wrapped is arms round Scott and, sort of, lay on top of im and said, all posh like, 'I didn't see anything and I won't say anything. Just don't hurt my child,' and that was it. We collapsed. We roared, man. We was nearly wetting ourselves and all the while I knew that the police would be getting closer. It takes less than five minutes a drive from Broadbury Road to Knowle posh bit if you goes flat out.

I stopped laughing when the reality it me.

'Jesus fucken Christ,' I shouted, 'shut the fuck up. Shut eht.'

Scott threw is arms up in mock orror. 'Please don't shoot me Mesturr Gangsturr man,' and they both exploded again, rolling around in the front. I reached over the seats, grabbed them both and yanked them up.

'They coppurrs are gonna be yur en two menehts an' thurr gonna be fucken tooled up, looken for an armed gang. One black face and two white, one wev a black eye.'

They stopped laughing. I couldn't believe ow stupid we'd been. At least we'd ad the sense a leave the engine running on the Astra so we didn't ave to ot wire it again.

'Scott, start driven now. No fucken around. Back streets down a the Baaff Road. Phel, get yer ead down onto Scott's lap. Pretend yer sucken em off. They coppurrs sees a black face round ere, wurr fucked.' I lay down on the seat. They done what I said.

We could ear the sirens now and no one said a word. When we turned down Talbot Road, a police car fucking flew past and I could ear more sirens coming.

'Don't you fucken move, Phel,' I said. 'Yer getten out en Easton. No one noteces a black face thurr.'

E never said nothing so I said, 'Yer quiet Phel. You gotta mouffuhl?'

'You shut the fuck up, man,' e said and e started a rear up so I said, 'Fucken get down, ya twat,' and I paused, 'or I'll fucken shoot yowe,' and we all laughed but it was a nervous laugh, look. We kicked Black Phil out on Stapleton Road where me and Scott were the ones what stood out.

'Get the bus, Phel,' I said. 'No one gets the bus back from an arm robbray.'

'See you up Scott's thes avo, yeah,' e said.

'Laturr, Phel.'

I got Scott a drive through town, through Old Market, past the *Evening Post* building, Temple Meads, Three Lamps, down St John's Lane and up through the back streets of the estate. E stopped off at is place and I took the gear in, then came straight back out again a join im. We took the Astra to the nursery school next a Shawnie's school cos you can't see it from the road look, and we torched it. Torched it good and proper. I loves torching cars, I done loads. We could see the black smoke rising igh as we climbed the fence out of the playground and ran down the lane leading a Leinster Avenue. We slowed down when we got to Jarman's and walked past the police station with its CCTV and its igh-tec security fence what they put up after the Sidney Cook riots. Fucking nonce.

Back in Scott's room, we emptied the bags and Scott's pockets: sixty-seven pound and some pennies, seventy-one packs of fags and two bottles of Gordon's gin. I'll settle for that. That and the memory of that posh bint cowering from my scary, scary finger. I could see er at the next dinner party: 'It was pointed right at Oliver. All I could do was cover him with my body and hope the bullet didn't pass right through me.' Gives you summat a talk about over the guacamole, don't it darling? Never mind making your day, I've made your fucking life I reckons. I always leaves the ladies with summat a talk about.

We split the cash and give the fags a Scott's Ma cos we knew she'd give us a fair price once she'd moved em. The gin was a bonus but Jesus Christ, that stuff was nasty. I'd never ad it before and I don't think I wants it again. It's what all they posh cunts over Sneyd Park and that drinks innit? They must be fucking mad. Mind, explains why they talks like they dooz.

'Pass that bottle, Scott,' I goes, 'maybe et gets betturr when you've ad a few.' It's like browns, isn't it? I always throws up when I aves that but everyone says if I done it more then I wouldn't. Well any time I wants a join the league of tedious cunts I'll bear that in mind, lads.

I took another mouthful and nearly chucked it up again, when we eard the front door. It was two o'clock and I knew that would be Black Phil but I was less than pleased to see e ad Carl with im. E's a druggy and a dickhead and it's one more person who can shoot is mouth off ain't it?

Black Phil said, 'E's cool, e's sound man,' so I knew e'd already told im what we'd been doing this morning, so I bit my lip and made sure I kept im on side. I give im two packs of fags (Silk Cut Lites, natch), tipped im a brutal glass of gin and said, 'Not a fucken decky bird a no one. Tha's no one,' and I give im the stare.

By alf past two the room was thick with smoke and we was wrecked and I was telling them about Siantell, me latest porking what I'd fucked from ere to eternity in the basketball court over Broad Plain, right opposite the police station.

'Fucken tets on that bit o' pork. She ehs orny as fuck and I tell you what, she don't need no fucken persuadehn.' Well they cunts were all, 'Fucken mental, man, fucken dog's,' and all that and eager for the gory details and I could tell they never ad a fucking clue what they was talking about.

'You ain't never fucken done eht, ave you? Not a fucken one,' I said. 'You ain't nevurr porked nuffen but yer right 'and,' and Black Phil goes, 'Fuck that, man, I went nearly all the way wev at Stevie-Jane, I mean I ad alf me fucken arm up er cunt and evrayfehn.'

'Well I'm glad you've mastered the delicate art a foreplay, Phel,' I said, loving it, 'but ef you ain't nevurr slepped er a lengf then yer stell a babbay ass, my son.'

Carl don't say nothing and Scott tries a look cool which is a waste of fucking time cos e's fucked and e's only stopping imself falling over by leaning against the wall. E smiles like a fucking alf-wit and gropes the air in front of im and says, 'Fucken tehts, man.' Jesus.

I thinks on me feet and I keeps stuff turning over in me ead an' all and I'd ad what I learned about Steve and our Ma on the back burner. I said, 'Boys, yer gonnal ave to get yer own fannay, but ef yer entrested in a 'and-job, I can elp you out for, say, one pack a twentay a frow?'

My words seemed to ang in the air and I filled up the pause with a long slurp of that fucking awful gin, then I took a drag on me fag to take the taste away but it never.

'What, so you wants a gev us a 'and-job?' says Scott One, giving me a dodgy look.

'Not may, ya cunt, what the fuck?'

'Eh's ehs Ma,' says Black Phil, laughing. 'Ehs Ma's gonna wank us off.' Then e bit is lip and looked at me.

I didn't take the bait. 'Betturr n that, Phel, betturr n that. Eh's arr Shawnay.'

'What, she dooz at?' says Carl.

'She's the fucken best, mate,' I goes.

'Ow the fuck jew know?' says Scott One and I give im that look what always shuts im up and said, 'I knows.'

They were fucking gagging for it, Carl and Scott anyway,

and I knew there'd be plenty more sad twats like them. I can't believe I never thought of it earlier. I mean, for fuck's sake, she ain't gonna be a brain surgeon is she?

Sweet. Money for nothing. Free fags for me and our Shawn and I got every local lad in the palm of me 'and. Well, the palm of Shawnie's 'and more accurately. All we needed was a small investment in tissues. All they needed was to nick some fags.

'You up fret, boys?' I said and I didn't need a wait for the answer. 'Less go ovurr mine.'

When we it the street, Black Phil peeled off and said, 'Enjoy yerselves, lads. I'll get me own pork, ta.'

Carl and Scott One followed me down the street, tripping over their tongues and leaving a trail of drool behind them.

STEVE

an itch to scratch

Thursday night and we'd nearly finished at the site down St Phillips. I needed to make sure I got some lads round to experience the Joy of Lisa the next day so I shouted, 'Oo's fer a pint then? First rahnd's on me.'

'Since yuh put it dat way, mahn,' said Norris. Three more of the lads: Lee, Michael and the new lad, Tone, were up for it an' all.

We downed tools. Some of the lads changed their shirts and sprayed their armpits and stuff. There was a load of verbals, most of it inept, and we piled into the Railway Tavern.

Tell you what, St Phillips is a bleeding strange area. Used to be industrial, with seams of slums running through it, more like a northern town. The industry's long gone and derelict now and most of the people have been moved out to the big estates south of the river, so there's fuck all left really except a few pockets of weirdos and no-hopers and the odd scabby pub like the Railway, crawling with ageing whores running out of punters and ageing hard men running out of people to menace. Big chunks of the area are being bitten out to make way for multiplexes, fast food chains, bowling alleys and all that shit that makes it look exactly like every other town in Britain. Europe. America. Singapore. Fuck it, wherever. We was doing the biting: clearing some old shit away and installing (you can't call it building) some new shit: a shiny new Easi-Fit Exhausts. It comes in a fucking kit from the company.

Bob the landlord smiled unconvincingly when I come up to the bar and said, 'Alright Steve, ya cockney cunt. What can I do you forr?' That's what I love about Bristolians, it's their ready wit and sparkling sense of humour.

'I'll ave two cold Guinness, two Kroneys an' a pint a rough, please Guvna. Yer a propah gent and no mistike,' I said in me best Dick Van Dyke. Rough means rough cider round these parts; it's better when it comes out than when it goes in.

'What's this, Steve putten es 'and en ehs pockeht? I can ardlay Adam and Eve eht,' went Bob and he starts pouring the Guinness, cackling at his own rapier wit. I managed a weak smile and thought, you go down the Fire Engine in White City pal, they'd have you on fucking toast.

'Wossa deal tomorrer night, boss?' asked Lee when I finally dragged myself away from the jovial banter. There weren't no need to ask cos he'd been there before. They all had except Tone.

'We are partyin Lay, my sahn. We are party animals, cept Michael ere, oo's a farty animal. Ain't that right, Michael?' and Michael went, 'Fock off,' and I said, 'Abusin the boss – I don't know fiy should let you shag my lahvly missus. Tell you what, sahn, you won't get a lot of jobs wiv perks like this. Ya up for it then, boys?'

Lee looked at the other lads. Michael nodded. Norris went, 'Ya mahn.' Tone stands up and starts towards the fruit machine. 'Wassa slag's name? Lisal ehs eht? I dunno boss.'

'Go on, Tone, she got tets like you nevurr seen an' be honest, eh's gottal ave been a while,' said Lee.

Tone's got L-O-V-E tattooed across the knuckles of one hand and H-A-T-E across the other. He's got little home-made jobs scattered all over any visible bits of skin. He's over six foot and built like a boxer. Number one hair-cut and a vein throbbing in his forehead like a warning light. Spent four years inside doing press-ups.

Tone swings back towards us with his eyes popping out of his fucking head.

'You tryna fucken say summat, beg man? You got a fucken point a make yurr?'

'Take et steaday, Tone, no fence like,' went Lee.

'Yeah, take it easy, Tone,' I said. He looked a right fucking head case, stood there with his twisted smile and his neck tendons popping. 'E can't elp bein a wankah, can e? Go on sahn, finish yer pint, I'll get you anuvvah.'

'Rough,' he said, calming down a bit.

No kidding. I said, 'Pint o' rough Bob, when ya ready.'

Blimey, you'd never guess he'd been inside, what with the facial artwork and the Noel Coward manners.

Tone took the pint without any thanks and started putting pound coins into the fruit machine like there was no tomorrow. He was getting sod all back and he was looking at the machine like he'd looked at Lee a while back. You couldn't relax with this head case about.

We was sat down, chatting at a table. Mostly about Lisa and what they'd done last time and what they were going to do next time but every two minutes Tone would yell something like 'betch' or 'cunt' and smack the machine so hard it rocked. After a few minutes of that, Bob the landlord calls over, 'Eh, mate. Do us a favurl an' take et steaday, yeahl? Ain't gonna pay out few upsets eht,' and Tone just keeps on playing and says, 'Go fuck yerself, ass-ole,' not very quietly.

'Wha's that you said, mate?' says Bob, cupping his ear.

Tone pivots round and moves in on Bob – scaring the varnish on the bar – going, 'I said, go fuck yerself. Maybe yer deaf as well as be-ehn a sad piece of peg shet. GO FUCK YERSELF – PAL,' and as he spat out the last word he chucked the pound coins he was holding right at Bob and you could hear them clattering into the bottles behind the bar and the pub went silent.

Bob's sorted out more nutters than I've had hot Ukrainian teenagers but he was backing off fast, even though he was behind the bar.

'So, ehs thurl a problem, then MATE? Ehs thurl a problem? EHS THURL A FUCKEN PROBLEM?' Tone's reached the bar and he's staring at Bob like the thyroid monster and I notice he's got hold of a Beck's bottle from a table on the way to the bar so I jumped up and said, 'Tone, take it easy mate,' but he ignored me. He'd worked himself into a frenzy now and he shrieked like a fucking madman, 'I ASKED YOU A FUCKEN QUESTION: EHS THURL A FUCKEN PROBLEM?' With that Tone shattered the bottle on the bar and gripped on to the jagged neck with white knuckles. We found ourselves all milling around behind him but doing nothing. It looked more like we was backing him up.

'Steve, mate. Step en now. Do summat,' said Bob.

Tone screamed, 'DO YOU WANT ME A CHANGE YER FACE, PEG FUCKURL? I ASKED YOU A CEVEL FUCKEN QUESTION: EHS THURL A FUCKEN PROBLEHM?' and he's hanging over the bar with his broken bottle and his face from hell. I noticed the bottle was in the L-O-V-E hand.

Bob's nearly wetting himself now but he manages to say, 'Thurr's no problem, mate.'

So Tone laughs and goes, 'Then everayfen's alright,' and he puts the broken bottle gently down on the bar, goes back to his pint and takes a long draw. I looked at him and he sat down at our table looking totally fucking relaxed like nothing had happened. He smiled at me. 'Thurr's no problem, boss,' he said and started rolling a fag – no shaking hands or nothing. Grade A psycho, no mistake – don't fucking mess under any circumstances.

Tone finished his roll-up and sauntered back to the machine. The other punters scattered like a shoal of little fish as he come towards them.

Bob whispered urgently at me from across the bar, 'Fer fuck's sake, Steve, get that nutturl out of ere.'

'No chance, Bob,' I went. 'On the site I tell im what to do and e's alright wiv at but once we've dahned tools, I ain't tellin im nuffink.'

We looked over to Tone, who was chatting to one of the tarts. I don't know whether this one charged or not but either way, I could see where it was heading.

'Looks to me like e got an itch to scratch, Bob, and I ain't gonna stop im,' I said. 'If I was you, mate, I'd quietly clean up that glass, leave the money e's chucked in a neat pile on the bar, and for fahck's sake let im scratch it.' Bob never said nothing, he just kept a frightened eye on Tone.

'C'mon lads, less make a move,' I said, knowing Tone would stick around with his tart. The boys were as keen to get away from that liability as I was but I said, 'You comin Tone? Up the Long Bahh?'

'Bezzy boss, bezzay,' he said.

'See ya tomorrah, Tone. Don't use up all your energy, mind,' and I forced a grin.

'Tara lads,' he says, grinning back.

Leaving Tone behind puts light in your life. We drank in the Long Bar in Old Market until nearly closing time and, talking of itches to scratch, I figured Lisa would probably be unconscious by now and I knew I could do what the hell I fancied, so I left the lads there and drove back to hers – I can't call it home.

I was desperate so I had a Jimmy against the old armchair outside the front door and let myself in. I could see that the lights in Lisa's room were on, which was unusual cos when she goes to bed, she's usually asleep in ten seconds. I figured I'd probably find her slumped and unconscious with a burnt out fag in her mouth but when I got in the room, her and Shawnie were spread all over the bed like dressed up water balloons, leaving fuck all space for me. Lisa had been crying but she always bleeding cries when she's had a few. So she's always bleeding crying. Shawnie had had her nose in the chocolate trough and there was wrappers everywhere.

'Ay ay,' I said, 'gels' night in, then?'

Lisa wiped her eyes and smeared her make-up round a bit more and Shawnie picked up the wrappers and chucked them into the empty Celebrations box while I took me clothes off. I left me undies on cos Shawnie was there and squeezed myself into a little sliver of space next to her. I think Shawnie tried to get out then but she don't move too fast and Lisa wrapped herself round the poor kid like an avenging jellyfish and grabbed any bits of me she could reach.

'I loves you Shawnay, I loves you Steve,' she went, half crying and half falling asleep. By the time I'd finished saying, 'I love you too, doll,' she was unconscious and starting to snore, leaving me and Shawnie lying there like fucking lemons. I'd been hoping for some sort of action with her ladyship, which was normally best when she was in the land of nod anyway, so there was a bit of stirring down below, if you know what I mean and that was kind of awkward cos I was forced to lie right against Shawnie.

I was just about to ask her if she wanted to get out, cos she was pretty much trapped in there, when, fuck me, she only grabs hold of me old fella who, I'm sorry to say, had reared his ugly head outside of me undies. I couldn't fucking believe it. She started wanking me off and, OK, I didn't stop her straight off. I mean, I'd been feeling horny and looking for a bit with her ladyship but this took me so much by surprise I didn't know what the fuck to do. I never asked for it or even hinted I might fancy it – this was one hundred per cent Shawnie's idea. What a fucking slag: I mean, first I find her giving her brother a blow-job; then she wanks off her own mother's bloke while her dear old Ma is snoring beside her. Fair play, she was good. Even spat on her hand when it got a bit dry down there. She knew what she was doing, no mistake – got enough practice in with the lovely Jason I suppose.

I had to take this all in so I didn't stop her for a minute or two and it had come this far so I thought, sod it, might as well enjoy myself and let her finish the job (I'd had a few, hadn't I?), so I pulled the duvet down and rolled onto me back to give her easier access. Shawnie takes this as an invite to suck me off, don't she? She clamps her lips around me knob and starts using her mouth like a fucking pro. Again, *her* idea. Nothing to do with me. She was seriously fucking good and I soon felt myself welling up and Shawnie must have felt it too cos she whipped it out of her mouth and finished me off by hand and I fucking come all over the shop. Fucking bomb in a yoghurt factory, it was.

It was kind of awkward then and I didn't know what to do so I said, 'Fanks, Shawnie,' and I put me feet on the floor to let her get out of bed. She didn't say nothing. She just wiped her hand on the sheet, rolled off of the bed and went to her room. I climbed back in and lay on the wet patch.

Most girls ain't got a clue what to do with a fella, make him come, like. Seems to me it's only young girls know what they're fucking doing, or care. Once they get older, they're just interested in their right to multiple orgasms, like blokes haven't even got the right to *one* of the fuckers.

Short of a full-blown shafting, that was the best I'd ever had; in fact it was better than any shag I could remember.

I lay on me back, next to Sleeping Beauty, just thinking. Thinking into the night.

SHAWNIE

boys and their willies

Willies willies willies willies willies. What is it with boys and their willies? I mean, I always knew they couldn't think about nothing else but I never knew what I could get just by using my right 'and. Couldn't get off school, mind. Couldn't get Siantell and er mates off me back. Couldn't get out of PE.

I ates Thursdays cos it's PE first and I'm crap at that. I'm crap at everything but especially PE. I ates the ole thing, starting off with getting your clothes off to change into the gym kit when everyone can see you. I mean, it's different changing rooms for boys and girls and that but it's still orrible being looked at. I wouldn't mind being in the boys' changing room anyway. I knows what a do with boys. There's only three other girls in my class anyway cos we aves really small classes in my school cos we're the divvies and cos there's more boy divvies than girl divvies. Toni, Siantell and Kerry-Ann they're called and all three of em's bitches what ates me, pardon me French. They gangs up on me and that. There was four others once. There was Kasha an' all and she was me mate but she was only in on the revolving door and she went back to Engrove, look. She got better or cleverer I suppose. Don't see er no more.

In the changing room, the moment I really dreads is taking me top off and I turned me back on them and tried to get it over with but as soon as it was over me ead, they was all round me and pointing and one of them prodded me left tit when I couldn't see and they all squealed and went, 'Urrl a'ss so fucken gross,' and 'Look at the fucken uddurrs on shay.'

When I finally got me top off Toni said, 'Shawnay, do us a favour. Come round arrs and lie down with yer arms and legs in the urr; it's me lettle bruvvurr's birfday an' e wants a bounsay castle.'

They thinks they're so funny. They started calling me 'Uddurrs' all through PE. The boys thought it was ilarious and they all started calling us that an' all. Hoo-bluming-ray, that's gonna stick then.

I ain't never got a PE kit so Mrs Taylforth always gets us an old school one and she done that but I swears it was made for an eight-year-old or summat cos I couldn't ardly get the shorts over me bum and I was scared stiff they might split. Me bum was splurging out all over.

We gotta warm up first – even if we're feeling warm already – by running on the spot and that and Kerry-Ann said, 'Watch out for they uddurrs – might knock someone out.'

When we did the stretching exercises, Kerry-Ann and Toni made sure they were either side of me. When Miss Teplakova told us to stretch our left arm up, Toni pretended a faint. When I lifted me right arm up, Kerry-Ann pretended a faint. They thinks they're so funny. Everyone laughed, mind. Except me. I wanted a cry but I wasn't gonna let em see that. Miss Teplakova moved them and split them up for the rest of the lesson.

Next we did some throwing and catching practice which was alright cos I ad Christopher for me partner and e's too thick a take the mick. Even *I* reckons e's thick so e's gotta be seriously bleeding stupid, pardon me French.

Then we ad a play bench ball, which I ates. You gotta get into two teams ('Ahh no, we got Uddurrs in our team') and one team aves the ball and they gotta pass it around and chuck it at the legs of someone on the other team but if they catches it they can chuck it back at your legs and if you gets it you stands on a bench. It's summat like that anyway.

Soon as we starts, someone shouts, 'Get Uddurrs first – you can't mess they thighs,' and, of course, they got me in five seconds flat, din em?

'Eh's like aiming at fucken tree trunks, enneht?' goes Toni.

Miss Teplakova blew the whistle and goes, 'You can shout someone's name if you want them to give you the ball but apart from that, we play in silence. The next person who swears will have to sit out.'

She's alright, Miss Teplakova.

We played a few games of bench ball and I got it first every time so I just spent alf an hour standing on a bench, which is better than aving to run round, I suppose.

We ad to shower after but there was no way I was gonna risk that. I took me shorts off and there were these deep lines around me thighs and Toni, Siantell and Kerry-Ann were like, 'Fat slappurr,' and that but I noticed that only Siantell ad a shower and the other two were too interested in looking at er to pay much attention a me. Siantell's a right cow and bluming lovely looking. She looks like one of they super-models or summat and she looks loads older than thirteen and the other two was bitching about er while she couldn't ear.

I took the chance a get dressed quickly and when I finished, Miss put er ead round the door and said, 'Girls, have you all had a shower?' and we said, 'Yeah,' and nodded.

Miss said, 'Well done. Well done Shawnie: changed already. Hurry up Siantell.'

I wondered if er or Mrs Taylforth, my LSA, would dare go into the boys' changing room. I could ear riots going on in there. Our Jason said that e used a ang round near the door with nothing on is bottom alf so if is PE teacher come in, e could call im a perv and lose im is job.

Mrs Taylforth worked with me for the rest of the morning. We were doing reading and writing and that. She was elping me make word cards for me word box. Only me and Christopher aves word boxes. I knows me letters *and* me letter sounds. I just can't seem to put em all together in words, they mixes themselves up. Mrs Taylforth reckons it might be easier to look at whole words and forget about the letters and I reckons she's right so I likes me word box and I can read loads of words now.

Mrs Taylforth's kind. I likes nearly all the teachers up Florrie. I ardly ever gives them a ard time. I started going when I was seven cos I wouldn't talk. They thought I couldn't but I could, I just didn't wanna. Never wanted a do no work neither so I never. Didn't do nothing except piss and shit myself – pardon me French – on purpose. Don't know why I done that. Used a put me arms up in front of me face all the time, especially if anyone spoke to me. And me knees. I can remember sitting on me backside, 'ands in me pants, or wrapped around me shins, staring through me knees, looking out through the cracks between them. The other kids just left me alone. So did the teachers after a bit. They got people a come out and see me and I wouldn't say nothing a they neither. My teacher, Mrs Birney er name was, said things like, 'What about SATS?' and 'Not on the scale' and stuff like that, like I was deaf or summat.

What was it our Dad used a say? 'Urr yowe deaf or fucken stupehd?' Well, I ain't deaf, and I ain't stupid neither. I thinks about stuff, I thinks about stuff all the time but I ain't never found no one a listen to it, what I thinks and that. You talks about summat other than football or telly or booze or, you know, sex, and everyone thinks you're a snob or summat. But I thinks, and I knows what's going on. I knows I didn't ought a be doing what I dooz with our Jase; I knows our Ma's trying a kill erself with cider; I knows Steve only thinks about imself; I knows our Jase loves me; I knows our Nan loves me; I knows our Dad's a bad man, I knows e's dangerous an' all and I'm glad e's inside and that. I'm sorry Ma but I knows Mrs Taylforth's the best person in the world. I knows Siantell's an evil cow but Toni and Kerry-Ann ain't alf so bad. I knows plenty. Just can't find no one a listen, or if I do . . . I can't find me voice.

I knows I likes food too much an' all but dinner was lush. We ad they potato waffles and loads of kids didn't eat theirs cos they said they were too greasy but that's ow I likes them so I got masses cos I ad Christopher's, Jason Mundy's and Curtis's an' all. And there was burgers and beans. Strawberry cheesecake for afters.

I'd sold two packs of fags from the load Jason gave me for me birthday so I ad money for the chippy on the way ome and I couldn't ardly think about nothing else.

After dinner, me and Christopher went round the back of the Terrapin for a fag. Teachers never goes there. You can ave a fag and watch the babbies in the nursery next door. Wish I was there. Big kids from our school dooz work experience there sometimes so when I'm a bit older I'm gonna try and get some of that: elp the babbies, look. I wants a work with littl'uns one day.

I was thinking maybe Christopher wanted a be my boyfriend. I ain't never ad a boyfriend. Reckoned I might let im. Once, round the back of Terrapin, e said, 'Show us yer tehts, Shawnie, I'll show you me deck.'

I said, 'I knows what *they* looks like, fank yowe veray much.'

E couldn't stop looking at me boobies, mind. We ad two fags before the whistle went.

I didn't do nothing all afternoon. I talks now and I don't ardly ide behind me arms and that but I never said nothing and I never done nothing cos I was just thinking about PE and the chips I was gonna ave after school. I ad enough for a battered burger an' all if I wanted. They dooz lush battered burgers over the Leinster chippy.

Mr Pope teaches maths what we aves last on Thursdays. Never did like men: they makes me nervous, look. E went on and on about fractions and apples and that and no one ad a clue what e was on about. Least I never. E kept on looking at me an' all; everyone keeps dogging me up. At the end e said, 'Shawnie, you're very quiet today.'

Well, that was true but I couldn't think of nothing a say so I never said nothing and I kept on walking. E said, 'If you need to talk about anything, Shawnie, I'll always listen and I'll always help if I possibly can.'

I was like, 'Right,' and I looked down as I walked out the classroom.

I was going down the path towards Leinster Avenue, which was normally the last danger spot, when I eard Kerry-Ann say, 'Uddurrs, ya fat fucken slag, watch out ya don't trep over yer tehts.'

'Least I got tehts,' I said. I don't know where that come from, I swear. I never thought. Next thing I knows, she ad me ead and Toni ad me legs and I was on the ground. Toni sat on me legs and Kerry-Ann sat on me face. She ad a short skirt on, like she always done, and a nasty scrage on er knee. She was rubbing er ass and er tuppence look, over me face. Least she ad knickers on and she never smelt too bad.

'Kess my ass, Uddurrs,' she said in a orrible voice, then she jumped off and they went up Leinster, laughing. Could ave been a lot worse. Stuff like that always appens to me. I suppose it's cos no one likes me: all the other kids ave got best friends and that, like I used a ave Kasha . . . least I got Mrs Taylforth. Steve says, 'She's bleedin paid to like ya,' but I reckons she do anyway. I sat on the ground and waited till they were out of sight then I went off meself. I was definitely aving that battered burger now.

When I come out the chippy I opened up the paper and I started off with some chips cos the battered burger ad just been cooked special like and I knew it would be really ot. I took two chips and put them in me mouth. Then I mixed the rest up so that the salt and vinegar wouldn't all be at the top. Alf the chips first, then alf the burger, then alf the chips what's left, then the rest of the burger, then the rest of the chips so that I finishes off with a salty mouthful.

I moved next to the big green bins to get out the way of the Connaught kids fighting and the cobby-looking teenage mums, swearing and pushing buggies through the scrum. They could fight and swear all they wanted. I was in chip eaven. I sucked me fingers and wiped me 'ands on the paper wrapper and put it in one of they big green bins cos I ates it when people just chucks litter in the street.

There'd be some Coke in the fridge to wash it all down with, that's if our Ma adn't drank it all with er vodka.

She wasn't too bad when I got ome and we was aving a chat when our Jason called me upstairs.

'Shawn, less ave a chat en yer room, lovurr.'

E give us a fag and we ad a chat. I tell you what, our Jason's a genius. E'd only gone and figured a way of getting us free fags, adn't e?

'You just gotta wank em off, Shawn. Twentay fags a frow – we'll splet em.'

I looked at im but I never said nothing.

'Tha's ten each, Shawn. Ten each. I gets the punturrs frew the door. You dooz a rest. I reckons we could charge double for a blow-job, sehs,' e said. 'Twentay fags for fuck all.'

'I ain't blowen yer scabbay mates, Jase: thurr dirtay so and sos and you ain't gotta swear.'

'Not for a packet each? Ef they washes first?' e says.

And I'm like, what? A packet each?

'Ef they washes first, then. I wants a taste the soap, mind,' I said.

'An' nuffen else, Shawn. They don't get nuffen else. I'll tell em and ef they asks or tries et on, they'll ave me a watch out forl an' I'll be outside,' e goes.

'Ef they tries *what*, Jase?'

'Ef they wants a go all the way – ef they wants a shag you, Shawn, yeah?'

I understood.

'I ain't aven that, Jase. I ain't shaggen no one.'

'I knows, tha's what I'm sayen,' e goes. 'Ef a punturr tries et on, gev us a shout an' I'll come an' rep ehs fucken deck off.'

'Stell swearen, Jase. Eh's dirtay,' I says.

'Life's dirtay, Shawn,' e says, which is right enough I suppose but that don't mean that we gotta go making it dirtier, do it? Well, I thought of that later but not at the time so I never said nothing.

'You got two punters waiting, Shawn,' Jason says. 'Scott One and Carl.'

I turns round and I'm like, 'What? Now?' But e've shouted a Carl already and when e come in, Jason said, 'Just a 'and-job, yeah?' and Carl nodded.

'She touches you, you don't touch er, right? I'm right outside.' Jason shut the door behind im.

Carl stood in me room, looking down at the carpet with wide eyes. 'Right Shawnay?' e goes, still not looking up.

'Right Carl?' I goes and I didn't see no point in anging round and Carl weren't gonna do nothing so I just put me fag out, walked over, undid is belt and button, pulled is zip down and let is baggy trousers fall down round is ankles. I could see e ad a boner already. I pulled is undies down and looked at is willy as it boinged from side a side, just like our Jason's dooz. Wasn't as airy as Jason's, mind. I grabbed old of it and pulled the skin up over the bumpy bit at the end. I knows what a do with a willy, don't I? I must be getting better because I adn't wanked im off for more than ten seconds before e squirted. Just like Jason except Carl made a noise like a dog with a toy, which was funny.

Carl pulled is clothes up and went all red and said, 'Nice one, Shawnay,' as e walked out the room.

I eard Jason say, 'Fucken ell, Carl. That uz queck,' and I was looking at Carl's squirtings on the floor when Jason said a me, 'Scott's just washen es deck, Shawn. E wants a blow-job. E've paid up front and that and I'll sort you out afturr. You alright?'

I nodded. Easy fags innit?

'Lesten out for our Ma, Jase,' I goes.

Scott comes out the bathroom and looks at Carl, who grins. Jason says, 'Straight en, Scott.'

Scott looked all scared an' all but I just took over and done the business. It was alright: I could taste the soap. And e zipped imself up and said, 'Tara Shawn, tahl an' that. See ya next time, yeah?' and that was that. Our Jason's a genius. E said e could get loads more an' all.

Jason and is mates went out and stayed out cos e didn't ardly sleep over ours no more. Me and our Ma spent the evening eating chocolate and watching telly but I ad loads more than er cos she kept falling asleep, so we finished off upstairs in er bed and she'd started getting tearful like she always dooz, when Steve come back.

Steve ad ad a few. E came in all red faced and jokey and as soon as e saw me in bed with our Ma e couldn't get is clothes off quick enough. Our Ma fell asleep almost on top of me and Steve climbs in the other side and starts rubbing imself up against me so I was bleeding trapped, wasn't I? Pardon me French. I mean, what could I do? Steve ad a ard-on you could poke someone's eye out with and I couldn't get out so what else could I do? I knows what fellas likes, don't I? Don't matter if they're young or old, rich or poor, black or white. I knows what they wants. They says I got learning dificulties but I ain't stupid. Well, I must be cos I goes up Florrie but I ain't *thick*, like, and I've learnt this well enough. Fellas, all fellas, wants a squirt: in your 'and; in your mouth; in your, you know, your tuppence (but I ain't aving that). They ain't fussed, long as they squirts.

So I gets old of Steve's willy soon as our Ma passes out and starts wanking im off. Just the same as our Jason and Scott One and Carl. You gets what you wants then, I knows that much. I wanted a get back a my bed. I didn't know what else *to* do.

Steve pulled the duvet down and turned onto is back just like Jason dooz when e wants a blow-job so I give im one even though e certainly adn't washed and it wasn't soap I could taste.

When e finally squirted (and e took for *ever*) e let me get back to me room.

The king-size Snickers bar I'd idden in me knicker drawer elped take the taste of Steve away.

LISA

every cloud and that

Friday was wild, Friday was mad. You don't ave to be mad to be me but . . . well, sad elps. Every cloud and that. Friday was fucking mint, until the end.

Steve said that there was some lads coming round after work. Four a them: Norris, Lee and Michael who'd been round before, and a new lad, Tone. Steve said Tone was a bit of a nutter but as long as I treated im right, e'd be a pussy-cat. I knows what calms the nutters down. I said if we was partying I'd need some money and Steve give me twenty-five quid. E said they'd bring the booze and turn up about nine but I figured I ad to get a few in to loosen up, look. I ad alf a bottle of Red Square stashed away anyhow.

Our Jason stayed over Scott's the night before so e wasn't there first thing and once Steve ad gone a work (e went early, look) and our Shawn ad gone a school, I sat in front of the telly and drank water cos that's really good for you, and coffee with a little vodka pick-me-up in it. I was thinking about ow to spend that twenty-five quid.

Trisha. Stuck up slag. 'Should I Let My Teenage Daughter Have Sex Under My Roof?' What, like our Shawnie? Chance'd be a fine thing, who'd ave *er*, I thought. Shawnie's a sweetheart but she ain't a looker. Bless.

I wasn't doing bingo look, cos it was Friday, so I just ad a go up Pipkins superstore over Melvin for the party stuff. I could get some of they Pringles and posh stuff like that as well as a few cans of White Ace (they don't do White Lightning up Pipkins, look) to keep me going. I could get some cheesy balls cos I loves they, and some Coke cos I knew they'd be bringing vodka back. They always do. Ooh, and some cheap lager. I don't drink lager but just in case anyone needed a break from the ard stuff. I'd ave to put them in the fridge cos no one wants warm lager. Especially the piss I was gonna buy. Ooh, and some eggs an' all for the kids' tea.

Pipkins ave got a concrete wall up the first five foot of it along the front cos of the ram raiders and it's got barbed wire or razor wire or whatever all along the top, below the boarded up flats, and you can't ardly see the wire no more cos kids ave chucked so many coats up there when they'd come out of school and picked on the crap uns. One of our Shawnie's was up there. Still is I suppose.

When I put me basket down, Sue at the checkout (I've known er for ever: she's Tony's cousin) looks at me twelve cans of White Ace and goes, 'Right Lees? Partay a-night?' and I goes, 'Evray night's partay night up arrs Sue, you knows at.'

'I ain't got the staminal a do that no more, Lees. A mug of Orlecks an' me meddle fengurr, tha's Friday night, look.'

'Sue, you gotta get out more lovurl, or come round arrs a-night: loads a shet ot fellas. Nuff a go round, like.'

'Our Dean might ave summat a say bout that, Lees. E's up the pub wev es mates but e won't ave may doehn nuffen by meself look.'

'You still getten a lengf from em, Sue?' I goes and the old dear behind looks at I queer, like.

'Ef e ain't pessed up an' ef the Cety ain't at ome an' ef thurl ain't no match on the tellay an' ef e ain't en a mood an' ef the keds ain't playen us up an' ef thurr's a zed en the monf, I might just get a teckle, Lees,' and we laughed – she's a laugh, Sue.

I 'anded a twenty over look, and took the change. Pennies. I knew she wouldn't come. 'Tara, Sue.'

'Tara, Lees. Ooh, Lees. Jew yer bout our Tonay?'

'Jus stop now, Sue,' I goes. 'I don't wannal earl a fucken word bout ay. Tonay ain't part of my life no morr.'

'I just thought you'd wanna know –'

'I don't wanna know nuffen bout that piece a shet, Sue. Whatever et ehs, et ain't gonna be good. E can rot whurl e ehs frall I currs.'

'Suit yerself, lovurl, an' enjoy yerself a-night. Don't do nuffen I wouldn't do, mind.'

'I can't fenk of nuffen you wouldn't do, Sue,' I goes. 'Fact, I can't fenk of nuffen you aven't done. Frall I knows, yer doen et now, look. I can't see beyind that tell can I and I noteced a funnay look en yer eye.'

'Cheeky bleeden murr,' she goes and turns to the po-faced old bat what was next. 'Right love? Tara, Lees.'

'Tara, Sue.'

Last thing I bleeding wanted was to ear about Tony. E's an evil piece of shit, no mistake. We were well shot of im. Any man what can touch up is own babby . . . Well, I blames meself. Still, if it wasn't for im there wouldn't be no Shawnie. Every cloud and that.

Tell the truth, there's a little bit of me what misses im. I mean, not all the orrible stuff an' that, but . . . well, in bed for starters. And all the stuff what e done round the ouse. E done us an en suite bathroom, breakfast bar, a barbecue outside the back what every bugger in the street was jealous of: it was beautiful. Still is but we ain't never used it in years now, not since e've been put away, look. Fucking rusty an' that now. Good with is 'ands mind, our Tony, in every way. I misses that.

There's a dear little playground over Leinster Avenue where some old mates of mine gets together and drinks cider when the weather's nice like it was that day, and a oarse shout of me name told me they'd started early. They Pipkins bags are thick and you can't see through em so I knew I could keep me cider and lager safe, look. I figured I could sacrifice the lager if I ad to.

'Lisa, you old slapper, come and have a chat.' That was Tom. E was sat against the fence next to the babbies' swings. Tom was posh, used a work in a bank and that but e was looking rough. E was looking like shit on a stick, truth be known: you could see all the redness in is face right through the wrinkles and the dirt and the creases and the tan e gets from sitting outside all day. It was ot but e was still wearing is suit, which was fucking minging and thick with black slime and crud and that. E ad they fingerless gloves on and some fucking awful tank top or summat what was fraying and unravelling and I didn't like to even think about what was underneath that get-up on a ot July afternoon. I mean I'm a sweaty Betty and that but Tom was a stranger to water these days and the smell coming off of im was ard to stomach, even in the open air.

Tom was with some scabby low-life I seen before: one a the Broad Walk cider-eads. Big fella, long filthy air coming down over is orange work jacket, used a be fluorescent. Didn't we all, lovurr. They were sharing a two-litre bottle of White Lightning and I could see that there was two more bottles in the carrier on the ground. I nodded at Tom's mate and went, 'Right Tom, sexay beast. Ow's et goehn?'

'Lisa, my darling, it's so good to see you. Tell me something, Lisa, have you got any booze in those carrier bags that you'd like to share around? Take a seat and . . .' Tom started coughing and didn't sound like e was ever going a stop.

'You looks like you ain't short of a drop, Tom,' I goes when e finally finishes acking is innards up. 'Sides, I'm fucken near on the wagon these days. I can just about afford the keds' tay. Gev us a go on yer bottle, Tom,' and I put the carriers down well out of is reach.

'Not if you're not going to share, Lisa,' e goes.

'You ain't aven the keds' tay,' I goes. 'I ain't got nuffen a fucken shurl, ave I?' and e goes, 'That's not how I remember it, Lisa,' and e's staring right at me tits. 'You could always be, ahh, how shall I put it, remarkably generous with your erm, considerable assets when you wanted a, a . . .' and e trailed off wheezing and trying not a cough.

'I can stell be genruhhs, Tom, ef you can,' I goes. This was too easy. 'Tell yuh what,' I said, yanking me top down to reveal a Cheddar Gorge of cleavage, 'you ansome young fellas can ave a go at one tetty each fer as long as I can ave a go at yer bottle,' and I didn't need a wait for an answer cos Tom's mate was thrusting the bottle towards me as I finished speaking. By the time I'd raised it to my lips, they were delving deep into me bra and grabbing old of me nipples like they was trying a get milk out of a dead cow or summat.

Good job there weren't no kiddies there. You never gets no kiddies in that playground. In less than a minute, I'd finished off the bottle – must ave been a good pint and a alf in there – and I'd ad just about enough of filthy rough 'ands trying a rip me nipples off.

'Thanken you, boys an' tha's all yer gettehn,' I goes as I puts the bottle down, burping.

'Stick around, Lisa,' goes Tom as I takes is 'and out of me bra and tucks me titties back in.

'Tom, you got plenty of uses fer that 'and, lovurl. I got business. Fanks fer the drenk an' that.'

What is it with blokes and me tits? I left Tom and is lovely mate in the playground. There's some rough buggers round ere, no mistake. All I got left really. Other night I told Steve I reckoned I was scraping the bottom of the barrel these days but e just turned round and said, '*You're* scrapin the bottom of the barrel? Ave a little fink about that one, gel.'

Steve didn't always want a share me round. Wanted me all to imself once. There was a time we used a talk, and kiss, and look into each other's eyes – all that soppy stuff. I can't imagine it now. Steve said e adn't never been close to a lady before, that e never knew ow to do it but e do. Did. I've thought about it, I've ad sleepless nights but I just don't know why e turned against me. E said, 'Jew know what, gel? I can't even be fackin arsed to ate you.' The more you thinks about ard stuff, the more you gotta drink and e've got me on a bottle a day now and that's before the cider.

E can't do kids, neither. E said e never ad a childhood really and that's why. I don't know what that means: it can't ave been worse than mine. Steve ain't interested in that. E just wants a talk about when e was a littl'un and that. E ad loads of the shite I ad but e didn't never ave the dirty stuff; least not much. It was my bleeding life. Least I ad me sisters, Janey and Cherry; Steve never ad nothing like that. No backup. Cherry's up London now with er flash fella and er new accent and Janey's doing alright over Bradley Stoke; they gets on with their own lives now.

The eat was getting up already and by the time I got up ouse that fucking armchair outside the front was minging. I wasn't a lot better.

I got inside and sat down on the settee and as soon as I done that I realized that the remote was over on the floor. Bloody Shawnie. As I ad to get up anyway, I got meself a can, lit up a Silk Cut and settled down for *Through the Keyhole*. I'd seen it before but fuck it, who cares? It was Nick Witchell and that Scouse prick snooker player what used a be in *A Question of Sport*.

Plenty of time a prepare for the party. White Ace ain't so good as White Lightning but it just needs a bit more cooling really. Well, it's a time thing, ain't it? White Ace's alright. *Through the Keyhole*'s alright. Steve's alright. Nothing a bit of cider can't sort out.

After a couple of cans at dinner (a large pack of Asda's prawn cocktail crisps, look: lush) I must ave closed me eyes for a bit cos when I opened them again it was gone three and the bleeding *Tweenies* was on telly. I knew Shawnie and Jason would be ome from school in a minute and Shawnie would want a watch *Sabrina the Teenage Witch*. *Sabrina*'s alright. I cracked open a can and made a start on the cheesy balls and they was lush an' all. I likes a split em in alf in me mouth and try and lick the cheesy bit out of the middle.

'Right Shawn?' I said as she come in.

'Right Ma,' she goes and she was looking a right bloody misery.

'Blige, Shawnay, summat crawled up yer arse an' died?' I goes. 'I fought you'd be appay an' that, what wev last day a term an' what ave yowe.'

'S'nuffen Mahl, I'm alright,' she goes, looking pretty fucking far from it. I thought I'd get it over with.

'Lesten, Shawn. Me an' Steve got some mates comen round a-night –'

'Aww Mahl, et ain't gonna bay anuvvurl a they nights, es eht?'

'Shawn, I don't stop you aven fun do I?' I goes. 'Fer fuck's sake, all we wants is a few drenks an' a laugh. S'not like –'

'Stop swearehn, e's dirtay.'

'Fiy wants a fucken swearl en me own fucken ouse I fucken well. Don't you fucken teach I a talk, tha's what I done a yowe. Don't teach yer Nan a fuck eggs.'

'MA!'

'Suck eggs. You knows what I means.'

Shawnie stared at me. 'Whatevurr you on about, Ma?'

'I don't even blooday know no more, Shawn. You ben such a pain en the arse you got me well riled.'

Shawnie shut up for a minute or two to let me calm down and we both lit up and stared miserably at the *Tweenies* singing, 'One finger one thumb, keep moving.'

'Ma?'

Merry and bright my arse. 'What?'

'You ain't gonna be all noisay an' that like last time arr yowe, Ma?'

'Lesten Shawn, when people gets a few drenks enside em, they aves a laaf an' they aves a dance an' they gets a bet rowday – you wannal ave a try sometime – sides, eh's Friday; weekend enneht? Lesten, Shawn, we got Prengles, cheesy balls, Chep Stecks . . .'

'Now yer talken, Ma,' Shawnie goes. 'That'll do fer starturrs. And I wants anothurl a they double Nesqueks a wash et down.'

'Cheeky murr,' I goes. 'You can ave a keng-size bag a Chep Stecks an' tha's yer lot.'

'Aww Ma. That ain't furl. I wants a Nesquek an' all.'

'Shawn, don't start, and lessen, you don't wanna bay comen down, lovurr. Thurr's some rough buggers yer a-night. I'll chuck in a carton o' Prengles an' all: salt an' venegarl or cream cheese and chives?'

'I'll ave cream cheese.'

'Double Nesquek the-morrer, right?'

'Alright, Ma. Whatchoo want fer tay?'

'Oo, I couldn't, love. Gotta beg night ain't I? Gotta squeeze inna summat sexay. Es our Jason ome a-night?'

'E's down town, Ma. E ain't back fer es tay a-night, and Ma – don't squeeze inta nuffenk tell I'm upsturrs, yeah?'

'Shawn, fex yerself summat, lovurl. I got you eggs.'

'I'll ave they burgurrs, Ma. They Asdal *economy* burgurrs. Everybody aves Birds Eye cept us, Ma.'

'Eh's the same bloody stuff, Shawn, just wev a deffrent lable on eht.'

'Ain't. Thur rubbesh, Ma.'

'SHAWN,' I shouted, 'don't start. And get us a can while yer en the ketchen, love,' and she glared at me but she got us the can anyway and I tell you what, White Ace ain't so bad when it's properly chilled.

I started on the other Pringles and watched *Ready Steady Cook* while Shawnie done er tea. They done some nice salmon fillets but they done them with red peppers what they burnt on the ob first until they was black and I reckons our Shawnie's tea was better than Ainsley's.

'Oo Shawn, ave they eggs wev yer burgers look, tha's lush.'

'Nice one, Ma,' says Shawnie. She'd stacked the cooked burgers on their edges all around the side of the frying pan so that she could put some new ones in to fry and finish off the packet.

I must ave closed me eyes for a bit cos I never saw the end of *Ready Steady Cook* and before I knew what ad appened, I found meself sat in front of *Robot Wars* which I ates so I switched over a *Vets in Practice* but I wasn't really watching it.

I started thinking about the party tonight. Well, it wasn't exactly going to be a party; more of a gathering for a few mates looking for a good time. Bloody Shawnie was taking the piss and ad taken alf me party nibbles up to er room but I couldn't face they stairs so I went into the kitchen for another can and started a think about what music a play. Tony ad got us a beautiful i-fi with a CD player and everything before e got put inside and Steve ad brought a lot of is own CDs down.

I was thinking about that and I never noticed that Shawnie ad left the burger box on the floor next to the bin (OK, so the bin was full of cans) and I toe-poked that into the side and went arse over tit into the cooker. On me way down I tried a save meself but only grabbed the frying pan our Shawnie ad been using (which luckily ad mostly cooled down) and pulled that down so as soon I it the floor it fell on me fucking belly and tipped oil and fat and that all over me clothes. I'd smacked me elbow summat wicked on the cooker and I knew I'd ave a ell of a bruise next day. Apart from that, I wasn't really urt: I got a bit of padding these days, look; cushions I from the worst.

I was shaken mind, so I didn't try and get up look, just in case. I sat up and leaned against the cupboard. I took the frying pan off of me and I was fucking lagged in grease; I could feel it soaking right through me clothes. I threw the pan into the corner and cussed Shawnie blind. I don't know if I'd it me ead or summat but I was feeling a bit groggy so I didn't try and get up. I just leaned over, pulled the fridge door open and got meself a can. After the shock I'd ad, that White Ace slipped down lovely, alf of it slipped down first go. Bloody Shawnie.

'Shawnay!' I shouted. I was riled. 'Shawnay!'

I could ear er lumbering down the stairs like a fucking ippo or summat. 'Ma!' she goes, when she come in. '*Ma*, what ave you done?'

'Et ain't what *I* done, girl. You done thes, laven yer fucken rubbesh on the floor. I could of died, Shawn.'

'Oh God oh God oh God. I'm sorry Mahl. Ehs anyfeng broke? Oh God I'm sorray Ma.'

'I don't know bout me arm, Shawn. Et don't feel good.' I drained me can.

'Whech arm, Ma?'

'Thes un love.' I touched it with me other 'and.

There was a long pause and I should of eard the cogs clunking in er ead.

'What, the one you just used a breng that can up to yer lyehn mouf?' she shouts. 'Thurl ain't nuffen wrong wev yer arm, yer just pessed.'

'I been sat ere fer ages, Shawn, I lost track of ow long. Et elps take the pain away,' I tried.

'Don't gev us that crap,' shouts Shawnie. 'Yer jus bleeden pessed. Get up!'

She must ave been angry cos our Shawn never swears. She grabbed me arms and started pulling me up. I knew it was time a shut up. Fucking urt, mind.

'Bleeden state of you, pardon me French. Whatever ave you got down yer front?' goes Shawnie.

I wasn't feeling too clever and I ad to lean against the cooker.

'Tha's yer burgurrs that ehs. Tha's yer fucken greasay burgurrs, and I got a fucken partay en . . .' and I looked at me watch but I couldn't make any sense of it cos me eyes were filling up by then '. . . I don't even fucken know ow long,' and the tears started rolling and our Shawnie looked like she was gonna join me.

'C'mon, Ma,' says Shawnie. 'Less get you up they sturrs an' ento the showurr.'

Shawnie put one arm around me as best she could and eld onto me with er other one. She never could stay angry very long. Not like our Jason: that's all e ever is. I tell you what, that girl is a fucking diamond. She's a gem. We got upstairs and Shawnie took me into the bathroom and switched on the shower. She ad to take all me clothes off for me cos I was crying so much and cos of me arm and that.

'I'll wash they the-morrer,' she said.

Shawnie elped me into the bath and told me a sit down cos I was feeling wobbly what with the crying and the fall and that. I let the water run over me body and it felt good.

'Wash yer air?' she goes.

'Fanks love.'

'Less get yer looken beauteful fer the partay a meneht, eh? Knock em dead, look.'

'Shawn, I'm a fucken washed up old slappurr covered en burgurr fat.'

‘Yer sex on a steck, Mahl, and stop swearen, eh’s dirtay,’ she goes and shuts me up by aiming the shower at me ead.

I knows she’s thick and fat and looks like one a they fish what lives in the mud at the bottom of the Bristol Channel, but I tell you what, there ain’t a fucking soul on this earth’s got a lovelier daughter than me.

JASON

a lettle chat bout mannurrs

'My mate wants a go on yer skateboard, pal,' I said to the wanker on Park Street. E'd just finished playing with is little mates on College Green where all the skateboarders angs out. Sad twats. E was waiting for the bus going back to Redland or Westbury or some poncey fucking ole like that. Nothing but cunts in they places. Little Skate Boy ad just rang is Mummy on is posh mobile: 'I'm at the bus stop, I'll be half an hour, yeah? Later Mum.' One of many errors, Little Skate Boy, first of which was getting out of bed this morning.

'It's American,' e said, stepping backwards. E shook is ead but is DC oodie never moved it was so fucking uge. E was going for the full wanker: Bolt three-quarters, Vans, frightened rabbit expression.

'My mate ain't prejudiced,' I said, motioning a Scott One who was starting a look menacing way too early. 'E likes Murcans,' I said, 'and e'd like a go on yer toy please.' I smiled.

'It's not a toy. My uncle bought it back from New York,' Little Skate Boy said and I swear, e was close a tears already.

'Wha's yer uncle called, Lettle Skate Boy?' I goes.

If you know what you're doing, you can beat people before you've even laid a finger on them.

'Adam.'

'Yer Uncle Adam's a nice fella, Skate Boy, so what ave you gotta do fer ehm?'

'He gives me things . . .'

'I'm sure e dooz, mate, I'm sure e dooz, yer a nice looken boy, but we ain't all got a rich uncle a suck off, ave way, so I fenks eh's onlay furr you shurrs yer good fortune wev they woss less fortunate than yerself.'

'I don't suck anybody off,' e goes, is bottom lip starting a stick out and tremble. 'I'm going now,' but Black Phil placed imself right in is path before e'd taken one ole step and Little Skate Boy went so pale, face a face with Phil, that they looked like fucking negatives of each other.

'You don't seem to understan,' I said. 'Less ave a lettle chat someplace morr privuht.'

I put me arm round is shoulders and gently guided im down the concrete steps that leads from Park Street towards the car park. I thought e couldn't get no paler but e went whiter than our Ma's fat ass at Christmas. E didn't seem to ave no bones a mention. Scott One and Black Phil followed us down.

'Summat else I needs a say, Lettle Skate Boy. Can't elp notecen you ain't at school today. I knows eh's the last day an' that but yer education's emportant.'

I loves this bit: it's the anticipation.

'It's an INSET day and I need to get the bus home,' said Little Skate Boy with a catch in is voice. Christ, e was beaten before I'd even started.

'I ain't stoppen you, Lettle Skate Boy,' I goes. 'I jus wants a lettle chat bout mannurrs first. Now, I fought, a well bought up boy like you . . .'

'I'm going home now,' e said, turning to go back up the steps and turning straight into Black Phil again.

'. . . would know a bet more bout MANNURRS.' And as I said 'mannurrs' I swung im round by the shoulder and drove me knee up through the baggy Bolts and into is bollocks. E bounced off of Phil, cried out like a girl and fell to is knees and I drove me other knee into is ead which fucking smacked back into Phil's knee coming the other way. Sweet: right then left, am I good or what? E slumped forwards and made a alf-arsed attempt a protect is ead with one 'and while olding is bollocks with the other. E ad blood coming from is nose where it mingled with the snot and tears into a fucking umiliation slick. I was wondering if I could completely fuck someone over only using me knees, when Scott shouted, 'CUNT,' and aimed a load of punches at is ead and the back of is neck but e only got glancing blows in or it is shoulders and that. It was crap; you might as well give the cunt a lie down.

'Ang on Scott,' I said, putting me arm out. Little Skate Boy's skateboard ad fallen down a few steps. 'Go get ehs skateboard, Scott,' I goes, 'we wouldn't wanna lose eht. Eh's Murcan.'

I was trying a sound calm but I could ear me breathing going twenty a the dozen and I adn't ardly done nothing.

Scott come back with the skateboard and I took it off of im. I give im me mobile and said, 'Jus make sure you gets the rest, right?'

Little Skate Boy was on is front with is knees tucked under im, fucking rigid with fear. Black Phil pulled is ead back by the air and reached into is front pocket and took out is mobile. E nodded appreciatively as e looked at it. 'Nice one.'

Skate Boy's terrified face shot down and is 'ands covered is ead again.

I couldn't believe it, I was fucking shaking. I tried a get control of meself.

'Sorry bout the unpleasantness,' I goes, 'but you wurr FUCKEN ME AROUND,' and the fucking red mist come down again and I stuck me size ten into is side, ard. The soft cunt lost all the wind in im and started gasping for breath. One more of they would ave opened im up but I wanted a make it last.

I bent down and put me mouth up close to is ear. 'You better say sorray, Skate Boy. You better fucken say sorray,' and e whispered, 'I'm sorry.'

'I can't fucken ear you, Lettle Skate Boy.'

'I'm sorry,' e whimpers.

'Sorray WHAT?'

'I'm very sorry.'

'Very sorray what?'

'Very sorry, sir.'

'TOO FUCKEN LATE, LETTLE SKATE BOY,' I goes, and I jumped up and kicked im so fucking ard that is top lip turned into mush and e cried out and fell on is side and then tucked up again, protecting is ead and bollocks. I stepped back, gearing up for another when Phil puts is 'and on me chest and says, 'We wants es money now an' maybay they trainurrs. We ain't tryna fucken kell em, memburr?'

Phil was right and I took a deep breath but I couldn't stop shaking and I nearly fucking nutted him.

'Monay,' goes Phil, 'monay.'

'MONAY, SKATE BOY,' I screamed and I put me foot on is ead and put me weight on it. 'YER FUCKEN MONAY.' E was crying and I wanted to an' all – fuck knows why. I was losing it. Little Skate Boy didn't do nothing except lie there gasping and that. I lifted up is skateboard and eld it over is ead like they dooz with they fucking towel-eads in Saudi only with an execution sword. You seen they fucking videos? Scott Two's got some. They gets em a kneel and bends em double fore they chops their fucking eads off. An eye for an eye and that: fair play. E looked like that. I bought it down on is ead and is face smacked into the concrete and got even more fucked up.

'WHURR'S YER FUCKEN MONAY TO?' but I never gave im the chance to answer cos I bought it down again.

And again. Scott was piling in an' all. Little Skate Boy screamed and took is arm away fast from is ead. Is 'and was anging at a fucked angle. I must ave fucked it up good and proper. I knew I could get an amazing ead shot in now and I brought the skateboard down again and it was fucking perfect. Is face smacked into the step and the edge of the skateboard took the skin from the back of is ead and stripped it down to is eyebrows. I'd scalped im, I fucking scalped im, man. You could see is skull and everything through the blood and the gore. Fucking dog's. I'd never felt so good in my life. Nothing come close: not even fucking a fat-assed bitch from behind with the biggest fucking line of fucking coke the world's ever fucking seen up me fucking nose. I ad a fucking ard-on, man. I lifted the skateboard over me ead again and Black Phil fucking barrelled into me, knocked the skateboard over the rails, eld me arms up in the air and put is face up close a mine.

'E's fucked Jase, tha's enough, mate. We gotta get out now.'

E kept on olding me. E's a strong cunt, Phil. We was face a face and I could feel me face shaking as I stared at im. E was right mind, I was losing it. Scott was bent double with is 'ands in is groin, saying, 'Fuck et, fuck et, fucken ell, man.'

Little Skate Boy was slumped face-first into the concrete with the white of is skull shining through the blood, looking like summat from the chamber of fucking orrors. The circle of red growing around is ead lost its shape when it started dribbling down onto the step below.

'We – gotta – legget – now,' said Phil, pronouncing each word by itself. I looked into is eyes and the red mist started clearing and things started making sense again.

'We'll ead down past the Pineapple,' I goes, 'and along the Otwells Road. Then we can go past the City ground or get a taxi ef thurl ain't no Escorts or Astras. Walken memburr? You nevurr runs.'

Me and Phil started down the steps but Scott was lingering, bent double and cussing.

'Scott, ya cunt, sheft yer ass,' I goes. 'Woss yer fucken problem?'

'Woss my fucken problem?' goes Scott. E looked shit. '*Yer* my fucken problem, Jase. You smacked me fucken 'and up wev that skateboard ya fucken nutturl. I reckons you've broke a coupla fengurrs.'

'Scott, we'll get et seen to back ome, not ere, now fucken move,' goes Phil. Solid man.

We walked towards Otwells as slow as we could make ourselves and I was feeling like a fucking god or summat but they was being miserable bastards.

'I ain't never doen anuvvurr job wev you,' says Phil after a long silence. E jabbed is finger at me (which was more than Scott could do): 'Yer a fucken ead case.'

'Yeah,' I goes, 'and?'

'That ked might be dead back thurl an' that makes may an accomplece a murdurl an' I ain't nevurr fucken touched em. First the Pakay, then Skate Boy. I ain't doing no more jobs wev you man, yer a mad dog. We gotta call an ambulance, man.'

'Fuck off,' I goes. 'E was a wankurl. E was fucken asken fer eht.'

'We can't let em fucken die.'

'E ain't fucken dyehn.'

'I'm callen an ambulance, man.'

'E ain't fucken dyehn Phel. Gev us that mobile.'

'You callen an ambulance?'

'Jus gev us the fucken mobile, man.'

Phil 'anded it over and I it redial.

'Ello?' I goes. 'Lettle Skate Boy's Mummay? Shut the fuck up, betch, and lessen. I'm sorry, ded that sound rude? Eh's just that I've broken yer lettle boy . . . Black DC ooday, red Van trainurrs . . . Tha's the one. Yeah, fucked em up good and propurr – I'm reelay sorray an' that . . . Well, you see, I destroyed es face first, then I scalped em . . . Yeahl, I scalped em . . . Yeah, tha's right . . . E's problay dead now but you might jus save ehm . . . Tha's right . . . E've lost a lot of blood, mind . . . E's on the steps goen down towards the Pineapple from Park Street, well, e ain't goen down, but ehs blood ehs, look. I'm ever so sorray, tha's jus what you gets fer be-ehn a stuck up betch wev a poncey fucken cocksuckurr fer a son. Ta-ta fer now.' I it the red button and snorted and looked at Phil and Scott but they were just staring at me like miserable cunts – never saw the umour like.

'Look, shay can call an ambulance and they can't trace us can em? I can't believe I jus got elp fer the cunt but at least I ad a laff.' What the fuck was wrong with they wankers? Going soft or summat.

'I ain't never doen a job wev you again, man. Yer fucken mental,' goes Black Phil.

'Me fucken fengurrs ehs broke, man,' goes Scott One. OK, I could see that e ad a grievance. Is 'and looked fucked. Maybe I was a bit over enthusiastic back there.

'Whech 'and, Scott?' I goes, although I knew. E showed me is right 'and an' is ring finger was anging at an orrible angle. Just olding it up made im wince.

'Thas yer wanken 'and, mate. You'll be needen our Shawnay,' I goes. 'Next un's a freebay, yeah.'

E tried a give me the thumbs up but just cried out and doubled up again.

Never did get that money from Little Skate Boy.

By the time we reached the Spring, Scott ad gone an orrible colour. Phil wasn't talking but e ad a fiver for the taxi. I needed a wank.

LISA

the lady in red

I felt so much better when I got out the shower. Shawnie wrapped the big Man U towel around me, took me into the bedroom and sat me down on the bed.

'You alright, Ma?'

'Getten thurr, Shawn, getten thurr,' I went.

'Ow's yer arm?' she said, peering at it.

'Et ain't good, love, but et ain't broke. I fenks I can dress meself alright,' I said.

'Ere,' says Shawnie going through me wardrobe, 'wurr the red un, Ma,' she goes, taking me little red dress out.

'Ooh, I dunno, Shawn. I uz fenken of summat a bet, you know, raunchiurr like.'

'Mahl, eh's lush and thurl be nuff a you comen out the top a thes a keep any fellal entrestehd,' and she put it up against me and started swinging er ips and singing. 'The laday en red, ehs dancen wev may . . .'

'Alright, Shawn, the red un et ehs. Anyfen a shut that racket up.'

'Oi, I got a lovelay voice.'

'Course you ave lovurr, course you ave,' I goes.

'I ave,' she goes, getting all igh-pitched. She walked to the door. 'I'll sort out that mess downsturrs a meneht.'

'Ta love,' I goes.

'Ma – clean kneckurrs, mind. Thurr's a purl en the drawurl, I done em meself.'

Fucking star, our Shawnie.

I put new knickers on and looked at me tits in the mirror and I reckoned I could still get away without no bra. I squeezed meself into the red dress. It's a mini with a bit of stretch in it so you can see every curve. I got a couple more than I used to ave, mind, but it's all there in the right places. I took the knickers off. I mean, if you ain't got your monthly or nothing, I can't see no point. I stretched the top down and shoved me tits up so there was some serious cleavage a look at. I took a look in the mirror and knew I'd still got it but me air was a right state so that was next. I thought I'd put it up to emphasize the flesh on offer. Then me make-up. Then me shoes: white eels I reckoned. One last look in the mirror – sex on a stick, ain't that what Steve says? Used a say. A little thought it me that I'd probably never look this good again, but that night? I was gonna make the most of it – no fella was safe.

I was bleeding parched but it was alright cos there was cans of White Lightning in the fridge calling me name. I went downstairs into the kitchen where Shawnie was just finishing off.

'Ma!' she goes. 'Put et away! Blige, yer more out than ehn,' and she started pulling the top of me dress up look, over me titties. 'Ma, you gotta lose some weight look, yer spellen out all ovurr.'

'Shut yer fucken mouf you cheeky murr. Sex on a steck, may,' I went.

'Stop swearen Mahl, eh's dirtay,' went Shawnie, on er knees and trying a pull the em down a bit. I took the chance to pull the top back to just above nipple level again.

Shawnie stopped tugging for a second and er eyes grew wide and she lifted the dress up on me left-'and side revealing an acre of snow-white arse and a flash of pubes.

'Ma! You ain't got no kneckurrs on. I tole jew, den I? Clean kneckurrs.'

'Well I ain't got dirtay uns on ave I?'

'You ain't got nuffen on. I'd soonurr you ad dirtay uns than nuffehn.' She was shouting now.

'I likes a feel the breeze round me behts,' I says, winding er up look. 'Eh's elfay.'

'Mahl, eh's ellegal. Few goes out like that you'll get restehd.'

'Well I ain't goen out, am I? Private partay, enneht? Fuck, they'll be yurr na meneht.'

'Ma, you can't –'

'Lessen Shawn, I ain't bloody changen an' tha's final. When yer oldurr you'll understan love, eh's what blokes likes enneht? I don't tell you what a wurr, do I, Shawn?'

'Ma, you wouldn't notece fiy was stark nakehd,' she went.

'I won't ear no more Shawn. Now lemme get me can.'

'Mahl, aven't you ad enough?'

'Will you stop blooday tellen I what a do? Can't I even loosen up fore a partay? No I aven't ad enough and I wants a can. Lesten Shawn, you best go upsturrs, look. They'll be yurr na meneht. Do some omework or summat.'

'I ain't got no omework.'

'What are they blooday doen at that school?'

'I tole jew: eh's the summurl oliday enneht?'

'Ohh yeah,' I goes. 'Shawn, thes ain't a partay fer you lovurr. Lessen, ave they pork scratchens an' all look, but pess off up they sturrs a meneht, yeah lovurr?'

Shawnie grabbbed the pork scratchings *and* some prawn cocktail Skips and stomped through the front room and up the stairs, making the light-shade shake as she went.

I got me can, lit a fag and started pulling some CDs out: Chris de Burgh for later; Westlife – can't go wrong there; Donna Summer – always gets them going; Michael Jackson, before e went weird. There was some good compilations an' all: *Ibiza Anthems* (try saying that when you've ad a few), we've even got a CD of *Music To Strip To* somewhere. That's got all sorts: 'Hey Big Spender', 'U Can't Touch This', all sorts, but I couldn't find it.

I put the Spice Girls album on cos it kicks off with 'Wannabe' and that always gets me in the mood cos it makes me think about when I was a teenager look, and I remembered the vodka (chasurr enneht?) so I tipped meself a big un and started bopping round the room, singing, '. . . tell you what I want, what I really really want . . .'

The next track was a slow one and I was shattered, what with the dancing and that, so I sat down and closed me eyes for five minutes. Fuck knows where Steve and the boys ad got to.

Little Shawnie's squealing and running through the paddling pool. '2 Become 1' is playing on the radio. Shawnie don't talk yet. She've only just turned four. She aven't got a stitch on and she's a skinny little sod. Our Jason's six now and e've got they little blue trunks on what our Ma give im. She give our Shawn a little pink bikini look, but I can't get er a keep it on when it's ot. They kids is looking fit and brown and lush. So's our Tony. E've got is City shorts on and nothing else which looks dodgy a me cos that charcoal on the barbecue aven't died down yet and there's fat and flames and all sorts. I got me Diamond White and Tony've got is Tennent's Super. E's alf pissed already (truth be known, so am I) and I'm worried they shorts is going up in flames, look. Be a waste of the best tackle in Bristol, that.

When I opened me eyes again I wanted to ear 'Mama' but I couldn't work out ow to skip tracks cos all they lights was blurring into a fuzzy mess. I ad a sip of me vodka but the bleeding glass was nearly empty. I reckons Shawnie must ave been pinching some cos there weren't no one else in the ouse and I've always got less than I should ave. I couldn't be bothered to yell at er again and there was still some left in the bottle next to the CD player. I managed to it eject and stop Sporty in full flow. I knew what I wanted: 'Everything I Do (I Do For You)' by Bryan Adams and a stiff one. In the absence of the boys it would ave to be vodka. Best way really. Must ave been nine-thirty and they still adn't got back.

'Look into my eyes . . .' You'd ave seen me filling up and I didn't know why.

'Evrayfen I do,' I sang, 'evrayfen I do . . .' and I drained another glass. Slipping down a bleeding treat it was. I was getting near the end of the vodka but I knew there'd be a load more coming and I ad plenty of White Ace in the fridge. I adn't even finished me can yet. It's alright, White Ace, if you chills it proper, look. It could wait. I tipped a big slug into me glass and splashed alf an inch of Coke in. God's own drink.

I needed a cheer meself up a little and I ad just the thing. It took me a bit of time to find it but when Bryan finished I looked through all the CDs and some of them went on the floor but I really didn't give a monkey's and I got the one I wanted in the end. I slipped it into the CD player and started singing along and practising me moves. Vodka dooz amazing things to your ips and mine were a-eaving from side to side in a way I knew would ave every fella in the room drooling.

'Oh my-y lurv. I can't take nuh nuh nuh nuh nuh-nuh. Oh my-y lurv . . .'

'Mahl, et sounds like yer be-ehn murdered or summat,' comes the shout from upstairs.

'Shut yer bleeden mouf an' eat yer pork scratchehns,' I shouts back and there's a pause before Shawnie yells down, 'Ow on earf am I supposed a do that, Ma?'

'You knows what I means, cheeky murr,' and I sings

twice as louder a drown er out. 'Deeply deppy ba ba-ba ba-ba, ba ba ba, ba-ba-ba-ba ba-ba. Deeply deppy ba ba-ba ba-ba . . .'

I moved me arse round in a big circle and bent over at the same time like they Jamaican girls you sees on Sky dooz. It looks dead sexy but I stumbled over a couple of times so I kept on practising till I got it right. I knocked me can over but I couldn't be bothered a pick it up cos I wanted a see what me arse looked like from behind so I went into the all cos there's a full-length mirror there but the only way I could see was to look between me legs and I got a right pervy glimpse before falling ead first into the wall which don't ave no wallpaper on it so I scraged it down the back. There was only a bit of blood and I figured that would be mostly idden by me air. Urt, mind.

I was knackered after all that so I sat down for a bit and lit up a Silk Cut and thought about that drop-dead gorgeous black fella Madonna ad in the church. (Our Ma wouldn't like *that* cos she always went on a Sunday, still do, far as I know.) I finished off the last of the vodka, splashed a little Coke in and sank right back into the chair. I was tired. Really tired. Of everything. I nearly missed me mouth but I still managed to drain me glass of the milk of eaven; elped stop me wondering where the ell Steve and the lads ad got to.

E've gone and burnt they burgers now. I bleeding told im, you gotta wait till the flames dies down and the charcoal goes white on the outside.

'Fuck eht,' e goes, slinging the burgers over the garden fence.

I'm lying face down on the big beach towel with Beavis and Butthead on it and I've got me little red bikini on and I ain't being funny or nothing but blokes can't take their eyes off of me when I wears that.

'You gotta wait a bet, lovurr,' I goes. 'Come and rub some suntan ento me back a meneht.' You gotta distract Tony sometimes, keep im sweet.

I must of closed me eyes for a bit cos when I opened them again I ad one of they fags made out of ash in me 'and an' the Madonna CD ad finished. I looked at me watch and the ash all fell on the carpet and it took me ages to figure out the time cos me eyes was bleary but it was really dark outside and I think it said ten to eleven. I checked me glass but it was still empty so I cussed Steve and is mates and walked to the bottom of the stairs.

'Shawnay,' I shouted, 'you a-bed?'

There wasn't no answer so she must ave been. I got a can of White Ace from the fridge, lit up a fag and put on a song that always makes me cry. Soon as I ears the first line, 'Goodbye English rose.' I knows it's about Princess Di and that but it's like it's for all of us. I was a bit pissed, truth be known and it seemed like it was just for me and the tears was fucking streaming down me face when I eard car doors and shouting and laughing and that outside. I rushed over to the CD player and it some buttons until the music stopped. I looked in the mirror in the all and I couldn't see fuck all but I ran me fingers under me eyes anyway to get the worst of the smears away. I'm waiting by the door. Check me air, check me tits. What the fuck were they doing out there? They'd stopped shouting but I could still ear laughing and that. I opened the front door and what did I see? One, two, three, four dicks. Three white, one black. All pissing on the old armchair outside. Used a be our Tony's chair.

'Fuck's sake, we do ave a toilet y'know,' and they starts sniggering and snorting and that.

'Well I ope you can manage betturr an that,' I went, looking down. 'Steck all they a-gevvurl and you might jus get one good un.' But, truth be known, I couldn't really see what they ad to offer.

'Right, doll,' goes Steve, 'you look a worse fackin state than us.'

'Ad a fucken pass the time some'ow. What fucken time jew call thehs?'

'Ah, we stopped fer a couple at the Railway, like, and we ad a bit a bovvah.'

'Right Lees?' goes Lee.

'Leesah,' went Norris, putting is dick away with one 'and and olding up a clanking carrier bag with the other, 'we gaht loobreecayshuhn.'

E made the word last for ever and I thought about the black fella in the Madonna video. Norris aven't quite got the body, mind: balcony anging over the toyshop these days. 'You betturr come en then, darlehn,' I goes. 'I opes yer ready a partay.'

'With you, always, Lisa my love,' and e planted a kiss on me cheek, squeezed me bum and came inside.

'Fucken smoov ur what?' goes Lee. 'Tell you what Lees, you looks fucken gorgeous,' e went, staring at me tits.

'A reeal womahn,' went Norris, eyes fixed on me arse as we walked into the front room.

'Yer quiet, Michael,' I goes. E always is and e stayed all quiet an' all cos e never said nothing which was a shame cos e've got a lush Irish accent, not like that fucking Paddy down the Venture.

Steve told me to fix some drinks while e sorted the music. E always likes a do that, it's a bloke thing, isn't it? Like cars and barbecues. I was doing the drinks in the kitchen, vodka and Cokes all round, and I eard the start of 'No Limit', 2 Unlimited. Me and me mates used a dance to this when Tony took us clubbing downtown. Our Ma would babysit and Tony would get pissed up and find a student to glass or stomp on. Always ad a spoil everything.

I used a get on with it: ave a drink and a dance and a giggle with me mates, but God elp any poor sod that come over a dance or chat me up. E ain't stupid, e always done it discreet, look. I saw im in action plenty of times but when e knew e could be seen e always eld back. This lush bloke ad been chatting to me once and I'd seen Tony's face and I saw im go into the Gents after im an' all. I knew what was gonna appen and I was only ten seconds after im but by the time I'd followed them in, this fella was face down in the urinal, with blood flowing over they little smelly, cubey things, Tony's foot's on the back of is ead and e ad a face what I never seen before. Never wanted a see it again neither. E was drinking piss through bursted lips and our Tony was smiling.

'We understans each uvvurr now,' e went and e grinned that fucking lush grin and put is arm around me and we walked out the door like we just ad tea at the Ritz or summat.

I used the Asda economy burgers box as a tray for the boys' drinks and it was wobbly as ell but I never spilt nothing even though I was moving to the beat already. Pays a get warmed up first.

'Get they down yer necks, lads. Oo's first fer a dance?' I started swinging me arse from side to side and waving me arms over me ead.

'No no, no no no no, no no no no, no no thurr's . . .'

'Dreenks can wait, mahn,' goes Norris and e jumps up and starts matching me ip gyrations. We turned our backs on each other, stuck our arses together and swung them both at the same time.

'Thurr's no lemeht.'

Lee gets up and dooz the same round me front so's I'm the meat in a sandwich. White and brown bread.

When I dances, the songs all merges into one and I loses track of everything but when Steve put 'Sex Bomb' on, I went over to Michael and gave im some good bump and grind a loosen im up, look. I started with me arse in is face (which must ave been quite a fucking view from is angle) then moved down south and did me lap-dancing routine. I soon felt some action down below and I turned round and said, 'Jus set back and enjoy, Michael, set back and enjoy.'

By the time Tom ad finished, Michael was the Lunch-pack of Knowle West. I sat down beside im, ran me 'and over is bits, stuck me tongue in is ear and whispered, 'Sort you out laturr, beg boy,' before jumping up, nearly falling into Steve, and shouting, 'Oo's fer anuvvurr?'

I don't mind saying I was a bit drunk but it was a party wasn't it?

I was aving a breather and a long cool one when Steve puts on 'I'm Too Sexy for My Shirt' and shouts, 'C'mon doll, less get fings movin ere,' and turned up the volume. I pulled up Norris and Lee. Lee was alf cut and started showing off. Norris began undoing is buttons and Lee pulled up is T-shirt to show off a beautiful little six-pack. Michael stayed where e was and said, 'Oi'm watchin the mineht,' in that lush accent of is.

'Less see what you've got, boys,' I shouted and finished Norris's buttons for im. E started rubbing is body like a stripper. I danced over behind im, pulled is shirt off and whooped. I grabbed is pecs from behind and rubbed is nipples while I moved with im.

'I'm a model, ya know whad I mean . . .' e sang and moved is 'ands over is fat belly and everybody laughed, even Michael.

'C'mon Lay,' I shouted and Steve started a 'Lay, Lay, Lay' chant. Well, it was just im and me really cos Michael was just staring and Norris was too busy groping imself.

Lee pulled is T-shirt over is ead like a footballer who'd just scored, and danced around blind for a bit. Lee's my age, twenty-nine, but e've got a lush body cos e dooz sport –

football and that. I moved in from behind and gave is abs and pecs a good seeing to. When e finally got is T-shirt off I planted me lips on is and we started the tongue dancing straight off.

'Where's mane den?' said Norris. 'Yuh wooden be leaven an old man to is oown devaces, now.'

I broke away from Lee, wrapped me arms around Norris's neck and whispered, 'Evray gurl knows the more mature man's the best lovurr,' and I give im some tongue an' all. E clamped is 'ands on me arse, groped around for a minute and broke away from me lips, laughing.

'Look at dis, boys,' e went, lifting me dress. 'Ain't a seengle ting keepen dis poonani warm,' and the others cheered.

'Not yet any'ow, eh Norrehs?' I said, pulling it down again. 'All en good time boys, all en good time,' and I noticed Steve ad put 'Like a Prayer' on.

I broke free and did the tit tsunami thing by jigging me ips and they couldn't look nowhere else and they kept cheering and whooping and that.

'Like a prayer, I will . . .'

I ran me 'ands up and down me body, then inside me dress and ooked me tits right out. They were all going nuts and I felt like Madonna or Britney. 'In the midnight hour . . .'

Outside of the dress they were bouncing all over the fucking shop and, truth be known, it was a bit painful but I kept it going cos of the effect it was aving on the boys. I shimmied over a Michael and bent over so's me tits were in is face and e grabbed one in each 'and. I thought I'd tease im a bit by yanking them out the way, turning me back on im and giving im the Jamaican arse dance. I bent right down so as me arse was me tallest bit and I don't know what appened but I just kept on moving and it was like slow motion but me face it the carpet and the rest of me followed and I was all over the bleeding shop.

'Like a prayer . . .'

Steve was pissing imself but Norris is a gent so e tried to elp but I couldn't seem to stop lurching around and taking im with me. E must ave tried loads of times but e couldn't get me to me feet so I sat on me arse and Steve goes, 'Gow on gel, you can do it,' and I reached up to Norris who grabbed me arms and pulled me alfway up and me legs gave way and next thing I knows, Norris is on top of me and everyone's wetting themselves.

Lee goes, 'Take et steady Norres, mate,' and auls me round and leans me against the settee what Michael was sat on and I ad to admit it *was* funny so I was laughing too.

'Less ave a breavurl eh?' I goes. 'Summat slow, Steve. Get us a vodkal an' Coke, Norres lovurr. Norry-babe. Nor-Norr.' We all wet ourselves laughing again. Norris got me drink and Steve put on summat slow by Robbie – 'Angels'. I closed me eyes and listened to the music. Taking it steady.

Little Shawnie's screaming cos our Jason ave splashed er but she's laughing as much as complaining and I just goes, 'Jason,' and lobs the Ambre Solaire at Tony who catches it and sits on me arse with is legs apart. E've got lush legs (e've got lush everything), you can see all is muscles and that but they ain't like a body builder's or nothing. Just – defined.

Our Tony squirts the Ambre Solaire onto me back and I just closes me eyes and listens to the radio which is playing 'Walking On Sunshine' – I don't know who it's by – 'and don't it feel good?' Tony squirts the suntan lotion onto me back and it feels ot cos it've been in the sun. E undooz me bikini top and I goes, 'Tonay,' but I ain't really moaning. E's rubbing it in and I tell you what, e knows ow a touch a lady. E've got strong 'ands and they goes all over me shoulders and me neck and me back and me arms and me sides and me arse and under me bikini bottoms and right into me crack and I goes, 'Anthonay,' and e whispers, 'Nevurr eard you complainehn lass night,' which is right enough but we was alone then.

'What about the kehds?' I goes and e goes, 'Thurr playehn. Any'ow, we ain't doehn nuffehn.'

E moves onto me thighs and e's going right up the top and e puts one thumb, then two in me fanny and I goes, 'Tonay,' but Jason and Shawnie are still playing in the pool and e moves onto me clit and I can't elp lifting me arse up a little to make it easier and fuck me, e knows what e's doing. The kids ain't seen nothing and Tony keeps going and going until I squeezes me buttocks together and grits me teeth to stop meself crying out loud when I comes.

'Yer a fucken bad man, Tonay MacCarthay,' I goes and e grins.

I says, 'I bet that barbay's readay,' but e don't ear cos e's calling to the kids: 'Jason, Shawnay, get yer asses ovurr yer, get some suntan on yer.'

Lee looked into my eyes. 'Yer back then,' e said, smiling. E must ave lifted me onto the settee.

'Fuck. Whurr's me fucken drenk to?' I went.

'Ere you go, Lees,' e said and e was groping me tits roughly with is other 'and.

'Take et steady, eh Lay? Ladays likes et gentle, look.'

'You want one Michael?' went Lee, pushing me left tit towards im with the flat of is 'and. Michael was sat on the other side of me and I couldn't see properly but I reached out and felt e still ad alf a ard-on.

'Ye carry on pal,' e said. 'Oy'll git moyn lader.'

Lee kept a-pawing at me and Norris went, 'C'mahn, yuh gotta shayuh, mahn,' and e gets up as Steve puts on 'I Will Always Love You' by Whitney.

'Can I ax you for de playsha of dis dance?'

I wanted a get away from the mauling I was getting but I wasn't certain I could stay on me feet, frankly.

'I ain't sure Norres. Fiy gets up I might fenesh flat on me back.'

'Tha's the plan, Lees,' went Lee.

'Don't worry, I'll lead.' Norris grins and olds is 'and out. I lets im pull me up and I wraps me arms around is neck.

'Ang abaht gel,' said Steve. 'Lift er arms up, Norris mate,' and e quickly pulled me dress over me ead and chucked it into the space behind the telly. I draped meself back around Norris's neck and rested me ead on is bare chest and e was a bit fat and that but it was nice. E was olding me up with one 'and and running the other over any bits of me naked body e could reach, especially me arse. I closed me eyes and let im grope me as we swayed slowly from side to side.

Tony's squirting the Ambre Solaire onto is left 'and, then rubbing them together and smoothing them all over our Shawnie's back and shoulders. Not missing an inch, massaging it in. Our Jason's watching and fidgeting cos e's getting bored already.

'Yer turn en a meneht, mate,' goes Tony as e delves into Shawnie's armpits, making er giggle. Then e slides is 'ands down er sides and over er little bum which e rubs and kneads for ages, sometimes letting a thumb slide right into the crack and making er giggle again.

You don't want a piss Tony off but I gotta say something. 'Tonay, she's only a lettle gurl.'

'She's fucken loven et, lestehn,' and e puts is thumb right between er buttocks and slowly over er arsehole and Shawnie squeals and giggles some more.

There's no stopping im in this mood: e's the orniest bugger what's ever lived.

E finishes the backs of er legs and starts on er front, paying loads of attention to er dear little nipples. Our Jason starts running off cos e's bored but Tony shouts, 'Jason, you fucken come yurr now an' watch. You'll be doehn thes a yer Mahl en a meneht an' I gotta learn yowe.' Jason's scared of im and e comes back.

'You jus done may, Tonay,' I goes. 'I don't need no more.' Wasting me breath, I know.

'E've gotta learn, aven't e? Ow a touch a laday, like,' and e's running is fingers, look, around Shawnie's little tuppence and she's giggling again.

'That funnay, Shawn?' E've got one 'and on er bum and one over er tuppence look, and is index finger disappears inside.

'Nice an' gentle, look lovurr,' e whispers and Shawnie ain't giggling no more and she just stares at im with big eyes. I daren't say nothing cos e'll just fucking swing for me or make me do summat vile.

E looks at what e's doing to our Shawnie and there ain't no sound except for is breathing.

'Nearlay yer turn, Jase, but we gotta lose some clothes first. Less play the ass smacken game. We're gonna smaaaack . . . SHAWNAY'S ASS,*' and e claps is 'ands near er bum and she runs off screaming and laughing. Tony pretends a lumber after er, really slow like a monster or summat, but really e's just making sure our Jason doesn't catch er too quick, like. Our Jason's giggling and trying a get round Tony. Shawnie's flapping along and stumbling. Tony catches our Shawnie just as she's falling and makes sure she don't urt erself. She lies face down on the grass, nearly wetting erself, and Tony smacks er left buttock, really gentle like.*

'You got the other un right?' e goes a Jason. 'Gentle Jase, gentle,' and Jason dooz what e says and just taps Shawnie's right buttock. 'Alright Shawnay,' says Tony, 'tha's eht, new game. Less smaaaaack . . . JASON'S ASS.*'*

Jason yells, 'NO,' and runs off, laughing like a maniac. Shawnie urtles after im but Jason's loads faster and she don't get close. 'Things Can Only Get Better' by D:Ream plays on the radio and I loves that song. Tony catches Jason and pins im down on is lap with is arse in the air and is feet kicking behind im. Shawnie squeals as she catches up and starts smacking Jason's backside. Tony goes, 'Ang on, Shawn, ang on lovurr. We gotta get ehs trunks off a meneht.'

Tony yanks them over Jason's backside. 'Pull, Shawn.'

Jason's shouting, 'Fuck off, fuck off, fucken betch,' but our Shawnie gets is trunks off and she's giggling like a loon (she've got a lovely laugh) as she drops them and starts smacking our Jason's little white bum while Tony olds is legs down.

'Fucken betch, fucken betch.' Jason's crying now.

Tony says, 'Tha's enough, Shawn,' and flips our Jason round so that e's sat on is lap. 'Fucken betch,' goes Jason and e tries to it Tony but Tony wraps Jason's little arms up in is left arm which looks brown and muscly and lush. Is right 'and rests over Jason's bits, look.

'Take et steaday, Jase, take et steaday, we aven't done everyone yet, ave way?' and Jason stops shouting when e realizes it ain't is turn no more.

'Less smaaaaaack . . . MUMMAY'S ASS,*' and I knows I gotta run and make a game of it or our Tony'll be angry so I starts legging it round the garden, and I don't ave no bikini top on so me tits is nearly knocking me out. I knows why our Dad used a call em knockers now. I can ear 'The Lady in Red' by Chris de Burgh on top of our Shawnie's squealing as she chases me. I loves that song. Tony lets the kids do the chasing while e sits in the middle of the lawn with a grin on is face an' is 'and down is City shorts.*

Our Jason's forgotten e's embarrassed about aving noth-

ing on and e've got old of me bikini bottoms and they're starting a come down when Tony sticks is foot out and sends me fucking urtling. I feels Jason's, then Shawnie's little naked bodies fall on top of me. They're laughing so much you'd think it was the best game ever.

'Get they kneckurrs off of er, keds. Gev er ass a good see-ehn to,' goes Tony.

I've got to let them. Our Jason pulls me bikini bottoms right off.

'Fat ass,' e shouts, 'fat ass,' and e's smacking it. My fat arse, really ard.

'Ass-ass, ass-ass,' goes Shawnie, in between giggles, and she's slapping away too.

I just gotta lie there, taking it, while Tony's 'and moves quicker in is shorts. Never seen nothing move so fast in City colours. I knows what's coming next.

'Less smaaaaaack . . .'

'I've never seen you looking so lovely as you did . . .'

I could ear the music. Me favourite song look, but it took me a little while to get me bearings.

OK. I was naked. I was on me elbows and knees. Me fat arse was sticking up in the air and me ead and me tits were all dangling onto the carpet and it felt wet and smelt of vodka and Coke. And cider. And filth. I lifted me ead up and, after a bit of struggling with the focus, I could see I was in me own front room; I could see Steve by the i-fi, drink in one 'and, mobile pointed at me in the other, grin on is face; I could see Michael on the settee, drink in one 'and, cock in the other, wanking imself off; I could see Lee letting is trousers and boxers fall to the floor and is lush cock was at ten o'clock already. That meant it must ave been Norris's cock I could feel inside me. E was pumping away from behind, slapping me arse with both 'ands as e done it.

'The lady in red is dancing . . .'

Well, I could remember dancing but not starting this. I tried a get in the swing of things. 'Bring et ovurl ere Michael, I'll do that fer yowe,' I went but e looked embarrassed and turned is face down. Kept on wanking, mind.

'I fink our Irish friend eey-ah likes to watch from a distance, Lees,' goes Steve, 'but Lee, e could use a 'and. Or a maaf.'

Lee waves is cock in me face and I knows what I gotta do so I grabs old with me mouth and starts sucking it ard. No point in nothing subtle when they're bevvied.

'Wot a maaf, wot a maaf, wot a norf an' saaf,' sings Steve, and e laughs at is own joke but no one else do.

I tries grabbing old of Lee's arse cos it's lush but Norris starts fucking me arder and I ave to put me 'ands on the floor again or fall over. Norris stops smacking me arse for a bit and moves forwards, grabbing me tits.

'Ahll womahn, ya mahn,' e goes but this fucks up the balance. I lunges forwards and Lee's cock goes alfway down me throat, right past me epi-whatsit and nearly makes me eave. I wrenches me ead to the side.

'Fuck's sakes, Norrehs. Take et steaday.'

'Leesah my love, apologees. Yuh perfic breasts were jus sweengen so provahcative,' and e gets old of me arse again and finds is rhythm. Comes natural to they, don't it?

I starts on Lee again, sucking, sucking . . .

'. . . DADDAY'S ASS!'

Our Tony's legging it slow motion round the garden. Shawnie's squealing cos she's getting over-excited but she's managing to follow im even though she falls over every twenty paces. Jason's showing a bit more nous and cutting corners and trying a ead im off.

'You'll never take I alive, coppurr,' goes Tony as e dodges our Jason again and makes sure e's close to our Shawnie

so that she can join in the game too. E can be lovely with they kids.

Our Jason's starting a get is air off and Tony sees this and knows e've gotta change summat. Shawnie falls over again and squeals on the lawn.

'Right coppurr,' shouts Tony, making is 'and into a gun and pointing it at Shawnie. 'On the fucken floor now or the betch gets eht.'

Jason dives to the ground, rolls twice and pulls out a pretend gun, pointing it at Tony. Fuck knows where e thought e'd been keeping it cos e never ad a fucking stitch on.

'Pkyow, pkyow,' goes our Jason, 'pkyow, pkyow, pkyow.'

With each 'pkyow' Tony tenses with pain, grabs a different part of is wiry brown body and gets driven backwards by the force of the bullets.

'Pkyow, pkyow.'

Tony sinks to is knees and Sharon next door smiles over the fence. I remembers that I'm naked but she never sees me. She've only got eyes for that lovely dad with the lush bod.

'Pkyow.'

Tony's face twists in pain as e falls forwards onto the paddling pool, dead. The water all gushes out the sides and our Shawnie slips in it and falls onto er Dad's back, laughing.

'Ass-ass,' she goes.

Our Jason's standing over Tony now with is finger-gun pointing straight at Tony's ead and is other 'and olding it steady. Just like e sees in Tony's videos. E sees allsorts in Tony's videos.

'Ass-ass.'

Shawnie's trying a yank Tony's City shorts down now and Tony sees Sharon turn away and go back towards the ouse so e lifts up is ips a bit to make it easier. Jason forgets is gun and starts elping Shawnie but they only goes down at the back cos at the front they're ooked over

Tony's erection. Tony reaches down to free them and Jason pulls them right off.

'Ass-ass,' shouts Shawnie and she's smacking Tony's lush backside. Our Jason joins in.

'RAAAAAGGGGHHHHH,' Tony roars and e flips over and grabs the kids who are both squealing now. It finishes with Tony calming things down by saying, 'Alright keds, tha's enough now,' and e sits there grinning in the paddling pool with an arm around one smiling kid on each thigh, gently rubbing their genitals. Our Jason's getting a little boner of is own and it looks so small and puny compared to Tony's grown-up cock sticking up between them. I knows e didn't oughta be doing that but I can't do nothing, can I, and e makes it seem alright the way e's sat there like, with the kids aving so much fun.

'Da-ad,' goes Jason.

'Eh's Tonay, Jase. I ain't yer Dad,' says Tony, 'but I loves you like I was,' and e kisses our Jase on the forehead, then e slaps them both on the thigh without listening to what Jason ave got to say and goes, 'C'mon, yer Ma's waiten fer er suntan.'

Tony jumps up and the kids runs over to me. I'm lying on me front on a towel, look, in case Sharon or er fella looks over again. I reckons they gone inside. No one ever sees what appens.

'I done er back,' says Tony, 'and I reckons eh's cooked. Whatchoo fenk keds?'

E puts is wet 'and between me shoulder blades and the kids puts theirs all over and I shouts out, 'Yurr, fer fuck's sakes. Yer fucken freezehn,' and the kids just laughs and Tony goes, 'Jus coolen you down, Lees.'

I sits up on me towel and keeps me legs together and tucks me knees up and covers me fanny with me feet and presses me tits into me thighs. It ain't like me to be bashful but I'm feeling it.

Tony goes, 'You gotta lie on yer back, Lees, and thenk of England. The keds'll see you right.'

I dooz what e says. You ain't got a choice, look.

'Shawn, thes ehs yer *job lovurr. You jus gotta drebble et ovurr er bellay a meneht, look,' and e shows er first, then e gives er the bottle of Ambre Solaire. Shawnie dooz really well and dribbles it all around me belly button, and Tony says, 'Right, nice one Shawn, tha's enough. Jason, you knows what you gotta do, don't yowe?'*

'C'mon Tone,' I says, 'e's only lettle. Anyway, I likes et best when you dooz eht,' and e swings is ead round and stares at me like some fucking ead case. I swear, is eyes looks like they're gonna come out of their fucking sockets when e loses it.

'You got summat a say, slag?' e shouts and everything stops and I ears 'Shine' by Aswad and I looks away and shakes me ead.

That orrible pause finishes when is face relaxes.

'Then everyfeng's alright, enneht?' e goes and smiles. On and off like a tap. 'Goo on, Jase.'

Our Jason starts sliding is 'ands around on me belly.

'Tha's a way, Jase, spread et round and rub et en, all the lettle nooks an' crannays, mind. Shawnay, squirt some on Mummay's boobays, look,' and she do cos our Shawnie understands loads more than what she says.

'Goo on, Jase. Shawn, come ere lovurr.'

My little boy's rubbing Ambre Solaire into my breasts. My little girl's being auled onto er naked Dad's lap. E puts er facing me so that is cock sticks out from between er legs like she've got a big ard-on. Shawnie likes to play with it, move the foreskin up and down and stuff. Tony likes it an' all. E starts olding er by the ips and sliding er along the length of is erection, then back again, 'Weee – eh's a slidurr, look Shawn.'

Shawnie giggles. I closes me eyes.

'Jase, yer a fucken starr, mate,' goes Tony with is 'ands all over our Shawnie. There ain't no stopping im in this mood. 'Jase, what yer Ma reallay loves, ehs when you feels er cunt, look. I'll show yowe.'

Tony puts Shawnie down and says, 'I'll be back wev you en a sec, lovurr,' and e gets up and I closes me eyes again cos I can't stand to look and I can't stop the tears. I feels 'ands split me legs apart and then start messing around in between and I guess Tony's guiding little Jason's 'and.

'Lettle man, what a fucken super-ero. D'worray bout er cryen, Jase, tha's what slags always dooz when thurr loven eht. What a fucken starr. SLAG – thurr's two good decks ere needs see-en to and you got two 'ands doen nuffehn.'

I gotta open me eyes to find little Jason's willy and e've got a ard-on same as Tony. I won't forget is face when e looked at me.

I felt fingers pinching me nostrils, stopping me breathing.

'Waykey waykey, gel,' goes Steve's voice. 'Grindin to a bleedin alt theyah.'

E stopped squeezing once I'd spluttered on Lee's cock and started doing the business again. Tell the truth, I'd ad enough and I was only fit for me bed now. Lee and Norris are lovely fellas and that but I was out on me feet and they was taking forever to come. I reckon our Jason's got a bit of a problem with that the other way look, cos that time e beat me up, then ad a wank look, e've shot is load in two seconds flat. Load of fellas dooz that.

Norris feels like e might be getting near mind, so I tries a tighten up, urry things along a bit. Lee always drinks more than Norris; I'm amazed e can get it up at all.

I closed me eyes cos I was getting sick of looking at Lee's airy belly. Didn't feel quite so sick with me eyes shut an' all. Lee's cock went in and out and in and out. So did Norris's. Shagging used a be a laugh, exciting look, but it don't do sod all for me now. When our Tony was slipping us a length . . . ahh, that was different.

Steve was singing along to the music: 'Olding back the years, chance for . . .' E've got a nice voice, Steve. Sounds like Peter Kaye in 'Amarillo'.

I likes Simply Red but Tony says Simply Red are shit and Mick Hucknall ad better fucking pray they don't run into each other. E wouldn't let me buy the CD. I couldn't do nothing without is permission: ave a can, turn the telly over, go see a mate, buy a Simply Red CD. I ad mates in those days but Tony couldn't be doing with that so e scared them off and made me stay in the ouse.

Our Shawnie's eating a burnt burger she've found next to the barbie.

'Shawn,' I says, 'get away from that barbay, love. You'll get burnt!'

'Lettle man,' goes Tony 'you are fucken Batman and Superman rolled inta one. Now watch thes; watch et close, mind.'

Our Tony makes me go down on me elbows and knees and e spits on is 'and an' rubs it around and e rams is cock inside me really rough a few times and I'm not even warmed up.

I thought, I don't wanna do this no more: this ain't fun, it ain't nice. I thought about our Ma. I thought about the nasty-tasting cock in me mouth. I eard Steve singing, 'Money's too tight to mention.' I could see im moving, dancing, even though I couldn't focus no more. I sucked arder and tried a tighten me fanny again to make it end quicker but it wasn't no good cos it wasn't never gonna end. Never gonna end.

Our Jason knows summat ain't right mind, cos I turns me ead round and I looks at im and I sees it in is face and there ain't tears in is eyes; there's summat worse.

'Fucken ell, you do et, Lees,' grunted Lee and e eld onto me ead and shoved is cock right down me throat making me retch. I looked up and I couldn't focus for ages but I started sucking again and when I got past the belly and the tangle of pubes I could see Jason's little face staring at me with that look only it weren't a little face no more and it couldn't ave been is dear little cock I could feel plugging me. Fuck knows where e come from. Steve was pissing imself laughing while I got me ead together and e put is arm round our Jason's shoulders and said, 'Fancy a gow, sahn? Everyone else as. G'wohn – is on the ahhs.'

I thought Jason might smack im one but e never, e just ran out the door and Steve couldn't stop laughing. He raised is face to the ceiling with is mouth open wide, unched is shoulders and done a little Michael Jackson move.

'Suck et Lees, I'm nearlay thurr,' goes Lee and e pushes is cock right into me throat again and that was when me body or me brain said, 'That's enough,' and me guts went into, whatsit, spasm like and I've just chucked me guts up. Emptied me whole fucking system. All over Lee: all over is bits, down is legs, filled is fucking pants for im. Last thing I knew was a load of swearing and a smack on me ead what must ave put me lights out.

Not a second too soon.

STEVE

a personal fucking request to the Almighty

'So this geezah right, walks into a bahh, and says, "I'd like a dooble ontondra, please," and the barmaid looks at im and says, "I'll give ya one."'

Nothing. Not a flicker. A broken church bell clanged in the distance and a tumbleweed rolled across the barren plains of the Bristol humour desert. Blank faces: Norris, Lee, Michael, that nutter Tone.

'Ya gotta streenj sense a umah bahs, no misteek,' went Norris.

Lee changed the subject. 'Tell you what, I'm well fucken pleased a see the back o' that Easay-Fet job,' he said.

I don't mind admitting that business ain't been too clever as of late. Seems like you're paying out as much as you're getting in and one cock-up, one ballsed-up order, one weather delay and your profit margin's out the bleeding window. Business had been pants and I'd been starting to wonder if I could make it through to when the money from Yeovil, my next gig, started coming in, but yeah, I was glad to get that fucking St Phillips job out the way an' all. That wasn't construction – that was a bleeding Meccano kit.

We'd finished on the Friday afternoon as luck would have it and it was on schedule too, thank God, cos you get all sorts of shit from Easi-Fit if you're even twenty minutes late on it. Me and some of the lads had piled into the Railway for a last bevvy. You should of seen Bob the landlord's face when he saw Tone was with us again, after last night. He glanced at his barman and put is hands on the bar, making me wonder if he had something underneath it.

'Right chief?' said Tone, all chirpy like but with a challenge in his eye. Bob didn't say nothing and Tone's expression hardened.

'Tone mate, grab us that table,' I said quickly. 'Pint a rough, yeah? Norris, Michael – cold Guinness, yeah? Lee – Kroney?' The lads were all, 'Nice one, cheers boss.' As I got to the bar I raised my hands, palms forward.

'Bob, don't look at me like that. It's a quiet pint, yeah? E's on a tight rein, right? No probs.'

'I ain't aven et, Steve. If that nutturr kecks off, I'm fucken aven em,' said Bob.

'Don't talk soft, Bob, but listen – nuffink's kickin off. Just take me money mate: two cold Guinness, two Kroneys and a pint a rough, and ave one for yaself, yeah?'

'Very kind Steve, I'll ave a Scotch. And you keep *that* on a lead, alright?'

'No probs, Bob.'

Tell you what, that first pint slipped down in no time so I said, 'Go on, Tone, s'gotta be yours.' Norris raised his eyebrows at me but when Tone got up I said, 'Listen, it's bettah nah than when e's got a few pints inside im, innit?' and I was right cos Tone got his round in and there was nothing more than a bit of powderpuff eyeballing and he come back with the bevvies.

'Nice one, Tone,' I said. 'Chiz. No problem wiv our mate then?'

'Why should thurr be a problem, boss?' he said, fixing me with those eyes, and I didn't like the way he said 'boss'.

'No reason, Tone mate, no reason. Jus gahn fra Jimmy, yeah?' and I left the diplomacy to Norris for a bit.

I was standing there in the khazi, dick in hand, when Michael come in. He's a funny sod: I've worked with a load of Irish and he's the only Irish I ever met who isn't known as Paddy or Mick. I mean, his name's Michael for God's sake. Says it all really. He don't talk a lot, Michael, which is alright with me but I wouldn't give him the time of day if he wasn't paying for whatever the hell it is he gets out of watching other fellas with Lisa; apart from repetitive strain injury of the wrist, that is. I guess it's like porn; live porn. Sex by proxy so it ain't threatening or something like that. That's assuming you find sex threatening in the first place, ain't it? Myself, I'd feel threatened by having a Sherman in front of someone else but each to his own and all that.

'Right Michael,' I went as he unzipped and got hold of his old fella, 'gettin some practice in then?' The day he cracks a smile at something I say, I swear I'll plant a kiss on his lips. The day I make anyone laugh in this humourless fucking town. And, come to that, I can't remember the last person I kissed. Just have a think about the sweat-soaked, ashtray-mouthed, stale-cider-breathed Lisa: well, would you snog it? Sometimes I think of me old Ma, on her deathbed – even then, she had more dignity than Lisa, although the last months weren't pretty. She wouldn't have social services in the flat so I had to nurse her till she went into hospital. That's no job for man – for a boy – but I done it. Compare that to the lovely Jason. I've come home early and found Lisa hiding in the bathroom with the door locked she's so scared of him. I ain't scared of you Jason, pal. I'm just waiting for a chance to make my move, and when I do . . . God help you, son, God help you.

Michael had vanished and I was just stood there with me dick hanging out. Sometimes the world stops still while me memory does overtime. When I got back to the table, Tone was leaning back with a roll-up and a sceptical look, listening to the others extol the virtues of the lovely Lisa.

'Skeen lake a peach, mahn,' said Norris.

'Tets like you nevurr seen, mate.' That was Lee.

'Aaah, de rollen cahntours of er backsade. Wahnce a man bin dehr, e can die wi a smale ahn ees face.' Norris liked getting poetic, especially about Lisa's arse.

'Spreads et about a beht, do shay?' goes Tone.

'She genrahs weeth de bounty Gahd bless er weeth,' goes Norris.

'So out of what, eleven men on the last job, ow manay's slepped er a lengf?' goes Tone, ever subtle.

'Woss it to you?' I goes, instantly regretting my tone. 'Ain't like you're intrested is it?'

'Nevurr said I wan't entrestehd, nevurr said that. I jus likes a know whurr a ole's behn, fore I gevs et one.'

'You up fer it then, Tone?' I said.

'Yeahl, I reckons eh's time I got to greps wev the best shag en Brestol.' Sarcastic wanker.

I had something to say to Tone and I was dreading it, so I figured that this was as good a time as any what with the other lads about.

'Tone, listen mate. Don't take this personal or nuffink but I can't use ya on the Yeovil job.' I'd sorted a job converting an old village school into yuppie flats. (Do they have yuppies in Yeovil?) Proper building work, not like fucking Easi-Fit, but I needed a smaller outfit who could work up until Christmas. 'Tone, it's economics, mate; I ain't makin fack all on the Easi-Fit job after I've paid you lot and this un needs some serious plumbin and electrical work an' all. I've gotta ave a smallah crew and you're the last in mate. Last in, first ahht innit? It ain't just you; I can't use Dean or Barry neevah. It's nuffink personal mate and I'll give you a bell soon as sumfink bigger turns up after Christmas.' I was babbling cos I was nervous and Tone was just fucking staring at me and not saying a dicky bird. 'Tell you what, Tone,' I gibbered, 'less call tonight a freebie, special introductry offah an' that. No ard feelins like.'

'I bet you knows all about ard feelehns, don't you pal.' It was Bob's voice from behind the bar. 'Like feelehn prisonurr FF8282's big black cock up yer ass.' I swear the pub went silent.

'Bob, fer fuck's sake . . .' but I didn't finish cos I didn't know what the fuck to say. I mean he might as well have just ripped his own throat out and be done with it. Bob was going to die and Tone smiled. Sweet fucking Jesus, Tone just smiled.

'Fuck it, Tone,' I went, 'don't let im get to ya, it ain't fuckin wurf it mate,' and I jumped up and slapped him on the shoulder: it was like slapping stone. 'Cahm on, less gow ovah the Midland. It's appy ahr nah.'

The others drained their glasses and got up sharpish. 'Yeah, c'mon Tone,' went Lee.

'Alright mate,' went Tone, 'jus taken me glass back.' He drained it.

'Don't worry baht that,' I went. 'Wossa fuckin bar staff for anyway?'

'Well, tha's jus what I was wonderen, boss,' went Tone, getting up. 'I'll be right wev yowe, yeah?'

Me mouth opened but nothing come out. Tone reached the bar with the glass in his right hand (H-A-T-E) just as Bob was reaching beneath it and I could see what both of them was planning and I could see that Tone had been set up. Still smiling, Tone thrust the empty pint glass towards Bob's face just as the half-sized baseball bat Bob had been hiding under the bar came swinging towards him. Bat and glass met over the bar and there was a fucking explosion of glass and blood straight off and Tone cussed and brought his hand sharpish into his midriff. Bob swung again, twice, and caught Tone on the head and shoulder and Tone went down. I noticed the other barman was holding a baseball bat an' all but he didn't use it.

Tell you what, Bob's a fat middle-aged yokel but he lifted that little hatch in no time, come through and got a proper kick in to Tone's head as he was trying to get up and Tone went down again with blood pouring out of his nose. That's when Lee got to Bob and pinned his arms to his sides. 'Leave et thurr mate, tha's nuff.' If he'd been Tone's mate he'd have lamped him and Bob was clearly relying on this. I'm not sure Tone's got any mates. It don't take people long to figure out what's bad for their health.

Tone was getting up but the fight had gone out of him cos even he could see that his hand was fucked up something evil. The rest of him wasn't too pretty neither, come to that, but the palm of his H-A-T-E hand was slashed diagonally through to the bones and an arterial spurt was spraying anything within three foot of him. Tone waves his hand at Bob, who still had his arms pinned, and he's still smiling and he says, 'Yer a fucken dead man, pal, a fucken dead man.'

I've seen arterial bleeds before and I know you gotta stop em straight off or you're in trouble.

'Tone, *you're* a fuckin dead man few keep wavin that 'and arahnd. Few wanna make old bones, sit on that fuckin chair, *nah*,' and he must have heard something in me voice cos he did. Lee had let go of Bob but he was still watching him warily. I said, 'Michael, 999 nah on your mobile, tell em it's an ahhterial bleed. Tell em e's dyin. Bob, I ain't fuckin kiddin. Less you wanna be done fer manslaughtah, give us a fuckin beer towel nah,' and everyone done what they was told. I rolled the beer towel up tight, got Tone to grip it as hard as he could and hold his hand up over his head. Then I grabbed his fist and squeezed it even tighter.

Claret was still coming down his arm but the worst of it was stopped and I knew Tone would be alright as long as the ambulance didn't take for ever. He was still smiling at Bob. 'Dead man,' he mouthed. I was thinking maybe I didn't fancy going down the pub with Tone again.

The world seemed to stand still for five minutes until the paramedics come and they were brilliant. None of that shit you get in *Casualty* when things get ten times worse as soon as they arrive. They had him strapped up and in the ambulance on the way to the BRI in less than three minutes.

'You can fucken clear out you lot, I don't want you en yurr no more,' said Bob.

'Believe it or not Bob, me old muckah, the feelin's mew-chul. Dunno baht you boys,' I said turning to the lads, 'but I could do wiv a double wiv me next pint. Midland?' They agreed. I was bleeding lagged in Tony's blood but that was alright cos I always keep a change of clothes in me car. I hit the Midland with a clean pair of kecks and a song in me heart cos I didn't have to put up with that nutter no more. Lee got them in and although I'd told Lisa we'd be back at nine, I figured she could entertain herself, what with the pony I'd give her this morning, so we had a good session and rolled out at closing time.

I know it's illegal and that but I tell you what, I'm a bleeding immaculate driver when I've had a few, straight up, I handle that motor like Nikki fucking Lauda. We piled into the Merc and I drove back to Knowle West, taking the Spine Road, Bath Road, Broad Walk route cos there's less chance of getting pulled that way.

Let's be honest here, Lisa's never exactly sober but the fucking state of her when we got back: she was rolling about like there was an earthquake; she'd been crying (natch) so there was mascara smeared all over; she was just about wearing this little stretchy red rag that would have looked amazing on a skinny fourteen-year-old tart but on her it just about covered the spare tyres round her middle and that's it; she couldn't hardly stay conscious for more than ten minutes at a stretch and the boys couldn't get enough. They must have sad fucking lives. Gimme a skinny fourteen-year-old tart any day. I kept meself well out of it and concentrated on keeping good sounds coming: Madonna, Whitney, Britney. Classy stuff that that scum-sucker Jason would heap scorn on but fuck it, who cares about him? He was too scared to even come home by this time.

I took a swig and allowed myself an indulgent smile; there's not many bosses like me but I reckon you gotta look after your workforce. The boys had had a few bevvies and now they were getting their money's worth: Michael giving himself a good seeing to (what does he get from that?), Norris going in the tradesman's entrance and Lee giving Lisa something to chew on. Everyone doing their favourite thing and all was right with the world.

I was sipping me vodka and Coke and mentally counting me rogan when it got even better; fuck me, did it get better. Tell you what, if I'd put in a personal fucking request to the Almighty it couldn't have been sweeter. I heard the front door go and in he walked: Jack the Blad, low-life of the year, the lovely Jason. His face was a fucking treat – I'd pay a hundred pound to see that boat again. He come in on his toes, all fucking Naseem Hamed-like and sees his dear old Ma getting roasted. I said, 'G'won Jase, ave a go, on the ahhs,' and I nearly fucking wet meself laughing until that filthy slag, that putrid fucking hunk of pig meat, only went and brought her fucking guts up. All over Lee. He jumped back saying, 'Fer fuck's sake,' and he had phlegm hanging off of his prick and second-hand vodka and Coke running down his legs into the trousers round his ankles. The only good thing was that Jason looked like he was gonna cry – again – and he ran out. At least he saw it but this was fucking serious; I mean, how could I charge money for that?

It's all a bit hazy after that to be honest but I remember Lisa was still retching and only semi-conscious. Someone was shouting something, I suppose it must have been me as I give her a smack. I hardly fucking touched her and if any tart had ever fucking asked for it, she'd fucking asked for it, but she went out cold.

'Fer fuck's sake, Steve,' went Lee.

'Lay, Lay mate. We'll get you cleaned up an' I'll make it up to ya,' I said.

'What you gonna do, suck me off?'

'Less tink about de ladee farst,' went Norris with his knob waving about in the air. He pulled his pants and trousers up, then felt for a pulse in her throat. 'She need to rest, we'll get her on de sowfa.'

'Fuck de ladee,' went Lee.

'We jus warr,' said Norris, 'fah Steve punch er lates out.'

'I nevah punched er – it was flat of me ahnd. I ardly fackin touched er.'

'Elp me get er on de sowfa,' said Norris and I did. Nearly fucking did us in an' all. 'She want a blanket or a duvet, now.'

Norris was getting on me tits but there weren't no point in arguing so I went up and got Jason's duvet and covered her up with it. She had drool and puke coming down her cheek. I brought down some of Jason's trousers and pants for Lee an' all cos they're about the same size. And a Man U towel to mop himself down with – seemed appropriate.

Michael was wiping himself clean with his hankie and I wondered which bit of that sordid scenario had finally finished him off.

Lee had changed and left his old clothes on the floor and he was heading for the front door, saying, 'I ain't fucken payen a be thrown up on, boss; sorry but I wants me monay back.'

I said, 'Lay, ang abaht mate, ang abaht.'

Norris said, 'Steve, Leesa can keep de vodka but I wahn me money back too.'

Michael didn't say nothing.

'Ang abaht boys, yer gettin previous. The night's but a puppy, my friends an' you'll get more than ya money's wurf.'

Look, I know it ain't on. I know. What the hell was I supposed to do? I mean, you can't let people down and Lisa had let em down big time. There was seventy-five sovs slipping out of me hands and I wasn't gonna let that happen. I had a good long think on it for about a second and a half and said, 'Cahm on boys, folluh me,' and we headed up the stairs.

JASON

Shawnie sucks

Scott One's 'and ad started a swell up summat wicked round the knuckles of is little finger and ring finger and e went a orrible colour like e was gonna throw up or summat. Fair play, e's normally that colour, but e got even worse, look. We dropped im at the Walk-In and started off towards is Ma's. I still wasn't getting nowhere with er but I adn't ad a proper chance yet and I still fancied me chances look, so I figured that maybe with Scott being out the way and Aimee round at er mate's (which she *always* was) I was in with a good shout.

'We den't jus ferget es monay, Phel,' I went as we turned the corner from Downton into Leinster, 'we never ad es skateboard neevurr. Bet thass wurf a few bob, ehs Murcan.'

'Well we couldn't reallay ang round, could us, be-ehn as ow you might ave jus kelled the cunt.'

'Don't talk shet, Phel,' I said, 'e jus needs a few stetches.'

'A few stetches?' shouts Phil. 'You fucken scalped em, man.'

'Aww Phel, be honest. That uz dog's – that uz fucken seprert.'

'Fucken seprert alright. I might bay an accessray a fucken murdurr now.'

'Phel, e ain't dead. E's jus aven a bad air day. I rang ehs Mahl an' that den I?'

'Yeah, that uz so kind. Yer seck, Jase, yer fucken seck. I means eht. I ain't worken wev you no morr. Yer gonnal ave may put away.'

It wasn't like Phil a lose is nerve. Im and Shawnie ave always been the only cunts I could rely on.

'Phel, you goehn fucken soft or summat? E was a cunt – e ad et comehn. Fenk ow manay cunts you done ovurr.'

'Yeahl, I done em ovurl. I beat em up, nutted em, kecked em. I never fucken scalped em, ded I? I never fucken destroyed thurr faces wev me size tens. That fucken Pakay we done, eh's onlay en the fucken papers enneht? Fucken *Evenehn Post*, page two.'

'Shut uhp! Fucken dog's, man. I gotta get one.'

'Eht ain't fucken dog's,' says Phil. 'They got our descreptions en em? Two white youfs, one black. Jamaican and local accehnts. One a the white cunts got a fucken black eye. The cunt what pestol-whepped the Pakay. Eh's down thurl en black and white. I don't even know why I'm fucken talken a yowe.'

'What the fuck jew mean, pestol-whepped the Pakay? I jus pointed me fengurl at the betch fer fuck's sake.' I couldn't believe that one. 'Lessen Phel, you don't sound vuray Jamaican a may. Don't you worray yer prettay ead mate. We torched the car, den us? They ain't got nuffehn.'

'That Pakay've got a smashed eye socket, Jase. E've lost the sight en one eye.'

'Sence when ded a bruvva gev a fuck about anay Pakay? E's a cunt, e ad et comehn.'

'You blinded the Pakay, Jase; you scalped the skateboardurr; you glassed that student outside the Enterprise; you repped that kedday from Cardeff's eyeled en alf, then mash up ehs face. You forgets a fucken rob em these days cos you jus wants a mash em up; yer a psycho, mate. You ain't sexteen yet, what you gonna move on to?'

'All outsidurrs,' I said. 'No cunt round ere messes wev I,

do em? What am I gonna move on to? Five yurrs from now, I'll be runnen thes fucken estate, Phel, an yer gonna be by me side, mate.'

'Ave you not eard of the McNabs? An' the Becks? Yer en cloud fucken cuckoo land, pal. Yer gonna be enside or sex feet underl an' I ain't gonna be by yer side or anywhurr fucken near you when you arr. Yer on yer own, mate.'

E was serious. I couldn't believe it. We were stood outside the Venture and I was just taking in is rant and I never noticed what was appening around us cos fuck me, before I knows what's what, Kerry-Ann, Siantell's mate, jumps out of fucking nowhere and starts fucking smacking me around the ead and screaming all sorts. I mean, she was ysterical, spitting and scratching and that. What was I supposed a do? You never its girls so I shoved er in the chest with the flat of me 'and (tiny tits mind) and she went back a couple of steps and then fucking flew at me again. What the fuck was I supposed a do? You gotta protect yourself, ain't you? I means that's the fucking law an' that so I give er a smack. *She* was attacking *me* for fuck's sake. I knows you ain't gotta it girls and ladies and that but *she* was attacking *me*. So I give er a little smack. Just the one but girls are crap at taking a punch and she went down like a sack of shit. Black Phil stepped between us and grabbed me by the shoulders and said, 'Fucken lave eht.'

I said, 'Fuck off Phel. I nevurr fucken done nuffehn.'

Kerry-Ann got to er feet and looked at the blood she'd just wiped from er mouth with the back of er 'and.

'Go on then, beg man. Tha's all yer fucken good forl enneht? Urten girls.'

She was mouthing off but she wasn't gonna fight no more. I looked past er and saw Siantell on the other side of the road outside the school. She was crying buckets man. She ad make-up all over er face and you couldn't ardly ear what she was shouting.

'Kehr, fucken lave eht Kehrl. I don't want a see ehm, I don't want fucken nuffen a do wev ehm. Lave eht.'

Kerry-Ann turns to Black Phil and shrieks, 'D'you know ow yer mate gets ehs kecks? Do yowe? Do you know yer mate's a fucken rapehst?'

She turns and crosses the road, back to er mate, without looking. Phil looks at me and I'm putting the pieces together in me ead, look.

Bang out of order. No way, no fucking way am I taking that. For fuck's sake, I never eard er complaining the other night. Well, a little bit at first but that's part of it innit? Girls like that likes a bit of spice. A bit of male dominance and that, but no fucking way is Jason Brewer a fucking rapist.

Siantell looked at Kerry-Ann's mouth and wiped some more blood away with a tissue or summat. They put their arms around each other and ugged and went off down towards Ilminster Avenue all over each other. Fucking dykes. Ell of a pair of tits on that Siantell mind, and just enough ass a get old of.

'Look at the fucken ass on that, Phel,' I went. 'Siantell mind, not Kerry-Ann. She jus fucken mental. Magehn that squirmen round underneef yowe.'

Long pause. 'Like I says,' goes Black Phil, all quiet, 'yer on yer own mate,' and e walked off the other way towards Inn's Court.

So there I was. On me own. I really wanted a see Shawnie but I couldn't risk running into that Cockney cunt so I eaded back to Scott One's ouse. I walked slowly while Black Phil strode off in front of me.

Sharon ad er keys in er 'and when I got back and she looked at me with er ead on one side and a disbelieving look in er eye when I tried to explain what ad appened.

'We were messen about on thes skateboard,' I said to er,

'and your Scott comes off awkward like, and urts ehs 'and, look. I reckons e've broke a fengurl or summat.'

'Oh e ave,' says Sharon. 'E've broke ehs lettle fengurl an' e've got severe bruisen of the knuckles, only *e* says e got ehs 'and slammed en a door and tha's what done the damage. Called I on ehs mobile, den e? Funnay that; I knew e was lyehn and I knows yer lyehn an' all. You wouldn't know the troof fet ran up yer trousurr leg and bit yer left bollock. I'm taken me lettle boy down the BRI now, Jason, and when I gets back, yer stuff's all gonna be packed an' gone an' so ur yowe. No argument. Bye bye.' Cobby bitch.

No chance of a shag then? I nearly said it. She slammed the door behind er. All I seems a see these days is the backs of people.

No point pushing it. I packed me stuff: clean and dirty clothes; one bottle of Gordon's gin; ten packs of Marlboro Sharon adn't shifted yet; fifty-five pound in cash she'd carelessly left in er kitchen drawer; two pairs of er knickers, for no reason I could think of; an iPod I knew I could fence easily; and a nearly full bottle of Baileys Irish Cream which I figured might elp that fucking awful gin slip down a bit easier.

Scott Two's a prat but I needed a place a kip and I figured I wasn't in a position to be fussy. E've ad the living crap kicked out of im by is stepdad for years now and on is sixteenth birthday e moved out and moved in with a bunch of druggies in a fucking ovel over Padstow Road. I don't like that end of the estate but I didn't ave no choice. Full a druggies. Druggies are the pits, druggies are so fucking dull they makes you want a die. They nicks anything that isn't nailed down and they can't think about nothing else and they can't talk about nothing else. This lot ad taken over this ouse over Padstow which Sarah and er old bloke ad started living in. I knew her vaguely from Merrywood. She was three years older than me and she ad a littl'un – boy I think. Er fella was long gone (can't blame im, she's a right slapper; decent tits, mind) and she was just living in filth, fucking shit-pit. Didn't ave a clue. The place was that fucking squalid that the whole tone was raised by a bunch of druggies moving in. I don't think they wanted a lose their more discriminating customers so they actually cleaned the place up a bit – give themselves somewhere decent a deal from. Sarah always done whatever she was told so she soon got into it. There was always gonna be someone she could suck off for a fix. Scott robs cars mostly for is. I-fis and CDs and that.

You never knew exactly who or ow many people would be dossing there but I knew Scott Two would be. I negotiated me way past the furniture and piles of rubbish out the front but when I got to the door it was all boarded up even though there were lights on inside. I knocked then stepped back and after a bit Scott Two's face appeared at the one window that the grille ad been kicked off of.

'Jason mate, come round the back, yeah, the door's fucked.'

There's a little archway shared with the ouse next door which I walked down, crunching on the broken glass. Scott opened the kitchen door and said, 'Jase, you finelay come round. Word's out yer Shawnay's doehn the business these days, Jase. Nice one. Might ave to come to an arrangement thurr.'

'Yeah, we'll sort summat. Scott, lessen,' I went, 'I ain't gonna bullshet you mate, I needs place a stay. Nuvvurr night round ours I might fucken murdurr that cunt Steve.'

'Jase, feh's jus the one night you got the floor mate, you knows at but anay more an' you gotta cough up like the rest of us.'

Right, cos you always pays rent on boarded up ouses.

'No problems mate, I knows a score,' and I did. E was

angling for cash or summat for imself but I wasn't giving that wanker fuck all. 'Ask us en, yeah?'

'Alright Jase. Lessen, Moxay and Sabrina fucked off someplace a week ago and they ain't paid nuffen for loads longurr, so far as I'm concerned thurr's a room but you gotta pay up front mind.'

'I ain't payen you a fucken pennay, cunt. Et ain't yer ouse.'

'Jew want a fucken roof over yer ead?' e went and then Jez appeared. Jez: posh once, Junky of the Year 2003 – gone down ill a bit since then.

'Jason, alright? I eard mate, I eard. Look Jason, you give us something up front, for Sarah yeah, cos it's her house and then there's no problem.'

For Sarah, right. I fished Little Skate Boy's mobile out and 'anded it to Jez.

'Posh or what,' goes Scott, 'fucken nice one,' and e tries a take it from Jez's 'and but Jez turns is back on im and keeps pressing the keys to make sure it's working.

'That'll do for starters, my friend,' e goes and e pockets the mobile and stands back so that I can get in.

'Keep these coming and we won't have to worry about rent. Up the stairs, first left after the bathroom.'

Jeremy my friend, you keeps forgetting a drop your haitches. We ain't in Sneyd Park now, pal, I thought but I said, 'Cheers mate, nice one,' cos wankers slumming it like im love being called 'mate' by genuine low-lifes like me. Makes them feel 'street', as Jez would say.

My room – for fuck's sake. Say what you will about Shawnie, she keeps the place clean. My room still ad Moxy and Sabrina's pathetic belongings in it: cheap tape player, no tapes; some clothes that were fucking minging and would ave to go, straight off; six Pot Noodles; a rucksack lined with silver foil (like no one's gonna see *them* coming) and a shit-load of little silver foil wraps, scattered round the floor like the opposite of confetti. The bed was a mattress on the floor with a duvet that I wouldn't sleep under if you put a gun to me ead. I made up me mind to ead off back to my ouse and pick up a few ome comforts while everyone was asleep. The duvet and the clothes went straight out the window and I opened all the others an' all cos of the smell. Council ad only put grilles on downstairs for some reason, like that's going to do any good. They dooz upstairs an' all these days.

I made a mental list of the stuff I would need: duvet; my booze stash; our Ma's booze stash; clean clothes (ow the fuck was I gonna *keep* em clean?); any cash that wanker Steve ad left lying around; food, if I could find any, and a ug with our Shawnie – I was missing that girl already. I ad everything else I needed except sounds but there was no point bringing me portable round, or CDs come to that. They wouldn't last the weekend. I'd ave to see if I could dig up some old cassettes for that shitty little tape player; you really couldn't sell that.

I sat on the bed, tipped meself a large gin and Baileys and lit up a Marlboro. The second it died, I stuffed it into the blackened Coke can at the side of the bed and lit up another to drown out the God-awful stench in that room and to take away the taste of gin and Baileys Irish Cream. Ave you ever tasted gin and Baileys? Don't. Tastes like girl's puke. Dooz a job, mind. After a couple of they, I was up for anything. I don't wear a watch but it must ave been the early hours and I reckoned they'd all be asleep, our Ma, Steve and Shawnie that is. I put me jacket on cos it was nippy for July.

I got downstairs and Jez and is mate were watching bad porn on Channel 5. Might as well ave been the *Teletubbies* for all they were getting from it.

'Jez, I'm off mate. I ain't got a fucken key a get ehn,' I went.

Jez looked up and took some time to focus on me. E nodded wisely and looked back to the telly.

'Jez, are you gonna be erel or what?'

Jez went through the focusing and nodding thing again.

I raised me voice and spoke slowly. 'Jez. Ur you gonna be ere when I gets back en an ourl or so?'

'No need to fucken shout at us, man. You can keep a civil fucking tongue in your mouth, can't you?' e slurred. 'Yeah, I'll be here.'

'I needs a fucken key, man,' I said and Jez started the focusing thing again. I eaded out the door before e got there. Life's too fucking short a wait for druggies to get their shit together.

I tell you what I was looking forward to most as I walked back to my ouse and that was that cuddle with our Shawnie. I was thinking about that and I didn't even check out the place before putting me key in the front door and going inside. That was when I eard that fucking awful music our Ma and Steve always plays and I knew I must ave been eard so I put a spring in me step and made a cool entrance into the semi-darkened front room.

I don't wanna even think about what I saw our Ma doing and I don't know why it came as a surprise, even with four fellas. One of them was Black Phil's dad, one of them I never knew, one of them was aving a wank just where I always sits a watch telly and one of them was that cunt Steve who was plastered and e put is arms round me and slurred some bollocks e reckoned was fucking ilarious. I should ave smacked im one but I wasn't gonna risk it with three of is mates there. Tell you what, mind, I was more certain than ever that e was gonna get some. Get it good.

I turned a walk out (which was all I could do – the gear would ave to wait till another day) and as I did, the pig dressed up as pork . . . ahhhhh, it's too fucking gross. Too sad. I don't even wanna think about it.

Our Ma. My Mum. Mummy.

Steve was still laughing as I slammed the front door.

The good thing about browns is, you just don't give a fuck. Don't give a fuck about nothing, not even yourself. Everything's alright, safe, sorted. I'd only done it twice cos I ates druggies, so the bad thing is, you chucks your guts up worse than our Ma with a mouth full of sweaty cock. There you go, I told you now.

Jez was so kind, bless; Jez was so elpful. E couldn't take me tenner fast enough and e was only too appy to cook up for me and share is scabby works. E kept them in a greasy money belt under is shirt.

'You want me to do it for you?' e goes and I nodded cos I'd only ever smoked it before. Sick as a dog both times but I reckoned I was probably gonna throw up that fucking awful gin and Baileys anyway so I didn't much care.

'This your first?' goes Jez.

'First wev a needle,' I goes.

'You've been pissing in the wind, mate,' e goes. 'You're in for a treat.' He tied some flex round me arm above the bend and tweaked a air or two in the knot. 'You'll feel a bit of a prick,' goes Jez and e snorts and falls forward into me shoulder and nearly bloody wets imself.

'Well you fucken concentrate, ya junkay cunt,' I goes.

'No need to get needled,' goes Jez. I eard is mate blow snot out is nose and I could feel Jez shaking with laughter.

'Fuck's sakes get on wev eht, Jez mate,' went Jez's mate. 'E'll fucken pass out wevout anay elp en a meneht.'

'Yeah, get on wev eht, Jez mate, fore way all dies laaffehn.'

I closed me eyes when I felt the needle enter the vein. Jez fucked around for a few seconds before I felt the needle come out again. E loosened the flex and pressed is thumb down on the entry point. E rubbed it gently and I felt the rush, felt the it, felt the total fucking relaxation of body an' brain, felt the nausea, felt the floor it the back of me ead, felt the wave overwhelm me an' it was just the best, like fucking Siantell from behind, multiplied by scalping Little Skate Boy, an' then some, an' then some. Dog's.

I eard Jez talking and is mate laughing and I didn't give a shit. This voice went, 'Fucken ell, fucken amachurrs,' and I didn't give a shit, just like I didn't give a shit about Jez, or is mate, Little Skate Boy, or the Paki, or Scott One, or Siantell and Kerry-Ann, or Black Phil, or Steve, or our Ma, or even Shawnie. Didn't give a monkey's about nothing.

Until the next day, when I woke up alone on the floor of me room and I felt like shit on a stick. I looked in the bathroom mirror and regretted it cos I looked even worse: me skin was pale and blotchy, me eyes were bloodshot with bags underneath and me 'ands were shaking. Saturday morning then. I ad puke on me shoulder and on the right-'and side of me neck.

I washed as best I could and when I got back to me room, I realized that the fags were gone, the iPod was gone, even the rest of that fucking Baileys was gone. Lucky I'd put the cash (notes anyway) in me trainer which was still on me foot. I was surprised they adn't ad that an' all. Thieving junky scumsuckers. I wasn't gonna make a scene cos I knew I'd never see that gear again no matter what. Live and learn.

I lay down on the bare mattress for alf an our, just a get me shit together, changed me top and it the street. Time a see if I could get some gear from back ome. On the way out I saw that Scott Two, Jez and is mate were still in the front room – watching *Football Focus*. OK, Saturday dinner-time.

Steve's Merc wasn't parked outside my ouse and you can see all the cars parked in Lurgan Walk. That was the good news but I couldn't believe me fucking eyes when I saw me ouse cos some cunt ad been spray painting the front. 'SHAWNIE SUCKS' it read. Then there was a smudged bit which looked like it might ave been a 'C'. Red spray paint right across the front, under the window, look. Badly done an' all, dripping everywhere like an old man's cock.

The smell of vomit it me as soon as I opened the front door. The curtains were drawn in the front room but when I looked inside I could make out enough to see that our Ma was unconscious on the settee (just for a change) under *my* fucking duvet.

'I come a get a fucken clean un. Not un that stenks of fucken slag,' I shouted as I ripped it off of er.

She was naked and the left side of er face was puffed out in an ugly bruise. I was about to chuck the duvet onto the floor when I noticed the puke and the empty glasses all over it.

'Fer fuck's sake, I don't wannal even stand en thes fucken shet-ole.' I threw it onto the armchair – at least that sicko adn't been wanking there.

'Fuck's sake, ahhhhh fuck. Jason, ahhhh fuck.'

'Lovely to see you too, Mummy,' I said, all posh. 'Hard night whoring?'

She sat up, feeling er face and looking down at erself. 'Fuck's sake, Jase, I ain't got a fucken stetch on. Geh's that fucken duvet.'

'Aw, does it bother you being seen naked, Mummy?'

'Why you fucken talken like that?' she goes.

'Because you raised me so beautifully, Mummy. Praps thes'll elp yer ya felthay fucken slag,' and I reached into me pocket and threw a 'andful of copper at er. I remembers Tony doing that when e wanted a make someone look small. A 2p bit stuck to the middle of er belly. 'Yeah, tha's about what yer fucken wurf.'

'Lessen Jase . . .' Why the fuck would I want a listen? What could she possibly ave to say that I'd wanna ear?

'I ain't lesnehn to a fucken word, Mahl, an' you know why? Cos en a town full a slags, yer the fucken worst. Yer the dirtiehst, most lowest piece of stenken fucken pork on thes estate.' I shoved er and she fell back on the settee, tits everywhere.

'Jason . . .' she said, getting up again.

'Shut et, slag,' I shouted and I slapped er. I know, I know, but she'd asked for it, Jesus fucking Christ ad she ever asked for it. I smacked er a bit arder but it wasn't on the bruised side, look.

'Jason,' she went again, crying now.

'SHUT THE FUCK UP,' I went, smacking er down again, not too ard, look. Then it appened again. It was funny really until she spoke. Until she opened er slag mouth. Until she said something so bad, so disgusting, so fucking unforgivable that I didn't just slap er. I punched er and I'm not ashamed a say it. I punched er in the belly and me 'and almost disappeared. And I did it again, and again.

I left er on the settee crying and retching and naked like the filthy slapper she is. Then I went upstairs to see Shawnie. I can't tell you ow good it was a see er – seemed like forever since I ad, not just two days.

I got me alcohol stash (Lynx Super, loads of our Ma's White Lightning) from me sock drawer and put it with as many clean clothes as I could stuff into me Nike old-all. I got me toothbrush, some toothpaste and me shaving gear. Downstairs, our Ma was still crying and gagging. I found two tins of ot dogs, a tin of Breakfast-Anytime-Bacon-Sausage-Egg-and-Beans, a packet of pasta in creamy sauce, five cans of Diamond White and a bottle and a alf of vodka. Fucking result. I bagged it up, got me duvet from the pig-sty, and eaded back a Sarah, Jez and Scott Two's. Mine.

Shit.

SHAWNIE

the first kehss

I got back from school. LAST DAY! I don't know why I was excited really cos I didn't ave nothing a do and anyway, I likes being with Mrs Taylforth up Florrie. She'd been spending loads of time with me and we just talks and talks: I can tell er anything and she always listens and gives me really good advice; like about me monthlies and boys and that. I mean, our Ma never told us nothing and when I started bleeding one day at school I thought I was dying or summat but Mrs Taylforth sorted me out.

On the last day of term, you never dooz a lot. Mrs Taylforth elped me with some word cards for me box: 'under' and 'over'. I finds them really ard cos I can't see no shape in them. I knows the letter 'O' which is the first letter and the first sound in 'over' so at least I can tell em apart.

Dinner was *amazing*. Amazing. We ad a choice of cheese salad or lasagne and chips. No choice then. School lasagne's lush: you can dip your chips in the goo and wipe your plate with the last two or three of them. You gotta use your 'ands so you aven't gotta let Mr Pope see you cos e ates that and e shouts. Funny a think e've got a willy too. Don't seem right somehow but I bet e's like the others give im alf the chance, even though e's posh. I sold three packets of fags after dinner (that was another trip down Broad Walk then, maybe Bedminster) and you'll never believe what appened then. I couldn't believe it. I was aving a fag with Christopher behind the Terrapin and we finished at the same time and chucked them on the grass and e just leant forward and kissed me. Right on the lips. Put is 'and round the back of me ead and felt me air (I makes sure it's clean now, don't I?) and kissed me. Never been kissed before. I can't even remember the last time our Ma kissed me. Our Nan dooz but I ain't seen er in ages cos the council moved er into a flat over Lawrence Weston which she ates, but that was me first *real* kiss, tongues and everything. E said, 'Yer beauteful Shawnay,' which certainly ain't true but I wasn't arguing so we kept on kissing and our teeth clacked together but it was alright cos e laughed so I did too. Can't remember laughing the same time as someone else. It was lush: I ad me arms around is back and I run me 'ands over is shoulders and e felt the back of me neck and run is other 'and over the fatty roll where me waist's meant a be and it was so lush. I was tingling; I was buzzing. E was trying a get is 'ands under me top but I pushed im away and said, 'I don't fenk so, Chrestophurr, not on the first kehss,' and e was a gent cos e never tried again, not till we'd been snogging loads more and when e did I pushed is 'ands away again and e weren't funny about it or nothing.

E said, 'C'mon Shawnay, you got the bestest tets en the wurrld,' and I could feel e ad a boner. I let im touch me bum up for a bit, then (luckily) the whistle blew and we went back into school.

After dinner, we just ad a video of *Titanic* which was really good but it was ard to follow it cos the boys was all mucking about and taking the mick. I mean, I knows the ship sinks and that but I wasn't sure what else was appening. Mind, I never knows what's appening in films. Didn't matter anyway cos now I knew ow Kate Winslet felt when Leonardo DiCaprio eld er close and kissed er when the ship went down. Lush.

Siantell and Kerry-Ann and Toni left me alone all day cos they were too busy bitching and whispering to each other and I floated ome with Leonardo's kisses on me lips, and then there was our Ma. Plastered. Rolling around all over the settee, cider all down er front cos she'd let er can fall. Fag ash on er thighs.

She was off er face. You wonders why I never drinks. I tell you what, I can see our Jason going down the same road an' all if e ain't careful. I tried a get some food down er but she wasn't aving none of it so I finished off the burgers meself. Asda economy burgers, mind. I ates they cos they got onion and they ain't like Bird's Eye. Our Ma don't give a monkey's and she just shouted at me. She'd got us some eggs mind and they slipped down a treat with they burgers and some red sauce.

Our Ma crashed out in front of the telly so I pinched a king-size bag of prawn cocktail Skips and went upstairs a finish them before she woke up.

I put some music on (Ms Dynamite – she's brilliant) and danced around me room while I tipped the Skips down me neck.

'Mess Dynamite-ee-ee.'

Next thing I knows, there's an almighty crash from downstairs and our Ma's yelling at me. She'd only gone and fallen over in the kitchen, adn't she? Getting a can from the fridge, I'll bet. Bought alf of our pots and pans down with er an' all. I found er in a pile of stuff, covered in oil, drinking cider and pretending she'd broken er arm. *And* pretending it was my fault. She was just plastered. She was a right state. I got me air off, I even sweared, I said, 'Ma, yer bleeden pessed.' I ates it when I swears; it means I'm just like everyone else.

She was all over the place so I took er upstairs and gave er a shower. Then, I got er to wear er red dress. I ad to get in quick, I mean, she looks a right slapper in it but you should see some of er other stuff. I pinched a load more of er nibblies and left er to it. I just sat upstairs, stuffing me face while she crashed around downstairs, pouring cider down ers.

I turned up me music and started sorting out me Barbie collection. I've ad em for years, since I was a babby like, and it seemed a shame a throw em away look, so I keeps em in that box what our Dad give us: it's really old and it's all different colours in the wood like, and it's got loads of little bits of shell stuck onto it. It's the only beautiful thing I got and I keeps all me Barbies in there with all their clothes and stuff. I mean it ain't like I still likes playing with them or nothing; I just keeps em looking smart, with their air brushed and that. Mrs Taylforth says they'll be worth loads one day, if I keeps em nice. I got twenty-three of them now: my favourite is Gymnast Barbie. She've got the most beautiful figure and er air's silkier and ain't got so many tangles as the others. I keeps most of the clothes in the packs they comes in so they stays perfect and I always uses the Barbie comb, not the Barbie brush cos that don't get the knots out, look. Mind, the brush is just right for Gymnast Barbie cos er air's so lush. It's a bit blonder than the others an' all. I ain't got no Kens.

I turned me light off and pretended I was a-bed when our Ma shouted up. By the time I eard Steve and is mates come back, I'd changed into me Krazy Kat T-shirt and I was tucked up under me duvet with a big bag of pork scratchings. Still cleaned me teeth mind. After look.

I fell asleep but they made a right racket and I got woke up by a load of shouting and I eard Black Phil's dad going, 'Yuh sick bwoys, yah man. I check on de ladee on me way,' and Steve saying, 'Norris mate, you are a pious fackin wankah pal, why doncha do us all a favour and just fack off?'

Next thing I knows, the light's spilling over me bedroom wall as the door slowly opens.

I was like, blige, what's going on, but it was Steve. I could ear there was other people outside. Could smell the beer an' all.

Steve said, 'Shawnie gel, yu remembah, uh, last night when you ah . . . when we got close?'

I remembered but I never said nothing cos I knows that was dirty.

'Well listen, Shawnie, few want a earn yuself a few bob, a fivah like, all you gotta do is the sime fing wiv a coupla mites a mine. Jest a 'and-job, like, and they're nice fellas an' all, Shawn. Swift one at the wrist and yer lahfin.'

I wasn't laughing but I'd seen Skateboard Barbie accessories up Broad Walk for £2.99, skateboard and knee pads and everything. That meant I'd still ave some spare for nibblies cos I was getting short even though I'd pinched a load off of our Ma.

So I wanked them off. Lee and Steve anyway. The other bloke, called Michael, just played with imself while I sorted Lee out, and I reckons that's disgusting. I mean, couldn't e wait?

It weren't no different to Jason's mates really. Old blokes just takes a bit longer, that's all. Lee wanted me to let im squirt in me face but I was like, gross.

When they'd finished, I cleaned meself down with the man-size tissues (200 for 49p over Londis) and put me fiver in me knicker drawer where our Ma wouldn't never find it.

Next morning, Steve come in for a blow-job, before going off to Yeovil, even though it was a Saturday. I finished im off, then I reached under the bed cos I'd stashed a bottle of Pipkins banana milkshake there (Pipkins banana milkshake is *lush*). When I finished it, I put the bottle back under the bed and ad a little kip, but I tell you what, I don't ardly dare go a sleep now cos I never knows what's coming next when I wakes up.

Before I knows what's what, there's our Ma crying

downstairs and our Jason's coming into me room. E just said, 'Shawn,' and climbed into me bed – never took is clothes off or nothing. E just eld me really close, so close that I couldn't see is face but I knew e was crying. E've never shown no interest in me tits or me body and that but I eld is face against me boobies look, and e snuggled in like a babby.

'You smells lush, Shawn,' e said, which, when you thinks about what I'd been doing was a funny thing to say. E smelt of last night's booze but e smelt of squirtings an' all an' that give me a cold feeling in me belly.

We lay there for a while and e never got a ard-on. I could ear our Ma making sort of puking sounds downstairs so I figured they must ave ad a really big fight. They always fights. Just like er and our Dad did when e was ere.

E wiped is eyes like e thought I wouldn't notice and got out of bed and said, 'Shawn, I don't want wanken off today lovurr but thurr's a fucken shet-load what do: I'm bringing Mikey an' at least two of ehs mates round on Monday, yeahl? After dennurr, mind. I ain't comen when that Cockney cunt's ere. Faverert firtayn-yer-ode,' e said, and e kissed me on the forehead and give me *that* smile before walking out the door. I couldn't wait till Monday, just so that I could see im again. I didn't care about aving to wank off is scabby mates; it's a job, don't mean nothing. I just dooz it and takes me fags and enjoys me time with our Jase.

I lit a Marlboro Light as I eard the front door slam. I always loves the first of the day: it feels lush. I even gets a bit light-eaded and I can feel all the muscles in me body relaxing, look.

Our Ma was still crying.

Jason brought the punters round on Monday. Then some more on Tuesday, and Wednesday and Friday. Just about every afternoon for the ole summer oliday in fact. In the evenings, Steve would bring is mates round and e paid cash. Fiver an evening, mind. I ad more fags than I could smoke and money for loads of lush food and Barbie stuff. I was getting fatter and fatter an' all but I just didn't care, don't know why. I ad willies literally coming out of me ears but I never ad our Jase, and our Ma started drinking even more, if you can believe that. She just drank and cried and shouted and cried and drank. And drank. And slept. I ardly saw er and when I did I wished I adn't. I just kept out of er way and kept the ouse neat and tidy.

Steve's mates thought I was great. They got me chocolates and everything. Steve said I was a bleeding diamond, loads of people said really nice stuff and that ain't never appened to me before and that feels so nice.

Some of Steve's mates wanted a go, you know, wanted a go all the way but I said I wasn't aving it and I told Steve. E turned round and said I'd get more money but I told im I didn't need it: I ad loads. Why should I do dirty stuff when there ain't no need?

Started doing more with Christopher, mind. Let him feel me tits and that, right under me top, look.

One evening, me and Christopher ad gone out and got some chips cos there wasn't any food up ours. I ad a battered burger and a jumbo sausage with mine and they was lush. There was a bunch of lads outside Jarman's; Jason's mates – a right rough bunch – and one of them shouted, 'Ey, fat birrrd,' and another made sucking noises and they all laughed but I knew I'd wanked two of them off, or sucked em or summat. They knew it an' all. Christopher didn't cos e didn't know nothing about all of that so e started moving towards em with is arms by is sides and is eyes opened wide like blokes dooz before they fights, but e ain't a fighter. One of the lads goes, 'Right spaz? C'mon then, fuck face,' and e was grinning and that and

Christopher turned towards im but I knew e didn't really want a do it and e'd ave got murdered anyway so I grabbed im by the arm and said, 'Leave et, Chres, they ain't wurf eht. Less go round the school an' fenesh they cheps, yeah?' E didn't take a lot of persuading. We turned away and the lads kept on jeering and shouting stuff that wasn't funny at all but I didn't care. I ad me chips and me fella.

We finished our chips but Christopher was still wound up cos of they ruffians so I started snogging im to take is mind off it and it was a bit salty and greasy which is the best sort of snogging really. E was still a bit funny mind and I could tell e was thinking about they lads so I ad an idea for taking is mind off of them. Works every time with blokes, don't it? You should ave seen Christopher's face when I pulled is tracksuit bottoms down and got is willy out. E've got a nice willy: cavalier, sort of long and smooth and not too airy. E squirted like a water pistol after about a minute.

E was like, 'Fucken ell, Shawnay. I fought you wanted a take et steaday.' E was all red in the face and is willy was still twitching when e put it away.

'Don't swurl, ehs desgustehn,' I went. 'Anyway, ain't like I'm goehn all the way ehs eht? You gotta show may commetment first.'

E never said nothing for ages till e said, 'I don't know ow, Shawn,' and I turned round and said, 'Few don't know, then I ain't tellen yowe,' but the truth is, I didn't know neither. Christopher kissed me and eld me tight and looked into me eyes and said, 'Yer amazen. I loves you Shawnay.' So there it is. Ain't just fags and money you can get by exercising your right 'and – it's love an' all.

I don't think I loves Christopher but e's dead sweet, look. E chased off some kiddie who spray painted 'SHAWNIE' summat, right across the front of the ouse, and then the letter 'C' which Christopher managed a pretty much rub out. That spray paint dries really quick mind, so we were stuck with the rest of it. Never did find out what the other word said. When our Ma phoned the council to ave it removed they said we'd ave to wait up to five months cos it was 'non-urgent' and ad we tried white spirit and a scrubbing brush? They never did come. We never did try white spirit and a scrubbing brush, neither. It's still there.

The oliday wasn't much of a oliday, truth be known. Our Ma was getting so drunk she really couldn't do nothing and I used a shout at er but it didn't do no good cos she'd either shout rubbish back or fall asleep or cry in front of the telly, so I ad a do all the ousework and the cooking cos blokes just can't can em? If I wasn't doing that then I was sorting out Jason and Steve's punters. Sometimes I'd ave four, five or six a day. It wasn't so bad. Least I got to meet people.

LISA

one a they dogs

I likes a start the day with a vodka now. Not just a vodka, mind. I aves a Russian coffee; that's vodka with a coffee in it, and I aves a big pint of water an' all cos they says that's really good for you, for your skin and your plumbing and that. Then I saves the rest of me vodka for later, evening look, cos I aves White Lightning when I'm watching telly or meeting Tom and is mates down the playground.

Our Jason beat the crap out of me. Seven shades. Not the first time neither, e've been doing it since e was ten or summat, but this was the worst. Just me body, look; e left me face alone except for a few slaps. Left me feeling rough, rougher for days, throwing up blood and that.

All the days seemed a merge after that. Steve would go off over Yeovil where e ad a new job on; Jason would turn up after dinner with is dodgy mates; I'd keep out the way; Shawnie'd stay in er room. Oo, she got a boyfriend an' all – Christopher – first love, bless. E ain't the full ticket and that but e's a lush lad, love im. Jason and is mates are orrible: they takes the piss summat wicked so Christopher never ung about when they were there. There was loads of them, Jason's mates that is. No one's got *that* many bleeding mates.

Steve told me what was appening at night. E said, 'It's only 'and-jobs, gel, bit o' maaf nah an' then. Some reason, the puntahs ain't bustin a gut to get frone up on. Bit of a specialized taste that. Listen, I ain't getting enough from the business to keep you in vodka, gel.'

I never said nothing but it bought me up short cos it was the same thing what appened to me at about the same age. Well, truth is, I was doing a load more by that time: I was eavy with our Jason by er age. Our Dad went nuts but I reckons that was just for show cos e was scared it might be is. Steve said it was only 'and-jobs to pay for my bleeding vodka and if I wanted that a keep coming I better keep it shut. E said e wouldn't let nothing bad appen to our Shawnie. I believed im but all the blokes what used to come and see me, used to party with the ostess with the mostest, mostly just walked straight past with a 'Right Lees'. Norris still come and see me, bless is eart: never could resist me arse. E even bought me flowers last time, I reckons e was feeling guilty for walking out on me the time before. Someone put me a bed, mind, and give me a duvet: I'll bet it was Norris. Steve wouldn't ave done it, e didn't give a shit no more. Slept in me bed and never done nothing *but* sleep. E'd say, 'I know where you fackin bin, gel.' E'd ave breakfast before I even got up, fuck off to Yeovil and come ome at alf past eleven stinking of beer. If e come back any earlier than that, it was with some scabby mates wanting a 'and-job from our Shawn. She gets all the flowers now. And the chocolates. She likes the chocolates best cos you can't eat the flowers. Not even our Shawn'd eat they.

I remembers earing some comedian or summat going on about ow you reaches a certain age and you becomes invisible. That's ow it ad got; I was invisible. They just walked straight past me, on their way to the younger flesh upstairs. Sometimes I got bitter and twisted like but I can't ate Shawnie. She's a diamond. Ain't er fault she's younger than me. Ain't like she's prettier, mind, and youth isn't everything. I bet she gives rubbish 'and-jobs. She aven't got the experience ave she? Blokes are so stupid. The feminists are right: I'd be a feminist if I could be arsed.

I ad to keep the upstairs tidy cos Steve took the punters straight up there more often than not. E went nuts if I adn't tidied, shouting and shaking me and smacking me about – not serious like – just a bit cos I'd asked for it. Only time e'd ever touch me really. E'd yell, 'Whatchoo fink buys at bottle yer swillin, gel?'

It's true, e got me a bottle most days – I fucking ated it when e never, I ad a build up reserves look but I kept on drinking they – said it was cheaper than rent, look. Soshe pays for me White Lightning. Soshe: no one says that no more, our Ma always used a call it that. Then it was dole and no one calls it that no more neither. Income Support or Job Seekers' Allowance or Credit or whatever the fuck it is.

I misses our Ma. There ain't a bus from ere to Lawrence Weston.

One dinner-time, must ave been the middle of August, I was sat in front of the telly and I'd closed me eyes for a bit (after *Wipeout* it's the news and I've given up trying a keep track of that) and next thing I knows the fucking can's being taken out of me 'and. I makes a grab for it and says, 'Fuck's sake,' and I sees our Jase with *my* can, drinking it look, and e takes a long swig, wipes is mouth and says, 'Ello Ma,' just like that Nick Cotton in *EastEnders* used to.

'Fuck's sake, Jason, yuh theeven lettle toe-rag, tha's *my* fucken can,' I goes and e smiles *that* smile what makes me blood run cold, takes another long swig and then tips the rest over me belly and me tits and that.

'There you go, Mahl, ave et then,' and is mates, four of them what I never recognized, sniggers behind im. They ain't polite like they used a be. I remembered what e done after e beat me up and I looked in is eyes and I could tell that e did an' all.

'C'mon boys,' e goes, and they went upstairs.

I keeps one can in the fridge now and our Jason always scabs that. I keeps the rest behind the cleaning stuff under the sink, Domestos and Mr Muscle and that. Shawn dooz most of the cleaning these days, look. Our Shawnie knows it's there but it ain't like Jason's ever going a look, is it? I keeps me vodka in a bag of light-bulbs under the stairs. I ain't stupid.

When Jason beats me up, do you know what? E gets a ard-on, a stiffy. E always ave. I'm is mother for fuck's sake and I can tell. I knows lads is age ave got an almost permanent bleeding ard-on but it's definitely smacking me around what dooz it. That's what appened the morning after the last party. That's why I said what I said (I was still a bit pissed I suppose). I only offered to elp, sort it out for im, take some pressure off. I'm is Ma for fuck's sakes, I knows what me little boy needs. I was right an' all cos when e'd finished going nuts and smacking the living shit out of me, before I even dared open me eyes and uncurl meself from the ball I was in, I could smell me little boy's come on me.

That kept on coming back to me, still do. I finds myself staring at the telly and before I knows what's what, it's a different programme and I've never even noticed.

The *Neighbours* theme tune bought me round, always do. 'That's when good neighbours become gooood friends.'

Yeah, right.

'Fucken twentay secuhns, ya cunt! You goehn fer a fucken record or summat?'

Shouting and laughing from upstairs. I fished out another pack of fags from behind the cushion I was sat on. B&H this time. I likes B&H. I pinched em from Shawnie. She've got bleeding thousands idden under er bed with er Barbies. Fuck knows where she gets them but it ain't like she's gonna miss the odd pack or nothing, is it?

I started coughing me guts up when *Doctors* come on: that's irony, ain't it? A right phlegmer and it urt like ell. I reckons our Jason must ave broke me rib or summat. I ad a bleeding disgusting mouthful but I washed it down with White Lightning and took a deep drag on me fag. Reckoned I might ave a little kip when it finished cos I didn't give a monkey's about *Doctors* really. I reckoned right. I woke up alfway through *Murder, She Wrote* with a wet bum cos me can ad upended and spilled right down the side of me, soaking into the settee and me jogging bottoms. Like Jason adn't tipped enough over me. I got up to get another and I felt me jogging bottoms clinging to me like I'd wet meself or summat. Sometimes I really dooz that. It's embarrassing. I started wondering if I ad done but I went into the kitchen and lit another B&H and got meself another can and when I eard the crack of the ring-pull I stopped worrying. Like one a they dogs.

STEVE

magical symmetry

I tell you what, the Yeovil job was a fucking pleasure after that Easi-Fit bollocks. This old junior school had been closed down and basically left to rot for twenty-odd years. Local education authority (Wurzel West) had fucked up its finances, overspent on the sheep-shaggers' helpline budget or something, and had to start selling off some of its assets. Former councillor I done a job for buys it up in his girlfriend's name, needs someone kosher to do the work. Look no further. Sweet.

It was an armpit: damp, vandalized and everything. The roof had gone right through in places and some of the floorboards wouldn't hold a four-year-old, let alone a grown man. Tramps and low-lifes had been using it as a doss-ouse and a toilet and God knows what else and we had to turn this shit-hole into bijou palaces fit for darling young professionals. Tossers, willing to fork out a hundred and ninety grand for a flat that can't shift the smell of tramps' piss.

It was proper building: we had to take off the roof and start again; most of the floors were unsound and had to go, we had to rip the bastards up anyhow and sort the drainage out; new lintels, purlins and RSJs throughout; windows and frames all needed stripping out and replacing with double-glazed uPVC numbers; internal walls needed jigging about and fire doors installing; there was this lovely old parquet flooring but most of it was fucked and rotten so we pulled it all up and done it fresh and it looked the business. New plumbing, total rewiring; poshest bathrooms you ever seen; chrome kitchen units and all that malarkey; all-over paint job. The whole fucking works and me with a tidy wedge in me pocket. Very fucking tidy wedge, truth be known. After Christmas.

Meantime, I had to supplement me meagre funds with, how shall I put it, outside earnings. What with Lisa about as popular as the Pope at Ibrox, that left me (with a helping hand from Miss Blow-Job 2005) to bring the corn in. Listen, I was keeping this family going, with a little bit of assistance granted, but there wouldn't be no punters if it weren't for me. Any dole Lisa was getting was going straight down her throat. And then some. I grown up with me Ma taking all the shit jobs – stacking shelves, cleaning toilets – just to make ends meet, putting meat and two veg on me plate. Tell the truth, she done what she had to do and she done the right thing and what did she get? Little pink pills and a date with the Grim Reaper. Lisa, on the other hand, has spent her life slagging around to make ends meet and her kids have pretty much brought themselves up. One thing they'll have in common though: an early death. Ain't no two ways about it, Lisa ain't making old bones. And who'll give a shit, eh? She's a grown up, ain't she? Me Ma left me on me tod when I wasn't much older than Jason and spent the last few years of her life making mine a misery. I know it wasn't her fault and what have you but after all I done for her? Didn't leave me with nothing but debt.

I'm gonna wring Lisa dry before she kills herself. It was costing me a bleedin bottle of vodka a day just to shut her up, and get use of her stinking house. And daughter. All I wanted in return, all I needed, was that she kept it a little bit clean and tidy. Ain't like she got nothing else to do, is it, unless you count falling unconscious in front of Aussie soaps as an occupation, but could she do it? Could she fuck. Drank me vodka right enough, that weren't a problem, but could she pick the dirty knickers and spilt ashtrays off of the floor? Could she fuck. I tell you what, she was putting me right off me dinner. Made me glad to be working in darkest Somerset.

The best thing about working in Yeovil, right, apart from getting away from that fat slapper Lisa: no Tone. No psycho in the shadows. No having to think about every single fucking dicky bird what come out your mouth just in case Mr Sensitive-Yet-Brutal takes it the wrong way.

Word had it, his hand was fucked long term. He couldn't even make a fist of it (bit of a major fucking blow that for Tone), couldn't grab hold of stuff with any strength, couldn't do most of the labouring work neither and he loved that work because it kept his body so lean and hard.

He was meant to be working in Bracknell, driving a forklift. He'd fucking hate that, Tone. He'd fucking hate Bracknell, anyway. Pits of the fucking world, Bracknell: I done a job there. Full employment, a Starbucks every hundred yards and a suicide rate to rival Moscow's. Not a genuine geezer in the town. You wouldn't want to bump into Tone there – or when he come back.

I reckon I should run a sweepstake on how many days Tone can stay out of nick. It just ain't in the likes of him. He don't give a shit. If he gotta do time in order to make his point with a blunt instrument then he'll do it. Just don't give a shit. Jason's the same: he ain't gonna get out of his teens before he takes a little break at Her Majesty's pleasure.

Lee's mate Ashley, right, passed on a whisper, and to this day I don't know the truth of it but he said it was a strong one; this whisper has it that it was Jason and his mates that done over that Paki shop off of the Wells Road.

I ain't so sure, I mean, shoplifting, fighting, doing cars over, maybe a bit of burglary – I can see him doing all that, but I reckon this was a bit out of his league. I mean, they had a shooter for fuck's sakes, pistol-whipped the Paki and everything. I reckon that's out of his league but that's what Lee's mate in the Cocks says.

That's the Happy Cocks. What's with the pub names round here? Used to be called the Fighting Cocks apparently, according to Lee, but they reckoned that give it a bad image so they rebranded. Call that place what you like, it ain't the name that gives it a bad image. It's dumped in the no-man's land between Knowle West and a dismal suburb known as Hengrove. A load of Hartcliffe boys drink there an' all and you better have a crew with you if you want any chance of enjoying your pint in peace. We'd stop off there for a few on the way back from Yeovil. Got a good few punters for Shawnie there.

Amazing thing, word of mouth. I got regulars from the site; from the Cocks; from the Venture; from the Railway and the Midland; from Lee's Downs League mates down Bedminster . . . and then mates of all of that lot an' all. Shawnie sucks like a pro, word gets about and before you can say Hugh Grant you got more punters than you got time to fit em in.

I tell you what, mind: I been having a good nose around the internet lately and there's some amazing stuff on there. Stuff with kiddies Shawnie's age and younger, way younger. They are doing all sorts, I mean all sorts. Really fucking shit-hot dirty stuff: makes me laugh. Shawnie don't know she's born, but I tell you what, it don't half give you ideas; didn't half give *me* ideas. I got this mate, Dave right, who knows how to set up a website that you can take credit card details on and everything. If a pig-ugly little slag like Shawnie can get such a loyal following in Bristol, just think what she, *we*, could earn nationwide, worldwide. If

I can get Shawnie online . . . then she can go global; be a virtual slapper. Ain't gotta be one fella at a time then, has it? Then there's mobiles an' all; how many fuckers across the world have got a mobile? It's a goldmine, it's a fucking goldmine. I was making plans, no mistake. I started building up a portfolio of ideas and pictures, obviously, you got to be business-like, haven't you? All I gotta do is get photos and videos and what have you . . . anyone's shy and they can just wear a Hitler mask or something. I can give them anything they want. That's the secret; that's successful business thinking. Don't matter if it's socks or sheep or pubescent slappers. Give the punters what they want. You ask Richard Branson.

They make me laugh, punters and what have you. They try and pretend it means something, loads of them anyway. They try and pretend there's some special connection between them and Shawnie, like it's romance or something. They get her chocolates; they tell her she's 'a lady', 'a princess'. Fella called Shaun, one of Lee's football mates from Bedminster, gets her bleeding great bouquets and writes her letters which is a fucking joke cos she can't hardly read her own name. 'To Shawnie, love Shaun', ain't that lovely? I read one of them and he even talked about the 'magical symmetry' of their names. Sad prick. That and a load of self-pitying crap about how she's the only one who 'really connects with him'. Why can't people accept things for what they are? He's a fella who gets his kicks by paying to have his knob sucked by a thirteen-year-old girl. End of story. No shame in that. What fella wouldn't?

I was getting it daily.

JASON

a people person

Sarah come back on a Wednesday and she'd managed to dump er littl'un at er Ma's. She was a bit cobby about me staying but Jez explained that Moxy and Sabrina ad fucked off someplace and I bought a wrap for er, peace offering look, and she never give a monkey's after that.

'Long as you pays yer fucken way, then I don't fucken gev . . . ahh,' she slurred, wagging er finger at me like a cartoon drunk. She was pissed and so interested in cooking up she couldn't be bothered to finish the sentence.

'Go on, Jase,' went Jez. 'You joining us?'

'I saves et for weekends, Jez mate,' I went (never forgot to get the 'mate' in). 'Thengs a do medweek, enneht?'

I'd settled into a routine for the summer: get the punters round for Shawnie, daytime; nick as much food and drink as I could while our Shawnie was doing the business and our Ma was out of it in front of *Ome and Away*; shift the fags straight after; over Scott One's ouse (is Ma ad forgiven me cos I got er a regular supply of dodgy gear, look – fags and mobiles, mostly, and I could ardly take em back over Padstow, could I?); go looking for a mobile or two if I ad the time; stop off at the chippy or the Millennium Raj; get back to Padstow to eat and get meself cleaned up (no point trying a cook or even keep food round there); sneer at the druggies and ead off out, sometimes down town, sometimes round a mate's with a few cans, sometimes up a nice bit of pork over the Bomby or somewhere. It's a good life if you got the balls to go out and grab it.

The mobiles were so easy. I got two MOs. One: you catches a bus – kids always uses their mobiles on the bus, 'I'm on the Wells Road, coming up to Gilda Parade, see you in a minute' – follow em off the bus, smack em into a wall, do what you wants to them, ave their goodies (mobiles and money); they never even sees your face, piece a piss. Two (this un's for when I fancied a bit more of the uman touch): ang round smoking in the park (Greville Smyth, Perretts, Redcatch, Vicky, Engrove, I always changes where I dooz it, look – always one step ahead), wait till some tart's finished gassing on er flash new mobile, chat er up, steer er into the bushes, turn er to jelly, just like Little Skate Boy, do what the fuck I wants with er, ave er gear. They never makes a sound they're so fucking scared. I likes the posh teenage slags best: they thinks I'm a tasty bit of rough, alf of them are well up for it. Then I scares em. Scares em with me words, scares em so they stays scared. If anyone comes along, I ain't done nothing ave I? I gets em so fucking terrified, I can do anything. Anything I fancies. I dooz plenty. They can't even cry out. I fucking loves it; I reckons they fucking loves it an' all, secretly like. Sometimes I forgets a take their mobiles, I loves it so much. Fucking posh pork deserves all they gets.

I was working by meself mostly. Black Phil was staying over St Pauls with is dad. Scott One panics too much, ain't got the bottle. Anyway, is finger was still fucked. Scott Two only dooz cars really – I done a few with im but I ain't into it, I likes a get out and meet people. I'm a people person, me. It's better by yourself cos you're your own boss.

I was doing alright: regular pork; plenty of rough stuff; designer gear (I even *bought* most of it); seeing Shawnie most days; much booze as I fancied and a nice bit of browns at the weekend – strictly weekends, mind, no druggy shit.

Sometimes I could get a shower over our ouse, if there was a gap between punters. I'd be washing meself down, look, and our Shawnie would come in and sit on the edge of the bath and she'd chat about 'When we was a family' and 'When our Dad was ere', and she'd make it sound like it used a be normal and nice, like any fucking thing about our family as ever been normal and nice. Maybe she don't know no better or maybe she's just kidding erself, but she ain't kidding me. Me and er's the only nice thing there.

One time, Shawnie was scrubbing me back, cos I gets a few blackheads there. I'm fine being naked with er; she's me sister, ain't she, and it's just my body, nothing special. Well, tell the truth it *is* a bit special, but you know what I mean. She was using one of they girly, scratchy things like an old slapper's beaver with a andle on the back, and she was talking about er Dad and that and I went right back. Stopped earing what she was saying cos it was shit anyway like it always was, bless, and it took me right back, right back to when I was about eight all over, all over again.

Shawnie's Dad, Tony: nutter. Didn't do fuck all towards looking after us except at bath-time. 'Daddy-time, Tony-time, they words starts wev the same letturr, dun em Jase?' Tony always loved bath-time. Our Ma was appy; give er the chance a tip a couple a cans down er neck. I wanted a bit of privacy in me bath by that time but Tony wasn't aving none of it: 'You shurr eht, I ain't payen fer two fucken baaf-fulls. Anyway, s'educayshnul, enneht? Gotta learn bout oppozet sex an' that.' E'd always take is shirt off, even in winter: 'I ain't getten splashed by you towe.' We never splashed. Least, we soon learned not to. In me mind, look, our Shawn's about six. E'd get er to stand up and e'd say, 'Currful you don't slep, lovurr,' and e'd old on to er; one 'and on er ass, one on er belly. E'd start rubbing er all over. *All* over, except er cunt. E liked a save that for last. E'd rub is 'ands over er neck, er throat, er shoulders, er arms, never missed a fucking inch, er chest (squeezing er little nipples), er back, er belly, er ass (sticking is finger right in, spending ages on it: 'Gotta take special curl a keep thes clean, en us darlehn?'), all round er cunt, then er thighs and er calves, back to er ass again: 'Nevurr get soap in yer tuppence darlehn, et'll steng yowe.' Then e'd ask me – ask me, *tell* me, 'Go on Jase, rub et en propurr, look.' I ated it cos it wasn't right but I ad to rub er all over. Made er giggle when she was little but after she was about four or summat she never giggled no more. I could see e'd ave a ard-on. E'd pull is City shorts up igh on is thigh and slip it out the bottom look, like we wouldn't notice.

'Keep goehn Jase,' e'd go. 'What a fucken starr, what a fucken superstarr. Tha's what Batman dooz a Catwoman, ahh fuck, fucken superstarr Jase, ahh fuck, tha's a way, Jase.' Fucking perv. When we was little, e'd wank imself below the level of the bath, like we couldn't see, but e'd stopped bothering by this time. 'Jase, you gotta rinse the soap off now, mate, so's we can wash er tuppence, look. You gotta be so gentle, Jase, wev a girl's tuppence,' and e'd 'and me the toothbrush mug and I'd rinse er down and then e'd start touching er cunt with is non-wanking 'and: 'Eh's a dirtay place, Jase mate, a dirtay place, you gotta be so fucken thururr wev eht.' E'd be going faster and breathing eavy, look, and our Shawnie'd just be standing there with er bleeding great eyes, staring at im. Sometimes e'd come there and then but if e was pissed, which was mostly, then e'd stand up, pull is shorts down and rub soap on is cock and say, 'Clean et, Shawn, clean eht,' and she'd ave to start and e'd say, 'Clean et Shawn, eh's dirtay, clean et fasturl, ahh good girl, fuck, fasturr Shawn, ahh fuck Shawn . . .' And she did. Didn't ave no choice, did she?

Sometimes e'd touch me an' all.

*

Jez said once you gets used to it, a tenner wrap's fuck all, just pissing in the wind. E said e ad a spare wrap and if I was up for it, e'd do me a good price on two: fifteen. Fair play, e was true to is word. Good gear an' all. No word of a lie neither; two wraps at a time is a different thing altogether. I was doing that well with the life of crime and that, money wasn't a problem.

Only one problem. Steve.

LISA

ain't got enough 'ands

'Dear Ma'? 'Dear Mum'? 'Dear Mummy'? I didn't even know ow to start the letter. Look, I ain't stupid and I knows when things are fucked up. So who do you turn to when things are fucked up? MaMummyMum.

I ain't that good with words, look, and I don't write letters a no one except the Soshe when they cocks up and won't take me calls no more, but I couldn't face seeing er or calling er and I needed summat, someone. I needed someone bad.

Dear Ma

Hows it going up your end? Evrything's fine her. Shawnie's doing well at school and our Jason's nearly ready to leave. I now you 2 never alway's seen eye to eye but he's a clever boy Ma and a good boy at hart, when he get's over his rebel thing he's going to make something of him self. Steve's doing rely well heve got a job over Yoevil that's going to get us thousand's and well have everything! People carier's and stuff. You remember Tom Rolfe from the bank? Posh Tom. He is living round are way now but he dont work at the bank no more. We meat up most day's now and chew the fat. Heard there was a ruck between the Knowle West boy's and the Larence Western boy's. Rough there mind.

I stopped and went over the cupboard under the sink for a can. Cider splashed me fingers when I pulled the ring-pull so I sucked them and wiped them on me T-shirt cos I knew I was gonna be lighting a fag next. Five left; so what? Loads more under Shawnie's bed.

It's ard to write when you're smoking *and* drinking cos you ain't got enough 'ands. I went back to me letter and stared at it cos I didn't know ow to get away from the small talk, so I just sort of blurted it out on paper.

Ma their aint no esey way to say this. I know he was never my real dad and evrything but Dad used to do allsort's to me didn't he. And you new it and you never did nothing becuse at least he wasn't doing them to you wasn't it. That's it isnt it. I been thinking about it for ages I been thinking about it for ever. You never done sod all parden my french and I never forgive you. Well I forgive you Ma cos Im the same as you now Ma. I can't believe it. I aint doing nothing now our Shawnie's getting it and I cant forgive myself but Ma I got to keep Steve hear cos I love him and that's were all the money come from. It's not like Tony because he was a mad man and Im sorry I stuck with him. Everything you said was right and he can rot were he is. I understan bout you and Dad now. Steve's so good to me and Shawn and heve got so much money coming. Our Shawn's getting so fat and she cant stop Ma she never stop eating and I now that's cos of what our Tony done you member what our Tony done? Evry day I thanks god he's in nick. He's an evol man Ma their aint nothing he cant do. Ma Shawnie's a big girl now shel be alright wont she?

I ad to light another fag. It's true. I do understand why our Ma never done nothing. Our Dad, well, e wasn't me real dad but e's the only one I ever knew, look; e was a wicked man. E was an evil piece of shit and e done the works a me and our Cherry and our Janey, especially me; the fucking works. And our Ma never done nothing. She'd pack us all off a school. Pink and shining we was: just about the only kids there who were scrubbed behind the ears and ad clean clothes on, cos it was poor round Knowle West in they days, mind. No one ad nothing, *we* never ad nothing, but everyone thought we was a cut above the rest even though our shoes and coats were always several sizes too big so they'd last and our clothes were falling apart like everyone else's. Thing is, they were always clean and we'd get a clip if we forgot our 'pleases' and 'thank yous'. I remembers when I was little, I was so shit scared that I used a put a please or a thank you in every sentence cos I thought you ad to. Then I'd get a clip cos they thought I was taking the piss. I didn't ardly fucking dare open me mouth in the end. Sometimes we'd get new stuff from Eastville market (our Ma's family comes from the Netham, look, before they was moved out to Knowle West) and we ad to keep it immaculate. We never dared play or nothing. We'd get such a fucking tanning if we come ome with a rip in the knee or summat. The kids at school used a beat us up for being posh, then we'd get another battering from our Dad when we come ome cos our clothes was messed up from getting beat up.

And no one knew, no one saw what that evil man was doing. No one ever sees. Long as we were turned out in Sunday best every day, everything was alright.

'Don't you be painten, mind,' our Ma'd say as she packed us off to school (Connaught Infants, over by the Venture). 'That stuff's murderl a get out. Speshlay the black, look. You dooz lovelay drawlehns, do yer Nan a lovelay drawlehn, look. No stecken mind, neevurr. That glue's a swine.'

I lit another fag.

Ma we was alway's turned out lovely and Ill alway's respec you for that but you new what our Dad was doing. Shawnie's a young lady now Ma it was her Birthday in july not that you membered.

Appy Birthday Shawnie, ave a shit-load of cocks.

Shawnie was upstairs with Christopher. I could ear the music. Bleeding awful it was but e's a lovely lad, Christopher.

Steve would be coming back with some of the boys soon but they were watching football in the pub so they wouldn't get ere before the end of the match so that'd be six at the earliest. Christopher would ave to go then.

I went to the cupboard under the sink, oping they didn't keep er up too late cos it was the first day of the new term back at school next day and our Shawn ain't worth knowing if she aven't ad enough kip.

I lit another fag. Ad another drag. Ad another swig. Cried another tear that splashed down on the page but it never smudged the writing cos I uses a Biro. I realized I would ave to get some more fags from under Shawnie's bed as soon as Christopher left and before Steve and the lads came cos I only ad one left.

Ma me and Shawnie need's you now. You got to ring or something cos it isnt good Ma it's messed up and it isnt good.

Love Lisa.

There was envelopes and stamps in the desk that Steve uses and I lit me last fag and went up the post box which is up the road over Melvin. It was still ot even though it was September now and I was panting like an old dog by the time I come back. Lucky I ad more cans in the cupboard under the sink.

The music stopped at about six and Christopher come down.

'Bye, Messehs.'

'Call me Lisal, alright lovurr?'

'Bye bye Lisa.' E sounded like a five-year-old with a really deep voice. Just the one can short of a six-pack.

'Bye bye lovurr.'

E closed the front door and Shawnie crashed back up the stairs all excited, look. Still no Steve so I got the Red Square out for when I finished the White Lightning; best part of a bottle left.

Telly's always shite on a Sunday, so I started on the CDs. I knows everyone thinks they're naff now but I still likes the Spice Girls; just the quality stuff, mind: 'Mama', '2 Become 1'. I ugged me own shoulders and swayed from side to side.

'Mama I love you, Mama . . .'

'Ma, that es *sad*,' goes Shawnie on er way to the kitchen, 'ave you gotta dance wev yerself?'

'Praps I'm *feelen* sad, Shawn. None of us can be appy all the fucken time can us?'

'Stop swearehn, Mahl, eh's desgustehn.'

'Shawnay, I'll say what I wants en me own ouse.' I turned up the volume to wind er up, look. '*Mamal, I loves you.*'

Shawnie muttered 'sad' again as she went into the kitchen and started clattering about with the frying pan. There was sausages.

I eard the sizzle as Shawnie put the first sausage into the ot fat and I was alfway up the stairs by the time she'd cut the second one off and put that in. When I got to er bedroom, I lay down on me belly on the floor and reached under the bed. Not too easy for me so fuck knows ow our Shawnie manages. Once I'd pushed the Barbie box to one side I could get me 'ands on one of the three carriers full of fags. She must ave been nicking loads: more than I ever managed. I didn't want to ang around in case she come up so when I pulled two packs out it was pot luck what I got: there was all sorts in there. I put the Barbie box back and stood up, breathing eavy. I caught sight of me face in the mirror and I adn't alf gone a queer colour. I'd done alright: one of the packs was B&H which I likes, the other was Silk Cut Lites which is like smoking tampons, but if you gets your lips round they little oles near the filter you can get a alf-decent drag with a bit of lung power.

I urried back into the front room, saying, 'Shawn, you'll burn they sausages, I can smell eht. Ow manay yowe got thurr?'

'I'm doehn em all, cos they goes bad. Eh's wecked a waste food.'

'Eh's wecked a fucken cook et the way you dooz, Shawn.'

'Someone's gottal en em? You want a couple, Ma?'

'I ain't ungray, Shawn.'

'You ain't nevurr ungray. You ain't eatehn, Ma. You don't eat nuffehn these days.'

'I reckons I can lev offa thes fra beht,' I goes, grabbing me spare tyre and shaking it about.

I puts 'It's Raining Men' on while Shawnie switches the ob off, puts all eight sausages on a plate and starts going upstairs.

I sings, 'Fer the first time en estoray . . .'

'Ma, yer doehn my ead ehn.'

Truth be known, I couldn't wait till it ad finished so I could sit down and ave a think and finish off me White Lightning. I must ave closed me eyes for a minute cos it was getting dark out when I eard the front door go.

Steve came in and e was getting set to go straight upstairs like e normally done when I shouted out to im. I can't remember the last time me and Steve, you know, made love. Last time e even touched me, look. Except to smack me one.

'Steve lovurr, come and ave a grope fore you goes upsturrs an' I'll wank you off special babe, like you likes eht,' I goes, sitting up and sorting me tits out.

E stuck is ead slowly round the door and looked at me like I was shit on is shoe. 'I'd soonah ave Lawrence Llewelyn-Bowen get is 'ands on me,' e says and e disappears upstairs. I could ear im switching on the computer e've put in our Jason's room. E don't know ow urtful e can be.

I sat down with Kylie playing but it never cheered me up any. I never let our Shawn see it but I was feeling low. I lit a fag and drained me glass and closed me eyes. Next thing I knows, the bell's ringing and Steve's urtling down the stairs and opening the front door. I'd forgotten there was punters coming. I forgets every fucking thing these days.

'Alright, ya fahnd it then? Cahm on in an' meet the misses,' went Steve. E closed the door and they come in the front room.

Ave you ever been so scared that it's like that fairground ride over Breen, where you're tootling along in your carriage thing and you're thinking this ain't nothing and you gets to the bend and the fucker drops away, and it's like a cartoon cos you literally fucking angs there for a minute look, then your stomach its your boots and the rest of you follows and there's fuck all you can do? Don't even come close. It was like someone was pulling me innards out me arse when I saw who walked in the door with Steve.

'Ello Lisa,' e said.

STEVE

for a glass of whisky

Front page of the *Evening Post*, 25 August: a half-page, grainy close-up of a face, barely recognizable as human, followed by:

Police were today looking for a man after pub landlord Robert (Bob) Beckham was savagely attacked as he locked up the Railway Tavern, in the St Phillips area of Bristol.

Beckham, 47, of St Annes, Bristol, sustained severe, multiple injuries to the hands and face in the attack which occurred shortly before midnight last night. It is believed that a hammer was used in the assault. He will undergo surgery today at Frenchay Hospital.

Police spokesman Detective Inspector Darren Head said: 'The attack happened after closing time, shortly before Mr Beckham was due to lock up and return home. He was found this morning by cleaning staff. In eleven years in the force, I've not seen a more brutal assault. Although Mr Beckham will need extensive treatment, his condition is stable and we have been able to interview him. Unfortunately, he has not been able to furnish us with any kind of description. We do know that the attacker acted alone and that robbery was not apparently the motive although a small quantity of whisky was taken. We would like to speak to anyone who was in the Railway Tavern or the Feeder Road area late last night and who might have seen anything.

'The attacker is extremely dangerous and should not be approached under any circumstances.

'Bob is a popular local character and we need to apprehend this maniac as soon as possible. Any information received will be treated in the strictest confidence.'

Anyone with information on the assault should contact Crimestoppers on 0800 555111.

They found Bob at seven-thirty in the morning, nailed to the bar and near bled to death. Lisa knows the cleaner as it happens, lady called 'Neet' would you believe. There's a family round here got all the cleaning jobs stitched up. A sort of cleaning mafia. Neet's in hospital an' all. She had the sceaming abdabs when she walked in and saw the state of Bob. He was unconscious, naked from the waist down and pretty much drained of blood.

Fair play to the geezer, Tone don't fuck around. He'd gone in just as the last of the bar staff had left, smacked Bob in the face with a hammer and locked the door after him. Too easy. Bob knows he's fucked already. Tone takes his time, working Bob over steady like, giving him a hammer blow each time he looks like he might be capable of standing or putting up a fight. Tone's wearing surgical gloves. Bob's face slowly turns into Italian food. Tone gets bored in the end, flips Bob over, sits on his back and, using the hammer, destroys Bob's left hand, just like he figured Bob done to him with his baseball bat. Didn't leave a bone intact; pulped it systematically. Slowly.

Bob's beyond begging at this stage but still conscious. Tone sits him up against the bar, takes a six-inch nail out of his jacket pocket and grabs Bob's right hand. Bob puts up a feeble struggle and loses the last of his teeth for his pains. Then he just lets Tone nail his right hand, arm outstretched, into the lovely old wooden bar. Barely even screams. Then the left, didn't hardly look like a bleeding hand no more. Tone pulls Bob's trousers and pants down, lifts his cock up and aims his hammer at Bob's bollocks, then says, 'Fuck eht, I'm en a good mood today.' Puts his hammer in his jacket, smiles, goes behind the bar and reaches up to the whisky optic. He pours himself a large one, sits down on the floor in front of Bob and surveys his handiwork. Tone's laughing; Bob would cry if anything on his face still worked. Tone watches Bob bleed for ten minutes, finishes his drink and jumps up.

'See ya Bob, mate. Ta fer the drenk an' all.'

The *Evening Post*'s got contacts in all the hospitals and they'd got hold of the picture the nurse took of Bob's face before they started treatment. The headline read: 'FOR A GLASS OF WHISKY.'

When the coppers asked him what happened, Bob answered, 'I fell.'

SHAWNIE

Dadday

I couldn't sleep the night before the new term started. New year; new school year. I always gets shaky first day back. Butterflies. Sometimes I even gets the runs: just nerves and that.

I opened a plastic bottle of Pipkins banana milkshake and it was lush. It went straight down so I opened another (I ad three look) and a bumper pack of Aribos and one of me Snickers bars. I likes to mix the flavours of sweets and chocolates and that cos you can make interesting new ones. I reckons I could do that for a job when I grows up. Making new sweets and tasting them and what ave you. That'd be the best job ever. I'd be brilliant at that cos I knows about sweets and crisps and there wouldn't be no reading and writing and that.

I was a bit scared but it wasn't so bad cos Mrs Taylforth was still going to be working with me (and Christopher) and I couldn't wait a see er. Some of me teachers would be different and that's always scary but at least Mrs Taylforth would still be there. And Kerry-Ann, and Toni, and Siantell. It ain't just fellas what urts you. Girls dooz it an' all. Everyone dooz it to me. I must be a orrible person cos everybody ates me and wants to urt me. Except our Jason and I only ever seen im when e brought is mates round for a 'and-job or a blow-job. That washing yourself thing ad gone right out the window: they was dirty so and sos I ad a suck.

Last night there was a worse blooming racket than usual and a load of shouting and then that orrible thing what appened and then it was just our Ma crying downstairs and I reckons Steve ad got took off in an ambulance. I eard it. There was no way I was going to sleep but I ad a do summat a stop me thinking about what ad appened. I spent ages brushing the air on me Barbies. Ow do it get so tangled when they been in the box, that's what I wants a know? I brushed it and combed it till there weren't a single tangle left in any one of them. Then I thought about what I'd need for school next day. I got me Nob bag from me cupboard (I ates me Nob bag – our Ma nicked it someplace cheap) and put me ome/school book in it. Me word box was still in there: so much for oliday omework – sorry Mrs Taylforth. I got me pencil case together (rulers and rubbers and that but *two* smelly gel pens, one of them vanilla ice-cream) and the file that Mr Pope likes us to use. Then me fags (two packs), a lighter, two bags of Quavers, a big bag of Monster Munch, a Snickers bar, a banana milkshake, a multi-pack of Mars Bars, a six-pack of mini pork pies (they're so lush, and you can stick em in your mouth whole so's the teachers can't see) and a Beanie Baby Tinky Winky what I always carries for luck.

I couldn't sleep and I couldn't stop crying so I done what I always dooz when I feels like that. I unwrapped a Snickers bar (Mars or Double Decker'll do but not Picnic cos it's too scratchy, look) and put it in me mouth but I never bit into it. I sat on the floor, curled up into a ball with me arms wrapped around me legs and me face resting against me knees. Then, if you rocks gently backwards and forwards, the Snickers bar goes in and out and in and out and it takes for ages before you finishes it. I can make it last for the first five songs on me Ms Dynamite CD (long as I misses out the swearing one at the start) and it's just a lush way of passing the time. I didn't ave no music on this time and I was just trying not to think but I couldn't stop meself.

I wish we ad a stop button and a rewind for when life's too nasty and you needs a go back and start again. Pause'd be good an' all, summat a give you time a think. And a record button, so you can just tape over the crappy bits of your life with summat better and it's like they never appened.

I got through that Snickers bar and four Mars Bars from an Aldi multi-pack before I realized that our Ma ad been knocking on the door and calling me name for ages. I sort of knew and sort of didn't. Never done that much rocking before. I stopped when she come in. She never said nothing and I never neither. Er face was red and puffy. I means redder and puffier than usual cos she'd been crying loads. She put er arms around me and give me a massive ug what I never wanted. Then she pulled back the duvet. I got in and she covered me up and lay down beside me, stroking me air till I fell asleep, just like she done when I was a babby.

When I woke up, I was alone in bed and I was crying. I felt rough. I put on a fresh pair of knickers; there was blood on the old uns and I threw them in the bin. I just pulled on me jogging bottoms and tucked me Krazy Kat T-shirt into them. I never ad no clean little white trainer socks so I put yesterday's on, then me cheapy trainers from Just 4 U up Broad Walk. I normally makes more of an effort when I goes a school, especially first day look, but I couldn't be bothered a think about it.

I checked me school bag again but, tell the truth, I couldn't remember what was supposed to be in there anyway. There was six Mars Bars left, so I ad one while I plucked up the courage to go downstairs for breakfast. I was right about Steve an' all cos e never come in for is morning blow-job.

When I walked out me bedroom door I could ear our Ma snoring. I went down the stairs and it was nearly alf past eight. I can tell the time when the clocks aves 'ands on them. I knew it would only take me five minutes to walk to school. I ad loads of time. The front room smelt of fags and booze like it always done. The kitchen was covered in blood. Dry blood. It was on the floor by the cooker; on the cooker, smeared down the front; on the wall by the back door. All over. The bin and the frying pan were on the floor. I couldn't make meself breakfast in there.

I guessed it was Steve's blood. Least I couldn't taste im this morning even though I adn't done me teeth. I always dooz me teeth, twice a day. Couldn't be bothered. Our Jase says, 'Can't be arsed,' and I tells im off.

No point staying there so I went to school early. Keener. I ad that big bag of Monster Munch on the way.

When I got to Florrie, Toni was outside the main entrance, waiting for Kerry-Ann and Siantell I'll bet. She made kissing, or it might ave been sucking, noises when I walked past er. I was like, so what? She won't do nothing by erself, don't give a monkey's if she do anyway.

Mrs Jay, who's the secretary and who always sits in the entrance, said, 'Hello Shawnie. How was your break? Did you do anything nice?' but I couldn't think of nothing nice so I put me ead down and kept walking. I was supposed to be at my tutor group at five to nine. I was early but at least I was safe. I walked into 2E. There was some other kids there but no Christopher so I didn't say nothing and found meself a space in the corner. I wished I'd ad a fag on the way. What was I thinking about? I opened me bag and sneaked a pork pie into me gob. I don't think anyone saw except Tinky Winky. E'd been looking after them.

Siantell and Toni and Kerry-Ann come in together. Siantell made a sort of fish mouth at me and the others copied and giggled. I looked down. Toni said, 'Right, Uddurrs?' and then something nasty about me Krazy Kat T-shirt. They were moving in on me and I just stared at the floor but

Miss Teplakova come in and said, 'Right, good morning. Welcome back,' so they left me alone and chewed gum.

It was PE after tutor group. They didn't oughta ave PE on the first day back. Especially first thing. I got meself over to the quiet side of the changing room, that's the side the other three girls weren't.

Mrs Taylforth come in and me eart started racing, I'd missed er so much.

'Kerry-Ann, Toni, hi. Hello Siantell. Shawnie, it's so good to see you,' she went. 'How's it going?'

I wanted a talk to er so much but I started filling up and I could only make a funny noise in me throat, nothing more. I looked down.

'I've got you a PE kit that should fit,' she goes, looking down at me body with eyes that said 'no chance'. 'You haven't brought your kit, have you?'

I stared at er shoes and made that throat noise again.

'So what have you been up to in the holiday, Shawnie?'

I couldn't talk to er. I'd been dying to see er for six weeks and when it come to it, I couldn't say nothing. She put er 'and on me shoulder and I looked down and didn't move. Toni said summat and they all laughed and Mrs Taylforth said, 'Alright, let's start getting changed now: I want to see those suntans.'

My body looks like it's made out of white sliced bread, soaked in milk. With the crusts cut off.

'Shawnie, I'll be with you for PE then with you *and* Christopher for English afterwards.'

Throat noise.

Mrs Taylforth left the PE kit and went off to find Miss Teplakova. Siantell, Kerry-Ann and Toni started pointing and laughing straight off. Siantell just stripped down to er bra and pants and she looked lush. She looks like she ought to be in *Cosmo Teen* or summat. She walked around the changing room like that, chatting to the other two and saying nasty stuff about me, for no good reason really. Just showing off er body I suppose. Toni and Kerry-Ann stripped down an' all and they were both lovely an' all, *so* skinny, but a bit more nervous like.

'C'mon, Uddurrs, less see yer suntan,' went Kerry-Ann.

Siantell stood in front of me with er 'ands on er ips. She was like, 'Yeah, Shawnay, I bet you looks luuush.'

I didn't ave a suntan. I never do. The sun gives me a rash cos I sweats so much, so I could tell they were being nasty really.

I was so glad when Mrs Taylforth come back in. I took off me Krazy Kat T-shirt and quickly put on the school PE top what was really tight. Siantell, Toni and Kerry-Ann were chatting to each other and giggling so I took me jogging bottoms down when I thought they weren't looking but as soon as I pulled them down over me bum, Siantell was looking right at me knickers and she stopped talking and just looked disgusted. I nearly fell over trying a get them over me left foot cos I'd tried to do it with me trainers still on and I ad to sit down and cock me leg like a dog to do it. Everyone followed Siantell (like they always dooz) and they was all staring right between me legs and I couldn't get the jogging bottoms over me trainer and I could feel the tears coming. Even Mrs Taylforth was staring.

Toni went, 'Fuck's sake, someone gev er a tampon or summat,' but it wasn't me monthly or nothing. Me knickers was soaked in blood. I finally got the jogging bottoms off of me foot and I wanted to run but there weren't nowhere to run to. I pulled me knees up to me face and ugged me legs and shouted, 'Make em stop looken make em stop.'

I can't believe I shouted at Mrs Taylforth.

She was like, 'Girls, I want you all in the hall, right now please. Right now, Siantell, shorts on now. I'm not listening, Siantell, shorts on now. Everybody move please.'

She got them out into the all in no time and stood in the doorway.

'Miss Teplakova will be there any minute, girls; ahh, there you are. I'm just helping Shawnie, Miss Teplakova. She'll be with you shortly.'

I got me Krazy Kat T-shirt back on again on top of the school one and it was so massive that with me legs tucked up, I could pull it right down to me toes and ide behind me knees if I wanted. I was iding, no mistake; I was iding behind me knees.

Mrs Taylforth closed the door and I could tell she didn't know what to say. I couldn't look at er. I felt dizzy.

'Shawnie, let's get this sorted, darling. Is it your period?'

I never said nothing and, straight away, she said, 'It's not, is it? Shawnie, I'm worried about the bleeding, darling. What do you think's causing it?'

I never said nothing and she never neither for ages.

'Is there any chance, Shawnie, that you might be pregnant?'

I was rocking, I couldn't stop myself. I wished I ad a Snickers bar or summat in me mouth. There was some Mars Bars left in me bag. I didn't know if I was crying. Alf the time I didn't ear Mrs Taylforth.

Ms Dynamite-ee-ee.

'Shawnie, this is really important, darling. I need to know, so that I can help you. If there's any chance, any chance you could be pregnant . . . Something is causing this bleeding, Shawnie.'

Ms Dynamite-ee-ee.

'Shawnie.'

She put er 'and on me shoulder and I stopped rocking. I didn't want er to touch me and I didn't want er to stop.

'Shawnie, has something bad happened, darling? You can tell me, Shawnie, you can tell me anything at all,' and she put er arms around me but I could only ug me knees.

She ad tears in *er* eyes now. 'Shawnie, I'm going to help you. Whatever has happened, I'm going to help. That's all I want to do, sweetheart. Please tell me what's wrong.'

I wanted to, I wanted to so bad. I wanted to tell er and she'd ug me and we'd ave a little cry together and she'd make it alright and I'd live over er ouse and eat posh food and visit our Ma and our Jason at weekends. I'd wear lovely clothes and laugh all the time and there wouldn't be a willy in sight.

'Shawnie, can you hear me, sweetheart? Shawnie love, you're scaring me. Please say something, darling.'

Nothing, I couldn't say nothing.

'Shawnie, I can see that you're very upset about something. Would you like me to contact your mother?' and I looked er in the eye for the first time.

I said, 'No,' and it was like somebody else ad spoke.

'Shawnie,' she kept on looking into me eyes, 'I think you might need medical help, darling. A doctor, I mean, but no one can help you if we don't know what's wrong. I know something's wrong, sweetheart. Whatever it is, I'll help. That's all I want to do. You're not in any trouble and I only want to help. Is there anything at all you can tell me? Just one little thing, you don't have to go into everything. Please tell me, Shawnie.'

She ad tears running down er cheeks. Then there was a silence what went on for ever.

'Shawnie, I'm going to phone your mother, darling, you're clearly very upset and I think you –'

'E FUCKED ME E FUCKED ME I BEEN FUCKED E FUCKED ME.' It came out as a sort of wail.

'I ain't a virgen no morr. I been fucked. E said I'm a beg girl now. E fucked me. I nevurr said yes, I nevurr, not like the blow-jobs an' that. E fucked me e fucked me pardon me French,' I went and I cried like no one's ever cried before.

Mrs Taylforth eld me in er arms and I eld onto er an' all. She smelt so clean. I sobbed. So did Mrs Taylforth.

I eard Miss Teplakova shouting for everyone to put the balls back and line up and I knew that PE was nearly over. They'd be back in a minute.

'Who fucked you, Shawnie?' Mrs Taylforth *sweared*.

There was another long silence and when the word come out it sounded wrong. I don't even know if I ever said it before.

'Dadday.'

LISA

eh's me name, enneht?

Never wanted a drink so bad in me life. I'd only been bleeding taken in for questioning, adn't I? Like any of this was *my* fault.

They come at twelve noon. There was me thinking I could ave a nice lie-in, what with it being the kids' first day back at school and that. They wouldn't stop ammering at the door. I tried to ignore it but they wouldn't stop so I sat up in bed and me stomach lurched and I shouted, 'Fuck off,' and they just turned round and shouted, 'Police,' right back at me, so I ad to go and answer it.

Fella and a slag. Plain clothes.

'Lisa Brewerr?' goes the fella, thrusting is card at me. 'DI Atyeo and DC Fell. We need to talk to you, Mess Brewerr. Can we come en, please?'

'No. Whatchoo fucken want?'

I was wearing the same tracksuit that I'd fell asleep in the night before. Night before that an' all if memory serves. Me air and make-up was a state and I'm betting I wasn't a pretty sight. Nor was the kitchen. No way I was letting them in.

'Et really would be better ef we could discuss thes endoors.'

It was the male copper doing all the talking. DC Slag was trying a look tough *and* understanding at the same time.

'You ain't comen en less you gotta warrant.' See, I'd learned summat from Tony. I'd learned plenty from Tony.

'Why would we want a warrant, Mess Brewerr?'

'You ain't comen en ere. Eh's my ouse.'

'I appreciate that, Mess Brewerr, but we really do need to talk to you. Would et be more convenient for you to accompany us to the station?'

'Orr, way could neck yowe,' goes DC Slag. Sounded Artcliffe.

'Well I ain't fucken done nuffen, ave I, so I don't know ow you could neck may.'

'Ohh, thurr's plentay,' she goes, smirking. Smug bitch.

'Well, let's ope thurr's no need fer that,' goes Atyeo.

I wasn't going to push me luck, mind. I took me keys off of the ook, walked out the door (still in me slippers, look) and slammed it. No way was I letting them see inside.

'Ouse ehs a mess an' I don't want the neighburrs chatten, do I?'

When I got in the back of Atyeo's car (Audi) some of them were standing at their doors and chatting and pointing and swapping theories already. They can spot coppers a mile off. It's a one-minute drive to Broadbury Road.

'Ef you wouldn't mind setten ere a meneht, Mess Brewerr,' e goes in the little entrance bit at the station. E keyed in is number and went through the metal security door. I was appy to sit down onto the bench, truth be known: I was feeling a bit dizzy. Number of times I polished that bench with me arse. Last time was with our Jason. Grim spot, mind: security screens and bolted down metal fittings with crap graffiti on em like 'FUCK DA POLICE' and 'SIANTEL SUCK'S COCK'.

I wasn't there two minutes before DC Slag, whatever er name is, sticks er ead round the door and says, 'Mz Brewurr? Thes way.'

I was shaking. It's scary in there.

We went down a long corridor, DC Slag walking in front of me, until we got to a door saying 'Interview Room 3'.

She opened the door and Atyeo was inside, sat behind a desk.

'Set down please, Mess Brewerr,' e goes, pointing to a chair on the other side. DC Slag sits next to im. I was thinking about Russian coffee cos normally I'd ave ad me first one by now.

'Zet alright fiy smokes?' I asked when I'd took a seat like they told me.

DC Slag dogged me up like Artcliffe slags always dooz and said, 'Police stations are no smoken now, Mz Brewurr, as you well know.'

Cobby mare. I knew it but it's worth a try cos sometimes they turns a blind eye, especially if they fancies one an' all.

'Mess Brewerr, you understand that you aven't been arrested and that you came ere voluntarilay?'

'Yeahl, I know. I seen eht on *The Bell*.'

'Tha's good, Mess Brewerr. Zet all right if I call you Lisa?'

'Eh's me name, enneht?'

'Lisa, I want to talk about your daughturr, Shawnie.'

'What about urr? Woss shay bloody done?'

Our Ma used a knit jumpers when we was little: orrible, chunky things but they kept you warm in the winter, look. Kids at school learned that if you could get old of a loose end, the whole fucking thing would unravel. DI Atyeo ad old of the loose end.

'I ave to tell you, Lisa, that your daughturr Shawnie as made a numburr of very serious allegations: namely, that she as been forced to ave sex by er father, Anthony MacCarthay, and that she has been seriously sexually assaulted by Steven Arden and a number of other men.'

When our Tony walked in last night I nearly died. I thought e was still in nick. E adn't changed, only e looked worse than I remembered. E was skinnier but more muscly. E was fucking covered in tattoos, ome-made jobs mostly, even on is face. Is mouth was smiling. Is eyes were cold, is eyes were evil. I couldn't say nothing.

E was cocky. Steve never ad a clue, e never knew me and Tony were an item; that Tony was Shawnie's Dad. Steve couldn't understand me face and why I couldn't talk. Tony was loving it.

'Ello Lisa.'

What the fuck was I supposed to do? To say? I never did nothing and I never said nothing. I wanted a cry, I wanted a run. I wanted me Mum.

'Am I missin somefink ere?'

'No mate,' goes Tony. 'I'm jus dyehn a first. Yuhl ain't gotta drenk ave yowe?'

'Course, I'll be right wiv ya, mite.'

E'd bought a bottle of whisky and taken it with im when e went up to our Jason's room to keep it away from me and to do whatever e dooz on the computer there. E went up a get it.

'Fuck may,' goes Tony, 'yer looken rough, gurl, you looks a right fucken dog.' E looked at me like I was summat what lived under a stone. 'Well, ain't you pleased a see may?' e goes. 'Don't I get a lettle kehss?' E was grinning. I was nearly wetting meself, I was fucking rigid. I never said nothing. Steve come back with the whisky.

DC Slag spoke: 'Lisa, can you tell us, en yer own words, what appened last night?'

I didn't say nothing.

'Ded Anthony MacCarthy come round to yer ouse?'

'Tonay. Yeahl, e dehd.'

'What appened, Lisa?'

After Tony ad drank a large whisky (Steve never give *me* one) e done Steve good and proper. I could see it coming, I knows ow e works. E turned to me and said, 'Lisal, I'll bet you could use a drenk,' and as soon as Steve turned a look at me an' all, Tony lamped im. I knew it was coming. Steve never. When Tony lamps, they stays fucking lamped. Steve went down like a sack of fucking spuds and Tony moved in with is feet. Steve curled up into a little ball look, and our Tony just fucking laid in. Really fucking im up, look. E kicked im in the spine and the kidneys and that. In the end that opened im up and then Tony went for is face, then is guts and is bits, look. Just like the old days. When Steve curled up again, Tony kicked im in the back of the neck. Steve was fucked. Tony never stops when they're fucked. E started jumping on Steve's ead. I never done nothing. Tony was laughing now. E was going '*Yeehah*' like a cowboy each time e jumped, look. Steve was fucked.

'They ad a fight,' I went.

'Why was that, Lisa?' goes DI Atyeo.

'Why jew fucken fenk?'

'Lisa, thurr's no need a take that attitude.'

'Ain't thurl, ain't thurr?'

DC Slag said, 'Believe et or not, Mz Brewurr, we're ere to elp.' Yeah, right. 'Whurr was Shawnay to when thes was appnehn?'

'Upsturrs, safe en bed.'

'An' Jason?'

'Woss et got a fucken do wev e?'

'Problay nuffen, Mz Brewurr, but we're tryen a build up a complete pecture.'

'Whurr is Jason, Lisa?' goes Atyeo. 'Hugo Smyth, Jason's Educational Welfare Officerr, says e asn't been a school since May.'

'E's about. I can't make em go a school, can I? E's at a friend's.'

'What's thes friend's name?'

'Scott.'

'Scott who?'

'I don't bloody know, eh's Scott Two, enneht?'

'Scott Two?'

I didn't know. I knew e wasn't at Scott One's no more and I knew that as long as e wasn't up ome, e was better off.

'We'll come back to that. Who won the fight, Lisa?'

'Tonay.'

'What appened next?'

Steve was in a orrible state. I seen our Tony do some numbers on people but this was bad. Worst *I'd* seen for a bit anyow. Steve was on the floor of the kitchen saying, 'Doctah, fuck's sake get us a doctah.'

You couldn't ardly ear what e was saying cos e was talking through so much blood and I don't know ow e was still conscious. Tony was squatted down over im.

'Lemme tell you summat, *boss*. I wants a tell you bout our mate Bob . . .'

E told Steve about their mate Bob while Steve was bleeding and retching and acking up blood on the floor. E's a twisted bastard, our Tony. Then e turned to me.

'I ben yurrehn all sorts bout yowe, Lees,' e goes. 'I ben yurren yer the best bet a pork en Brestol.'

I couldn't say nothing. I just looked down.

'They ur sad cunts. I wouldn't touch yowe wev a pointay steck even few was the last bet a pork on the planeht. Might fucken catch summat.'

I thought about lying to the police but what's the fucking point? Why should I protect Tony?

'After e done Steve e said, "Look after e, an' no phone calls tell I comes down," and e went upsturrs a see Shawnay.'

The mood changed in the room.

DI Atyeo said, 'What did Tony do when e went upsturrs?'

'I don't know; I was looken afturr Steve.'

'You never called an ambulance?'

'I couldn't, could I? E'd ave bloody kelled may.'

'Ow long was e upsturrs for, Mz Brewurr?' goes DC Slag. Being nice to me now.

'I don't fucken know, do I? I was tryen a stop the blood comen out a Steve, wunn I? E wuz fucked.'

'We ben en touch wev the BRI, Lisa. We know ow Steve es.'

'Es e alright?'

'You aven't spoken to them? Well, you'll need to speak to the docturrs but I thenk they'll be keeping em en for a few days. E'll lehv.'

Steve's face was a right fucken mess. Is eyes ad totally closed up. Is left cheek was ripped down over the bone where our Tony ad jumped on it. There was blood pouring out of is nose and mouth. E'd lost some teeth. There was blood all over im. E was ardly conscious but e kept on retching and coughing up blood. E was trying not a cry and e was writhing around, moaning, trying a find a position that didn't urt im, look.

DC Slag said, 'D'you know what Tony was doehn upsturrs?'

I knew what Tony was doing.

'No I don't. But I can guess.'

'What's yer guess, Lisa?'

Maybe e was playing Ungry Ippos with er. That's what dads dooz with their kiddies, isn't it?

Tony come down and told me to ring the ambulance. When they come I ad to tell them that Steve ad got beat up in the street by kids. E told Steve e gotta say that an' all. Then e put is arms under Steve's armpits and started dragging im out.

'Open the fucken doorr, slag.'

Steve was crying out in pain. Tony dumped im in the street, just outside the ouse, and strolled off towards Melvin like nothing ad appened. When the ambulance come, I told them what I ad to.

'I fenks e was aven sex wev ehs dorturr.'

'You don't know? Dedn't you talk to Shawnie afturr?'

'I put er a bed. Tha's what muvvurrs dooz enneht? I put er a bed.'

'So you dedn't talk to er, last night *or* thes mornehn?'

'I nevurr sawl er thes mornehn. She got erself a school.'

'You were asleep?'

I never said nothing and neither did they for fucking ever.

'Lisa,' goes DC Slag in the end, 'beforr lass night, ow sexually experienced would you say Shawnay was?'

Another orrible long pause.

'I dunno.'

'Would you know ef Shawnie was a virgehn?'

'Oh yeah, she's a virgehn. She's only firtayn, look.'

'Yer quite sure of that?'

'Certuhn.'

'Lisa, you didn't look very surprised when we told you that Shawnay ad accused er father of rapen er but you never got en touch wev us. Do you ave any reason to be afraid of Tony?'

Well, I laughed. I'm sorry, but I laughed.

'Ave you met em? Ave you seen Steve's face? Ave you looked at Tonay's record?'

'Yes to all three of those questions, Mess Brewerr,' goes Atyeo. 'E's currently under arrest and being eld at Trinity Road. E'll be charged shortlay.'

Trinity Road – Tony was inside again so I told them everything. About Tony, Steve, Shawnie, not our Jason. I told them about Steve's mates coming round and what they got our Shawn a do. About Steve's computer. About im itting me. The works, the fucking works. Truth be known, I just told em what they wanted to ear cos I needed a get out and get some vodka inside me.

'Lisa,' goes DI Atyeo, 'why ded you let thes carry on? We could ave elped you a long time ago.'

Cos I was getting a bottle of vodka a day.

'I don't know,' I goes.

DC Slag ad changed er tune: 'Lisa, you and yer daughturr are vectems of serious domestec violence. You were doehn the best you could. We understand why you dedn't feel able to come forward.'

I lifted my eyes.

No you nevurr, darlehn. No you nevurr.

STEVE

the Shawnie brand

OK. This was the plan. I couldn't keep Tone away after the Bracknell job. He was ringing me, ringing the lads. Happening to meet us in the Cocks and all that, so I was gonna bring him in. Look, I'm no hard man. Never pretended to be. I'm a bit fly, I can duck and dive with the best of them but I leave the rough stuff to fellas that can do it right. Fellas what love it. There's plenty. Every town, there's plenty. Trick is, to get them on side. That's what I figured I'd do with Tone. If the Shawnie brand was gonna go global then first off we'd be needing some brains: someone to handle the accounts, the computers, the marketing strategy, all that malarkey. Look no further. Then we needed someone to provide some protection. A bit of muscle. An enforcer. Take a bow please, Mr MacCarthy. Perfect. No probs with the money. I knew this would be a big earner for all of us. I was just scratching the surface. That was the plan. Until Tone come calling.

So Mr Arden, may I call you Steve? Excellent. Steve, how would you evaluate your business plan?

Well, I would say, all things considered, weighing up the pros and the cons, at the end of the day, it's a total fucking disaster. A nightmarish abortion without a single fucking redeeming feature.

I was staring up at the whitewashed ceiling, trying to work out which bit of me was in the most pain: me face, me fingers or me ribs. Just two other people in me room. Ward. Whatever. One was some middle-class tosser in his forties who'd come off his motorbike (a big Harley – nice) and the other was a shit-for-brains office worker from Sun Alliance who'd fallen off a chair while painting a ceiling in his three-bed Barrett home in Bradley Stoke. Oh yeah, I know all about it. Every fucking detail. There's a guest room what's gonna be a nursery when they decide to have kids and the back room's just right for entertaining, but in time, it can be turned into a play room cos it goes out onto the garden . . . There's more if you want it.

I assessed the damage: doctor said I had a fractured jawbone, two broken fingers, three cracked ribs, four lost teeth, five gold rings. Partial hearing loss, bruised kidneys, multiple face wounds and severe bruising to the torso. Well, that's enough to be going along with. Tone don't fuck around. Saying that, I reckon I got off light. I know what happened to Bob; it's a bleeding miracle he's alive. Yeah, I got all the details from Tone. We had a nice little chin wag while I was bleeding half to death on the floor. They shoot rabid dogs, don't they? Tone's psychotic, he should be put down. I got off light.

Last time I felt this rough was the day I learnt I wasn't a fighter. Some things you gotta learn the hard way. My old stepdad, Stan – stepdad bollocks, that fucking arse-wipe what shacked up with me mum, then fucked off when he found out she was ill – used to knock her about, knock er about something cruel. The usual shit: come home pissed and give her the benefit of the flat of his hand. He'd have me when he fancied an' all.

I was fifteen before I plucked up the courage. The courage to do him, that is. He come back rat-arsed and I said to him – I'd had a couple meself – I said to him, 'Right, Staan,' and he was leering whisky fumes into me face and I was scared shitless cos he was a grown man but I'd made up me mind and I had it planned and I made like I was gonna say something and he leaned forward grinning and I nutted him but he must have seen it in me face or something cos he dodged to one side and I only caught the side of his face and his shoulder. I knew I'd had it as soon as I'd fucked up the head-butt: get in first and you're laughing but it was Stan who had the smile on his face as he took me down with a body shot and fucked me over like a pitbull with a cat. Made a right fucking mess of me he did, made it last, humiliated me. I didn't show me face for a few days after that, I just hid in me room and listened to Stan take it out on me Ma. Like he needed an excuse.

Seemed like she never got over that cos she went into a rapid bleedin decline from that point on. Doctors said she was terminal, Stan showed a clean pair of heels, guess who was left holding the baby. Just for a change. Once we knew she was on the way out I tried to get close to her, tried to find a way through. She wasn't having none of it until a couple of days before she passed when she give me a hug: first one in a hundred years and she managed to do it without hardly touching me, made me feel even further away, more like the opposite of a hug . . . Ah fuck it, she's long gone. Who gives a flying fuck except me? Some things you gotta put behind you.

I tried to work out what the fuck was going on. Tone and Lisa clearly got history; ain't no doubt about that. I reckon he's Shawnie's Dad. Or Jason's. Oh, he gotta be Jason's Dad: cut from the same tree them two. Maybe he wanted to take over the Shawnie franchise, maybe they both did. Shit, that'd be it.

I figured I couldn't hardly go back to Lisa once I got out of hospital. Unless I had Tone taken out. Maybe I had too much time to think but that's what occupied me mind for the rest of the day. That and the fact that I was pissing blood. Who to use. How many to use. How far to go – shit, Tone's such a fucking loon you'd probably have to kill him. If you just do him some damage, he waits until he's fit again, comes back and does ten times worse to you. He'd proved that with Bob. Bob the landlord, can we fix him? No we can't. Bob lost his hand in the end and he'll spend his life under sedation, too scared to put his nose out the front door. Bob's physically and mentally destroyed. Tone has that effect on people.

I was lying flat on me back, trying to figure out if I had the bottle to take Tone out for good. Have someone do it, I mean. I'd be doing the world a favour, no mistake.

I kept on staring at the ceiling until the nurse come in with our tea cos I'd sooner chew the fat with Tone than with them two fucking dullards I was stuck with. Not that I could fucking chew Dairylea, state of my face. Solid food ain't much good for me, what with me boat being held together with wire and suchlike, and my tea was a sort of khaki-coloured pea soup and a thin round of white sliced cut into soldiers. Yummy.

Course I wasn't gonna fucking kill Tone. All I had to do was get Shawnie out. And Lisa I suppose. I nearly let myself grin at the ceiling when it come to me. I nearly laughed out loud. It's domestic violence, ain't it? One well-placed phone call, they'd be put up in a nice little hostel by the sea for a bit, then straight to the top of the housing list. We could start up again in Southmead, or Lockleaze, maybe Barton Hill. Sweet.

I finished up spending two days and two nights of purgatory in the BRI while they checked for concussion and while I got over the operation. I wasn't exactly match fit when I pulled me blood-stained clothes on (thanks for the visit, Lisa) and I took a glance in the mirror and there was some sort of fucking gargoyle leering back, but fuck it; I wasn't gonna wait to be discharged. Stuff to do.

Didn't even bother saying goodbye to the two wankers I'd been banged up with, although to be fair, the conversation had got a lot more lively since it'd moved on to carpet tiles.

I pushed open the swing door. Two coppers.

'Steven Sidney Arden? I'm arresten you on suspicion of . . .'

SHAWNIE

implications

Sometimes you just wish you'd kept your mouth shut. Mrs Taylforth was brilliant. She was great. She gave me big ugs and said loads of nice things but she wasn't gonna leave it alone. She's always talked about 'implications' and I ain't never been sure what that's meant but I knows they're always bad or they makes bad stuff appen.

'Shawnie darling, there are implications here.' She made them sound like ghosts or summat. 'After what you've told me, Shawnie, I have no choice but to speak to Mr Bayliss and Mr Pope. What happened was wrong. None of this is your fault, darling, but all those things you told me are terrible, terrible and you don't have to do them any more. You really don't have to do them any more.'

Mr Bayliss is my eadmaster. E's alright but I didn't want im knowing about me private life. Or Mr Pope – I don't know what it's got to do with e. I was trying to think ow a say this but other people always thinks faster than me, dun em, and gets in first.

'I'm sure Mr Bayliss will speak to the right people, Shawnie, maybe social services, and stop all this happening.'

You should ear what our Ma says about social services. I couldn't say nothing. I kept trying. I kept failing like I always fails. It was out of me 'ands. Like everything always is, but maybe a bit of me, just a little bit, knew this was gonna appen. Miss Teplakova said sometimes you gotta make things appen and I don't think I ever done that before but maybe this time I'd made something appen, not just waited for it.

Mrs Taylforth stayed with me after she'd spoken to Mr Bayliss and Mr Pope. First we went to the school pond (which I loves) and we sat next to it on the big stone and she told me about stuff like newts and dragonflies. Then we went inside and looked at books together. She read me *The Twits*. That book's so funny. I likes the bits about Mr Twit's beard and all the food stuck in it and that. The police come at dinner-time. Didn't matter, I wasn't ungry – first time in me life. It was a police lady who never ad no uniform and a lady called Theresa who said she was my 'key worker', whatever *that* is. Maybe she's trying to unlock summat.

They asked a load of questions, really personal stuff. I was nodding and shaking but I couldn't get any words out with them there, I starts a stutter and that so I just shuts up. It was lush Mrs Taylforth stayed with me. We were talking in the Geography room which didn't ave no kids in it but it was really ot cos it ain't got no windows neither.

They asked me all sorts. They asked me if I knew what sex was. Duh. They asked me if I'd ad sex. They asked me who with and if I wanted to and if I'd said yes. They asked if I'd ad a bath or a shower since the last time. Really personal stuff. I just nodded and shaked me ead. The only time I spoke was when they asked who'd ad sex with me and I said, 'Me Dad,' in a really quiet voice that sounded like a little kid's.

'Do you mean your real dad, Shawnie, or do you mean Steven Arden?'

They kept asking if our Ma joined in or ad summat to do with it. They kept asking about Steve. They never asked me about Jason and is mates and I wouldn't ave said nothing if they ad cos I knows e'd ave got in trouble.

When they'd finished asking questions, the police lady said, 'Thank you, Shawnie, you've been really brave.'

Then I ad a go up Broadbury Road and it wasn't alf as bad as our Ma and Jason says. It's skanky out front but they put me in this nice bit where there was two rooms that was all for me. They was all light purple and that – big comfy sofas. Tell you what, I could live there, it was *loads* nicer than our place, but I ad to leave Mrs Taylforth at school and I stopped nodding and shaking once she weren't there. They made me take off me clothes and put on this tiny little nightie that didn't ardly cover nothing. A lady doctor I never seen before ad a good nose around. She was personal, I mean really bleeding personal, pardon me French. I suppose she was looking at what our Dad done.

E done dirty stuff. E was sweaty and e smelt of whisky. E said, 'Yer a beg gurl now, Shawn. Thes ehs what beg gurls dooz.' E put one 'and on each of me knees and split me legs open as far as they'd go.

There's woodchip on me ceiling and it's yellow with big rings around the light cos we ad an overflow in the tank in the attic, look. I remembers me Dad fixing it while the light spluttered and our Ma rushed around putting pots and bowls and what ave you down to catch the drips.

'Aaahh, what a fucken starr, Shawn. Dadday's so prowd a yowe.' E got faster and rougher and it urt. Really urt. I couldn't look at is face. Not when e was doing it and not after neither. E made a orrible noise when e squirted.

Big girls can keep it.

'Shawnie. Shawnie. SHAWNIE. You can put these clothes on now. We got you some clean ones.'

They weren't mine. They never fitted.

People kept talking a me. I didn't know who they were.

'Shawnie. We're going to get in touch with your Mum and you'll see her really soon, but we need to speak to her first.'

All the bad stuff appened while our Ma was at ome. She never stopped none of it.

'Shawnie, we need to make sure that no more bad things happen to you and we don't know if your house is a safe place to be yet, so Shawnie, you're going to be staying with a really nice couple called Sophie and Simon. Sophie and Simon Clydesdale. It's not permanent, Shawnie, that is, it's not for ever, but it needs to happen for a bit. It's in Redland so it's still Bristol. It's a place of safety, Shawnie.'

Both they names starts with a Sammy Snake, sssssss. Mrs Taylforth learned us that.

'Theresa will go with you, Shawnie, and make sure that you settle in alright. We can get clothes and other things from your house tomorrow, but we need to get you to a safe place first.'

Miss Dynamite-ee-ee. I was ugging me knees. I think I was rocking again. Alf the time I eard voices talking at me but they never made no sense. I knows they were being nice and that but I just wanted me Ma. I dunno if I was crying. I don't think so.

They were going on and on about an 'Emergency Protection Order'.

'We have to keep you safe, Shawnie.'

I wasn't sure what an Emergency Protection Order was but they said it ad implications so I didn't like the sound of it.

They were talking about loads of stuff. I can't remember it, I couldn't understand it. Truth be known, I couldn't ardly ear it.

'Shawnie. Shawnie. SHAWNIE.'

I looked out between me knees and saw Theresa.

'Shawnie, we need to make sure that Jason is safe too. Where is Jason, Shawnie?'

It felt like she was trying to stare me out. I closed me knees together and it was just like when I was at infants' school and all these posh people would be talking at me and they might as well ave been talking French or summat but I just put me face behind me knees and I never said nothing.

'Shawnie. SHAWNIE. Shawnie, you want your brother to be safe, don't you? Where is Jason, Shawnie?'

I stared at them over me knees.

'Do you know where Jason is, Shawnie?'

I shook me ead.

JASON

top man

I was meeting Jez, is mate Connor and that tosser Carl over Melvin, outside the Venture. It was their first time with Shawnie for Jez and Connor and when I turned up – late of course – they were stood there, trying a look cool but Jez was acting nervous as ell. Nice to ave the upper 'and on Jez for a change.

'Jez mate. Alright? Ope yer feelen ornay, mate, you got a fucken treat en store. Eh's Connurr, yeah? Right Connurr.'

E nodded and never said nothing. Arrogant cunt or out of is depth, I couldn't quite figure it yet.

Carl struts up from up Galway. E raises is fist and makes me meet is punch alfway with mine.

'Right Jase? Top man.'

E did the punching thing with Jez and Connor.

'Connurr, Jez. Long time, boys.'

We eaded off over Lurgan. It's only three minutes from there. Carl used to get is gear from Jez but e was moving with a different crowd now so there was a bit of needle at first but they were soon talking about a 'welcome back' deal. Jez reckons e's a bit like BT: might not always be the cheapest but you knows it's a top service and reliable, like. Reliable's a big deal for druggies. Jez was always carrying and I've ad some right fucking shite off of other dealers, never Jez. E knows I'll come back. Not that I'm a druggy like, but for weekends, look.

By the time we got to my place, they were new best buddies.

'What the fuck's at, a fucken advurrt?' goes Carl, laughing. SHAWNIE SUCKS. Fucken ell, man. What the fuck you got *that* wretten on yer ouse forr?'

'I never fucken wrote eht, ded I?' I goes. 'Sides, ain't my fucken ouse, ehs eht? Some cunt done eht.'

'You nevurr urrd a white spereht, Jason?'

First fucking words Connor ever says to me and I'm thinking about aving the cunt already. Sounded Artcliffe an' all. 'Like I says. Ain't my fucken ouse, ehs eht? Jew want that fucken blow-job or no?'

'Take et steaday, mate, I'm just sayehn –'

'Jus sayehn what, pal?'

'Jus sayehn, that can be cleaned off of yer ouse easay.'

'You fucken deaf or stupehd? Eht AIN'T – MY – OUSE.'

'Alright mate, alright. No fence, yeah? Less go see the luvlay Shawnay, yeah?'

Fucking smart cunt.

'Connurr, mate,' goes Carl, 'she ehs good. She ehs fucken dog's, man.'

I turned me key in the lock and opened the front door.

'Shawn? SHAWNAY?'

Not a fucking dicky bird.

'Ma?'

It was nearly four o'clock. First day back at school and that for Shawnie but I figured she could get a 'andful in before the Cockney cunt come back. Connor was staring at me with a little smile on is face. Seriously fucking embarrassing this.

'Lesten,' I goes, 'set down an' I'll find us all a drink. Our Shawn'll be back en a meneht.'

I checked upstairs but when I come down Carl and Jez ad moved on, they'd been making plans. They'd forgotten about their cocks already. Druggies can do that.

'You're alright, Jase mate. No worries. Listen,' goes Jez, 'we're just cookin up. Don't suppose you'd be interested?'

'Fuck off, Jez, you ain't fucken cooken up en ere. Shawnay's back any fucken meneht. Eh's me Ma's ouse for fuck's sakes.'

Fucking junky cunts.

'Whoa, Jasuhn, don't spet yer dummay out,' goes that Artcliffe cunt, grinning.

I smiled back at im. They three'd never seen me in action. Connor was sat on the arm of the settee.

'Connurr, mate,' I goes, strolling towards im, 'thurr's summat I gotta tell yowe . . .' and as I said 'yowe' me Nike Air connected with is chin summat wicked. I eard a crack, which might ave been tooth or jawbone. Is ead smacked back into the wall and I decided to finish im off with knees and elbows. When you're fighting up close, you gotta forget about fists and feet, you'll never land em. Up close, you needs your ead, your teeth, your knees and your elbows.

I ad Connor against the wall and I wasn't gonna let im fall. I kept me right knee going into is bollocks and me elbows going into is face. Is ead smacked against the wall again and again. E was fucked but e couldn't go down. Is blood and spit were spraying out onto me and e was making noises like a fucking girl. E fell in the end when Carl and Jez got old of a shoulder each and pulled me back. When e went down, I aimed a kick at is face which, unluckily, just missed. E ad blood coming out all over. E was fucked.

Carl and Jez ad to elp im outside, fuck knows what they did with im. Couldn't give a shit. I felt so fucking good I was buzzing, man. I felt so fucking good, I ad to celebrate with a wank in the kitchen sink, Jesus, didn't ardly need me right 'and. I just ad to remember the sound is ead made on the wall. And the look in is eyes.

I started looking for our Ma's booze stash.

There was a can of White Lightning in the fridge as usual and I figured that would be a good starting point so I took it out and turned round and saw the dried blood, smeared and spattered all over the kitchen. I didn't know what ad appened but I was scared for our Shawnie now. I guessed it was our Ma's. Whatever, I knew it was time a sort Steve out once and for all so I got the big spanner from under the stairs, found our Ma's vodka stash, cracked the can open and sat down on our Ma's settee. Can in one 'and, spanner in the other. The springs in the settee were fucked – fat slag. I put the telly on and it was *Countdown* but I wasn't watching anyway. I was thinking about that spanner going into Steve's ead just like it done with Keiran's ead all they years ago. Catch the London cunt by surprise. Won't know what's it im. Long as you stays ahead of the game, you always ends up on top. Keiran comes around all the time to score off of Jez. Right fucking loser.

That can lasted about five minutes. I started on the vodka. I was mixing it with that fucking awful Aldi Coke.

By six o'clock, I'd ad almost alf a bottle (no problem, bottle and a alf left) and not a fucking soul turned up. I knew there was summat strange going on but I never knew what.

I done some chips. Dry blood on the microwave – there's some serious fucking ygiene issues in this ouse, no mistake. Just for a change. I sat on the chair with the spanner and the chip box on me lap. Lurgan Walk's a quiet street and I knew I'd ear Steve's car when e come back.

When I finished me chips I lit a Marlboro and tipped another vodka and Coke out. *Buffy* on the box. Shite. Wouldn't kick er out of bed, mind. One good thing about Steve, and it's the *only* fucking good thing about im, is that e've ad Sky put in. If no one came back, I figured I could kill time with Everton v Villa. Match started at eight.

The bollocks before it with Andy Gray and that started at seven.

After a little kip I thought I'd waste alf an hour or so checking out what Steve ad been doing on the computer e'd put in me room (like I couldn't guess) but the cunt ad tied it up with passwords and obscure usernames and what ave you and there was no fucking way so I went back down, tipped meself a massive fucking slug of vodka with a little splash of Coke and switched to Sky Sports. Richard Keys was doing is usual crap, talking shit-loads and saying fuck all. We got a big mirror in the all and I practised some moves with the spanner while e prattled on.

I rang Shawnie's mobile but there wasn't no answer. Our Ma's a sad fucking slapper and she ain't got one now cos she dropped ers down the fucking toilet and I wasn't gonna ring that Cockney cunt. I started watching the match. Bit of a fucking contrast after watching the City. Premiership's like a different game. I mean, it's not like you're talking about two top sides ere but the difference in class is obvious straight off. Ball control, movement into space, stuff like that. Everton went one up through Marcus Bent on the hour mark.

I filled up the ashtray with dog-ends and me belly with vodka. Me old mate, spanner, sat on me lap.

I must ave closed me eyes for a bit cos I missed the end of the game and the next thing I knows, I'm earing a key in the front door. It was dark, except for the light from the telly. I slipped me fingers round the small ead of the spanner. The front door started a swing open. I tightened me grip as I id in the shadow of the sitting-room door.

STEVE

never done nothing

Tell you what, it's a while, it's a fucking while since I been down the cells. Last time was bleeding years back: drunk and disorderly in Kilburn; I mean, who isn't? Nothing come of it. I ain't never done time but I done a hundred and twenty hours' community service for handling stolen goods. Videos: small beer, kids' stuff. This was serious.

I didn't have no company which is always a fucking relief. You never know what sort of drunken scumbag or drugged-up nutter you can end up with in there. It was a square cell and there was wooden benches on three sides of it. It was clean, you could smell the disinfectant, but you can never shift the stench of piss and puke and assorted body fluids that have been swilled and spilled, spattered and smeared around in a cell, year after year.

I lay on the middle bench and stared at the ceiling. I wasn't gonna sleep, was I? My mind was doing the 2,000 Guineas. What the fuck was going on? I was the one who'd been offended against for fuck's sake so what the fuck was I doing in this shit-pit? I couldn't believe Lisa or Shawnie would say anything but they must have bleedin done. You look after your own but anyway, why the fuck would they risk getting Tone even angrier? Didn't make no sense. Fuck it, coppers didn't have nothing. My word against theirs, a half-wit kid and a stinking drunk.

What if they looked at me computer? Fuck it fuck it

fuck it. Of course they would. Fuck it. Course they fucking would.

Look, just because I got them pictures on me hard drive, don't mean I'm some sort of fucking perv or nothing. I just needed to do a bit of research, didn't I? I mean, you don't set up a new business from scratch, do you? You check out the market.

And what was the purpose of this research, Mr Arden? Fuck it. I was in trouble.

The bastards charged me: living off of immoral earnings, gross indecency with a child and unlawful sexual intercourse with a female child. So far, they said. Big trouble. Big fucking trouble.

That ain't never fucking right, mind. I never had sex with her. I mean, it's got to be penetrative for intercourse and that, ain't it? She's only a kid for fuck's sake. Wouldn't be right. I wouldn't put a kid through that. Not before she's ready, like. She just done oral. It ain't like that's gonna hurt her, is it? Ain't like she needs no persuading neither. She just had to suck on the lolly.

I knew it wasn't gonna be good. I knew I was fucked even though I never done nothing. I hadn't, I hadn't done fuck all. Just kept a fucked up family going, that's all, and I was gonna get crucified for that. Shawnie started this anyway – it was her idea from the start so how the fuck can that be *my* responsibility? Some teenage slapper chooses to suck you off and suddenly you're a criminal. British justice – contradiction in fucking terms, ain't it. For fuck's sake: stitched up by yokel slappers, beaten up by a yokel psycho, banged up by yokel filth. You seen that film, *Southern Comfort*?

I tell you what, none of this shit would have appened in London. I've shagged loads of teenage slags there: Philippinos, Ukrainians, Albanians, Scousers, local skirt. Philippinos are best, they'll do anything (I mean anything), no comeback, they know the fucking score. They know what bleeding side their bread's buttered. I never even fucking shagged Shawnie and suddenly I'm Public Enemy Number One.

I was fucked and I knew it. I ran me hands over me face and it felt like someone else's. I ran me mind over me life and it felt the same.

The cell door opened. PC Gummidge sticks his stupid, yokel face around it and says, 'Arrden, DC Atyeo wants a lettle chat. Enterview room one.'

LISA

my lovely boy

Nearly fucking ten at night when they finished with me cos it wasn't just the police, it was social services an' all and they just went on for ever. They were at it, on and off, all day. Atyeo, DC Slag and Theresa (my new social worker) taking it in turns.

'We need to make sure you and the children are safe, Lisa.' That was Theresa. Ow many fucking times did she say it? Never said what they was going to do mind, not until way later.

'Lisa, we've taken out an Emergency Protection Order for Jason and Shawnie. That means a judge thinks that for their own safety, your children have to be taken into immediate protective care.'

'Whatchoo fucken mean, protecteve curr? You ain't aven my kehds.'

'Lisa, we've already picked Shawnie up from school. It seems that Jason didn't get to school today and he's not at your home so we're still looking for him. Perhaps you could help us –'

'Fuck off, fuck off. You ain't aven my blooday kehds, thurr mine. I wouldn't blooday tell you whurl e wuz fiy knew.'

'You don't know whurr your son ehs?' goes DI Atyeo.

'Well, I sees em, don't I? I sees ehm most days, but e ain't sleepen ovurl ours.'

'And you nevurr asked em whurr e *es* sleepehn?'

'E wouldn't tell I, would e? E don't tell I nuffehn. What you done wev our Shawnay? Whurr's my lettle girl to?'

Atyeo looked at Theresa, who said, 'Shawnie is safe, Lisa: she's in temporary foster care with a couple in north Bristol. Lisa, this doesn't have to be –'

'You FUCKEN BETCH . . .' I lost it, completely lost it. I went for er. I didn't know what I was doing. I adn't ad a drink all day, they'd let me out for *two* fag breaks for fuck's sakes. They'd taken me daughter. It's lucky Atyeo and Slag were there cos I went mental. DC Slag ad to put me arm behind me back and press me against the wall.

'Do you want me to andcuff yowe? Do you want a be charged with assaulten a police offecerr?' she went, and I was fucking ashamed of meself cos I stopped fighting and started crying. I ates crying in front of other people, especially coppers, but I couldn't elp meself. I dooz it all the time these days.

'Lisa,' goes Theresa, 'Tony has been arrested already and Steve will be shortly. We don't know if they'll get bail and we don't think you are in a fit state to look after your children at the moment.' DI Atyeo glared at er.

I sniffed and wiped and got me shit together. 'Whatchoo wannal arrrest Steve for fer fuck's sake?' I goes. 'E ain't done nuffehn.'

'*We* don't intend to arrest him, Lisa, the police do, but according to Shawnie, he has sexually abused her on a daily basis. He also . . . hires her out to other men for sexual purposes. These are very serious offences . . . allegations, Lisa.'

I couldn't say nothing. I knew that our Shawn was doing a few favours for Steve's mates but I was doing loads worse when I was er age. Look, money don't come from fucking nowhere, do it? When I was our Shawn's age I was taking it every which way and I never got fuck all for it; just kept out the way of me stepdad's 'ands for a bit. If I was lucky. Brings the cash in, don't it? Ain't like it's urting er or nothing. Not like what our Tony done. That man's evil. E never could keep is 'ands to imself. E'll grope anything, shag anything. I'm just glad we never ad a dog.

'So what you done wev Shawnay?'

'I said, Lisa: she's in temporary foster care.'

I'd been shaking for a bit but it was getting worse now. 'Tempray? So I'm getten er back, like?' There was sweat running into me eyes.

'That depends on whether we can ensure Jason and Shawnie's safety. On whether we think you're in any state to look after them.'

'Course I can fucken look after them. Done et fer fifteen yurrs now en I?'

'Lisa, there are clearly substance abuse issues. With alcohol . . .'

'So I aves a fucken drenk, just like anyone else. Don't mean I ain't a fet fucken muvvurr, do eht? I looks after me kehds, always ave. I jus –'

'That's what we'll be assessing, Lisa. Whether you are able to look after your kids, and yourself. We'll also be offering you help with alcohol abuse, which I strongly urge you to accept. The judge –'

'I don't fucken abuse nuffehn. I jus likes a drenk like evrayone else. I jus wants me kehds.' I just wanted a drink. I likes a drink. Or two. Yeah.

'You *can* get them back, Lisa. It's up to you, love.'

'Don't you fucken "love" may. *No one* loves may.'

I knew ow stupid it sounded soon as I said it. It's amazing ow clear things can be when you aven't ad a couple. It's amazing ow much you sweats an' all.

'Lisa, we've feneshed ere,' goes DI Atyeo. 'We'll talk again tomorrow. Don't make any attempt to see Steve. You won't be allowed to anyway.'

Theresa leant over and 'anded me a card. 'This is the number of social services at Broad Walk, Lisa, and you can get me there. If I'm not there and it's urgent, there's always a duty worker, and I can be reached so that I can ring you back at any time, Lisa. I'll be in touch anyway, tomorrow. We're on your side, Lisa.'

'That's nice to know, Tresa, cos I don't thenk no one's evurr ben on my side beforr,' and she never got me sarcasm cos she put er 'and on me arm and give me a squeeze and what was meant to be a smile.

'Lisa, et's dark. We can get a patrol car to take you home.'

'I'm alright.'

I ad twenty quid in me pocket what Steve ad gave me for food the day before. The Venture's on the way ome.

'Lisa,' goes Atyeo, 'we need to find Jason. We need to make sure e's safe.'

'E's en Tembuctool an' you can stop usen me name everay fucken sentence.' I was getting cobby.

'I'm sure you care more about Jason's safety than anyone, Lisa. Please talk to us if you've got any information.'

They walked me to the front desk. There was a lad our Jason's age asleep on the bench: baggy jeans, no shirt, skinny body, baseball cap. Shit fat mum like me next to im, looking weary cos she'd been there too often.

'We'll be en touch, Lisa,' goes Atyeo.

'I'll see you tomorrow,' goes Theresa. Yeah, can't wait.

It took me two minutes to get to the Venture, five seconds for me a talk to Paddy, fifteen seconds for im to put the glass in front of me, three seconds to 'and me twenty-pound note over, two seconds to get a lovely double vodka down me neck. Lovely ain't the word. There ain't a word. I knows it can't get through to your system that quick but I felt me whole body relaxing straight off.

'Fock may,' goes Paddy.

'I ain't got the time or the enclanashun, Padday. Don't bother about change, jus keep they comehn tell me monay runs out,' I went, lighting up.

'Rate ye are, Lase.'

'Padday – glass ehs emptay.'

There was a fight at the pool table – 'Feftay pay thurr. You fucken blind or summat?'

'I ad money down fore you was even fucken yurr.'

'Whurr's et to, beg man?'

'You callen me a fucken liurr?'

Bish bash. Blood. 'E ain't wurf eht' and all that. Who gives a fuck? Don't mean fuck all, do it? The vodkas kept coming, there was a special offer: £1.80 a double.

'Yer, Padday. Any chance of a descount fer bulk?'

'Sure, yer not that beg, Lase.'

'Cheeky cunt.'

Woman shouting at man, 'Fuck off ya fucken bastard, bastard, you ain't got . . .'

And so on and so on. Next double slipped down a treat an' all. And the next. I ad an hour a spend twenty quid but it weren't a problem. It was like the fucken Wild West that night. It was like one a they John Wayne films me stepdad used a watch on a Sunday afternoon after *The Big Match*.

I just sat there. Sometimes you knows you ain't gonna get urt. I kept a good grip on me drink, sat on me stool and leant against the bar while the insults, blood and glasses flew past. The Venture was getting alf-eartedly trashed. A couple a fights ad merged and they rumbled on with no one really wanting a get urt so it was mostly shouting and shoving and that. Thank Christ our Tony wasn't there. Paddy kept serving, God was in is eaven. Everything was alright.

I got me neck wet and never thought about fuck all.

'Tha's yer twenneh gahn,' goes Paddy before closing time, giving me 20p change. Fuck.

'Tara, Padday,' I went.

They were taking the piss when I walked out the door, especially that wanker Garry. Went a school with the cunt. 'You worken, Lees? Ang on, I'm sure I got feftay pay ere somewhurr.' They all laughed. I turned on im.

'I knows about yowe, Garray. Ain't no fucken point en yowe payen feftay pay or whatevurr, way all knows thurr won't be no fucken return on *that* envestment.' I looked at is bits, look. Laughter all round, except Garry. In the net.

'Fucken slappurr.'

'Oooh, that urts.'

It's only two minutes back ome and it was a lovely night. Clear skies, more stars than you could shake a stick at and a tiny bit of autumn chill in the air. I don't like ot summers – I sweats too much. And it's always good when the kids goes back a school; time's me own then.

The telly was on but the lights were off when I got back. I couldn't think who the fuck would be watching telly. I opened the front door and startled meself with me reflection in the big all mirror. The front-room door was alf open so I pushed it and walked through and fuck me, there was a spanner chopping down through the air and it damn near scared the living shit out of me but it weren't actually a problem cos it missed me by a foot and a alf and our Jason went crashing into the i-fi after it.

E was fucked.

'Cocknay cunt,' e went from the carpet.

'Jase, eh's may. Eh's yer Ma.'

E rolled around swearing for a bit. E couldn't get up. E looked like e was going to puke, e was so pissed.

'Jase, eh's may. Eh's yer Ma.'

'Cunt,' e said and threw up on the carpet and started crying. I give im a ug and pressed im into me bosom. It's what e needed. E cried and just said 'Ma' a lot. Our first ug for seven years. Fair bought a tear to me eye. We stayed like that for ages and it was lush until I felt im starting to retch again and I pointed im away from me and the CD player.

'Come on lovurr, you needs yer bed.'

E wasn't ardly conscious by this time. I noticed that even though e'd obviously found me stash, there was still almost a bottle of vodka left next to me chair. I got me 'ands into is armpits and auled im up.

'Ma?'

'What, love?'

'Ma?'

'What, love?'

'Ma . . .'

Ave you ever tried walking with someone that drunk? I'd ad a few meself. We must ave looked a right pair going up they stairs.

We fell onto the landing slo-mo and I lay there giggling for a bit but our Jase just closed is eyes.

'Jase, nurrlay thurr, lovurr.'

'Fuckfuckangfuckun.'

'C'mon, darlehn.'

I got im into is bedroom, where e belongs, and let im fall onto the bed. E was asleep when e it it. I took off is shoes and socks and they didn't smell too clever. I took off is T-shirt and is trousers. It's really ard undressing someone when they're a dead weight. E was lying there in is boxers. My lovely boy. Is face looked like it did when e was a babby. So peaceful. E was on top of the duvet what's a double look, so I just folded it up over im, kissed im on the forehead and said, 'Night, beauteful.'

My lovely boy.

JASON

on me own

I kept me eyes clamped shut cos the sun was fucking streaming through the window.

It come to me, slowly, that I was in me old room over Lurgan. I was feeling like a tramp's turd and me ead was fucking splitting so I concentrated on not moving anything except me right 'and.

You know what it's like when you're alf awake and alf asleep. I ad a ard-on like the Leaning Tower of Pisa as I went over and over a job I done last week in Vicky Park. Fucking dog's, it was.

It ad been another ot day. What a fucking eatwave. There was flesh everywhere and most of it would ave been best kept under wraps truth be known, but it was the fag-end of summer and most of it was brown at least and there was a few lumps of pork worth sniffing.

I'd strolled around, staring people out, waiting for me chance. Cock getting ard at the thought of it. So much pork, so little time.

Posh Pork was lying there fucking begging for it. She was in the bushes, couldn't be seen from three directions. Little stretchy shorts, Nike sports bra top, sweat trickling between er tits, which were fucking tasty. I mean, not Jordan standard but well worth getting your 'ands on. Couldn't see er ass cos she was lying on it but I knew it would be good. Smooth brown shiny skin with wispy fine bleached airs on it. Bottle of mineral water. Top mobile clamped to er ear. My kind of girl.

'You are such a liar. You are such a bloody liar . . . I can't believe . . . Charlotte!'

She kept the mobile clamped to er ear and give me a right eyeballing as I walked past.

'Charlotte!'

I stood on the other side of the bushes and listened in.

'Oh right, and it's not like he does. Have you ever met a bloke that doesn't?'

I thought about er nipples. I figured they'd be little firm brown ones on the soft white skin what the sun adn't got to. I ad to put me 'and down the front of me trousers – when you got a cock as big as mine, it can be fucking murder when you gets a ard-on – and I rearranged meself while she finished er call. Not much pubic air I reckoned and I reckoned right.

'You are *such* a liar, Charlotte, I'm not . . . WHAT? CHARLOTTE! I'm not listening to another word. I'll see you tomorrow, half ten yeah? Food Street, yeah. See ya.'

Now you're seeing me. 'Right, sweeteart, I'm the bet a rough frum yer drames. Alright fiy sets next to yer?' I went, and sat meself down without waiting for an answer.

Thing is, with posh birds, they're all gagging for it. They're used to they public school wankers what breaks out in a sweat and a stutter when a alfway decent bird gets within ten foot of them. I can't understand ow the middle-class manages to reproduce itself.

'Um, I was just wondering, well pondering really, well . . . I just thought I'd . . . well, not *ask* exactly but . . . it's just that I thought it might be awfully good fun if you and I, that is we . . . um, if we . . . er, not to put too fine a point on it . . .'

Meanwhile some dodgy fucking rogue like me steps in and shags the fucking ass off of er.

I was leaning on me elbow, looming over the tastiest bit of pork this side of the river.

They got a little water maze over Vicky Park that I used a love when I was a kiddie. Our Nan used a take us up there. You can see the trains from there going someplace better. It was just up the ill from there.

'I ain't be-ehn funnay or nuffehn, but you got the best boday en Brestol. Ow about I rubs some suntan ento yer?'

Thing is, with posh birds, they always pretends they're not interested. It's what they dooz. You just gotta fucking ignore all that and give em what they fucking wants.

She said, 'Look, I'm just looking for some peace and quiet until my boyfriend arrives; he'll be here any minute . . .' Yeah yeah. I ignored er and grabbed the factor fifteen. I squirted the suntan onto me 'ands, put me face tonguing distance from ers and slid me 'and inside er Nike bra top.

Posh Pork put er 'and on mine but she couldn't stop me. She was saying, 'Fuck off, fuck off, my boyfriend's coming,' but fuck that, they always says that.

I ad me 'and on er right tit and I was nearly bursting me zip open and I could tell she was well turned on. Posh birds always gets the ots for me. Bit of rough innit?

'You dooz what I sez darlen and you dooz et quiet look or yer boyfriend ain't nevurr gonna wanna look at you again.'

I took er nose in me mouth, really gentle look, and gave it a little bite.

'I can do whatevurr the fuck I wants wev yowe, darlehn.'

She shut up complaining then and I worked me left 'and inside er little shorts. She only ad skimpy little knickers on and I got two fingers up er straight off. 'Open they lovelay legs up, darlehn.' She ad a face like our Shawnie's, aged five, when Tony was touching er up. She looked me straight in the eye the whole time so I looked down at me 'andiwork and said, 'You are a fucken superstarr, darlehn.'

I tell you what, open-air sex turns me on summat

wicked. Only took a minute of that and I've shot me load in me pants, look. Well, you can't ang about when you dooz it in public, can you? I left Posh Pork trembling, like I always dooz with the ladies. She never even noticed I'd ad er mobile.

I don't like anging on to bent gear so I'd took it straight round to Sharon's, then went back to me armpit up Padstow Road. Sometimes I reckons there ain't no fucking limit cos whatever I wants I just fucking dooz it: rest of the world's too shit scared. I ain't scared of fuck all. You just needs the bottle.

A loud rapping on the door stopped me 'and going up and down and brought me back to the ere and now. I opened me eyes and the sun nearly fucking blinded me. The noisy cunt at the door started ammering again.

'Fuck eht,' seemed the only reasonable thing to say so I said it and staggered over to the window. Rough or what? It was like someone ad pissed in me brain.

I saw the patrol car outside.

'Fuck eht.'

There were so many reasons I didn't want to talk to the Old Bill. I was in me boxers but I found me clothes neatly folded on the chair at the bottom of the bed. I was still trying to figure out what the fuck I was doing there and what I'd got up to last night as I pulled me clothes on double quick. Shit on a stick, man. I clattered down the stairs and saw our Ma, unconscious, in the front room, vomit all over the carpet. Ahhh, I'd missed ome life. She was fully clothed, thank Christ; fag in er 'and, burnt down to the butt; lights still on, CDs scattered all around er; lying on the floor with er ead propped against the i-fi which was well smashed up. Filthy fucking slut. I thought about aving a little puke on er meself cos I needed one but there really wasn't the time. I could see two woodentops through the glass of the front door and I guess they must ave seen me but I wasn't stopping for they wankers.

'POLICE,' they shouted. Never.

I never even ad time a nick nothing. I went out through the kitchen, macheted me way through the back garden (our Nan used a get er mate's orse in to sort it out in the old days) and was up over the back wall, into the brambles in the path out back. The path leads to Glyn Vale and I ran there with a ammer smacking into me ead each time me foot it the ground. When I reached the pavement I threw up skilfully, ardly breaking stride, over the pretty flowers in some cunt's front garden and started walking up towards Donegal Road. I knew I could dive back down the lanes if the coppers come but they never. Always one step ahead.

I lit a Marlboro and tried to figure out what the fuck was going on as I walked back over Padstow. Me brain wasn't working so well. I was feeling rough as fuck and I was acking me guts up – some right phlegmers. I got to Melvin and a police car drove past but I was cool. I just carried on walking with me ead down. I couldn't fucking remember, I really couldn't. I knows our Ma wasn't there. No one was when I turned up. She *was* in the morning. Nobody else, mind. Where ad Steve and our Shawnie got to? I couldn't figure it. I remembered Everton were beating Villa 1–0 but I'm pretty sure that wasn't the final score.

Jez, Carl and Connor fucked off someplace. I remembered what I done to Connor alright. Gobby cunt, ad it coming.

I chucked me fag in the gutter and thought about our Nan and our Ma. And our Shawn. Black Phil, Siantell, Jez, Scott Two. Every one a they cunts ad turned their backs on me. And me Dad, I suppose, wherever the fuck e is. Whoever the fuck e is. I probably knows im – I knows all the faces round ere. None of em gives a fuck, mind. No one gives a fuck. Fair play, I don't give a fuck about none a they neither. I don't give a fuck about no one and no one gives a fuck about me. I should write a song.

I couldn't go back up Padstow, not if the filth were looking for me. I lit another Marlboro and the breeze blew the smoke down Galway. I was on me own.

SHAWNIE

what I done and what I said

I was really scared cos they said I couldn't go ome cos of what I done and what I said. Everybody wanted a look at me bits and talk about, you know, sex.

It was nearly dark and Theresa was driving me through town.

'Sophie and Simon live north of the river, Shawnie. They live in Redland.' I'd never been to Redland.

I likes going through town at night. I ain't ardly never done it so it was really exciting. Bright lights and loads of posh cars and thousands of people. Pakis and black guys and loads of really tall people – really, they all looked like models or summat. They got new fountains in the centre, just oles in the ground look, and there was loads of drunk people in them. They looked like our Ma, rolling around there in the water. They wants a put a fence up or summat cos the likes of our Ma just falls in and can't get out again.

Theresa said, 'How do you feel, Shawnie?'

I felt really excited. I wanted a see me Ma but Theresa said I'd see er soon. I didn't want no more of our Dad and Steve and is mates and that. Jason's mates an' all. That willy train kept on chugging in and I was sick of it. I didn't know what was appening with our Jason mind, and that was scary. 'Whurr's our Jason to?' I went.

'We don't know, Shawnie. We were hoping you could tell us. We're worried about Jason.'

Don't you worry about Jason. 'E's alright.'

'How do you know, Shawnie?'

'Look,' I went, and I pointed at the big ship in lights. Like the *Titanic* except it don't sink. I loves that ship. Makes me think of that song we ad in the infants: *the big ship sailed on the ally ally oh, the ally ally oh, the ally ally oh*. Never did understand what that meant. I remembers when our Nan took us for a pizza and we went in a taxi and I saw that big ship up in lights and it gave me a feeling in me guts what I can't explain. It's almost like being scared but sort of nice. That was ow I was feeling but I couldn't explain all that so I never said nothing.

There was this fella who was as drunk as our Ma gets, being dragged across the road by is mates. Theresa ad a slow down quickly and she said summat nasty what I couldn't quite ear.

The shops were so posh. I never said nothing but I was thinking about walking into them with loads of money like Paris Hilton or Coleen whatsit or summat and buying this and buying that. Clothes and jewellery and posh chocolate and stuff.

We left the shops behind and started driving past some really tall old ouses, a bit like the ones over the other side of the Wells Road except there's loads of big cars parked outside these uns.

Theresa parked the car and got out and I just sat there so she opened the door for me and I got out like Lady Muck but I didn't wanna.

'This is Sophie and Simon's house, Shawnie. *Your* house now.'

I saw the curtains twitching and a woman's face look out the window. It wasn't my ouse.

Theresa walked up to the door and I stayed two steps behind er.

Sophie answered the door and she looked sort of old

but nice. She smiled a lot; she smiles all the time. She got purple bits in er air and I knows she dyes it cos no one's got purple air in this country. She wasn't wearing no shoes and er clothes was lush, like you gets in magazines, posh but not showy, like. She ad black streaks going through er air an' all which must ave been weaved in or summat. She says sometimes she aves different colours in it and sometimes she just dyes the whole lot a different colour an' all just when she feels like it. She curls er eyelashes with a eated eyelash curler. She's so cool.

Sophie moved towards me like she wanted to ug me or summat but she changed er mind and dropped er 'ands to er sides and said, 'Shawnie, you must be hungry, darling. Can I make you a sandwich? We've got ham, mackerel paté or Cheddar. Salad of course. Or maybe just a drink? We've got Coke.'

I never said nothing.

This fella come down the stairs. E was a bit fat and e ad this baggy white tracksuit top on with summat written on the back. Sophie said it says Real Madrid. E said, 'Sorry I wasn't here to say hello, I was on the computer. You must be Shawnie. Welcome to our humble abode, Shawnie. We weren't quite certain if Jason was coming with you.'

I never said nothing and no one else did neither so there was a silence what made me look down to the ground till Theresa said, 'We're hoping to bring Jason here soon.'

Sophie and Theresa talked for ever and Simon tried to join in an' all but you could tell this was something that Sophie and Theresa ad been planning together and they were stuck with letting im join in as well. Like when I used a tag along with Jason and is mates when they were trying a do boys' stuff. Killing frogs and stuff.

I wanted me Ma and I cried a little bit but I never made a sound and I don't think no one noticed.

'Shawnie, come on in. This is your house now, darling;

treat it as your own. The TV's through there, you can use the computer in the back room any time you want but don't touch Simon's whatever you do. I'll show you your room.'

They gave me me own room: it's lush. It's got a big window what looks out on the garden and the garden's not so big but it's dead nice cos it ain't got no brambles but it's got flowers and an apple tree and a little pond and it's even got black bamboo. They got real green beans growing there an' all and we aves em for tea but, tell the truth, you gets sick of they after a bit. They got two guinea pigs and they uses em to cut the lawn: Simon says e never dooz it. Sophie says, 'Guinea pig shit's just as good as horse shit for the flowers.' I likes looking out the window and listening to the guinea pigs going 'weep weep'. They're lush. My room've got a double bed and proper curtains and everything. There ain't no carpet but it's got these wooden floorboards what's all black and polished and an amazing rug what's really thick and woolly and you can cuddle up into it and I can do stuff like that cos Sophie and Simon always knocks before they comes in. I spends loads a time in there and they just leaves me alone. I got me own bathroom and toilet an' all cos Sophie and Simon ave got one in their bedroom what they uses. I got olive oil soap and it smells queer, look, but it's alright.

Simon said me duvet's made out of real goose feathers, and me pillows. I'm like, 'Ain't that a bet tight on the goose?' and e laughed. E's nice really. E don't get me a do nothing dirty. E just chats and jokes and I gets a bit shy but that's alright. They pillows is lush. You just sinks into them and the duvet feels like a cuddle.

I tell you what, there's only one bad thing about staying ere: they ain't got no crisps, they ain't got no sweeties, no cakes, no chocolate, no Nesquik, no nothing. Sophie gives me almonds and dried apricots when I says I'm ungry. She says, 'Dried apricots are lush,' but it don't sound right when she says lush. Sooner be bleeding ungry, pardon me French.

Sophie or Simon drives us over Florrie every morning and e've got this massive big car and I feels so posh.

Christopher's still me boyfriend: we snogs at dinner-time and that and sometimes I sucks im off behind the Terrapin but it's ard when you lives someplace else. Ard to ave a proper relationship, look.

Sophie lets me use er nail varnish and she's got *seventy-three* different colours! She talks about sex, loads. She talks about sex like it's summat everybody dooz. I told er about Christopher, well, not everything. She said e could come round if I liked. She drinks loads of wine but she never pukes up or passes out or spends all evening shouting and crying like our Ma dooz. Sophie's got snake-skin shoes and leopard-skin knickers. Sometimes she wears they knickers what comes over the top of your jeans (I can't wear they) and I reckons er ass is a bit big for that but she says, 'Fuck it. If they don't like my fat arse they don't have to look at it, do they?' Sophie swears loads but somehow it don't sound so bad.

Sophie says, 'This is *your* house now, Shawnie. I don't know all that's happened but I do know you've had a hard time. Any time you want to talk, I'll listen, darling, but if you don't want to, that's fine too.'

Sophie works doing circus costumes and stuff. She've got a work-room in the ouse which is *so* messy. It's got cotton and bits of material all over the floor and boxes and funny-looking dummies that are like, naked people what ain't got no eads and arms and legs an' that; beautiful and skinny, mind. There's framed photos on the wall: ladies dressed in next to nothing or as spiders and that but you can still see loads and they're out in the street and what ave you. You gets like, massive flowers and jellyfish and stuff, what she've made, all over the room and all over the ouse and after a bit you gets used to it and it don't look funny no more. When people comes to the ouse mind, they gotta think . . . well I don't know what they gotta think, but she've always got stilt people and circus people and that coming round. I ain't got a clue what to say to em so I just goes to me room, look.

Sometimes Sophie gets me to dress up in a costume to try it on, look. I been a scorpion and a flower and a sun thingy. I didn't fit into the flower. Sophie said, 'Sod it, I'll have to change the harness,' but I thinks she was just being nice cos they circus people are loads skinnier than me. Everybody's skinnier than me. I thought blokes wouldn't like me if I was really fat but it don't put most of them off. Nothing do. They just gotta do it, ain't em?

Sophie dooz stuff with druggies an' all: painting and pottery and that down Totterdown. Can't see ow that's gonna elp but she reckons it's really important; makes a difference and that.

Simon works all the time. I don't ave nothing a do with e really but e's nice. E dooz summat with computers at that place what dooz they cartoons with that dog and the cheese and that. I don't talk much a Simon but e says that's OK, we'll chat when I'm ready.

Sophie's got a belly-button ring. She says she can't let er Ma see it cos she'd be so mad. Our Ma'd never notice. I'm gonna get a belly-button ring.

JASON

last fucking supper

I lit a Marlboro and looked out the window onto Wilder Street. I reckons I'm the only white face in the street but that don't bother me cos coons are cool. I tell you what, it's fucking amazing for gear around ere, I mean I'd ardly been ere for ten minutes and I'd been offered all sorts; you name it. I thought Knowle West was easy but St Pauls is fucking ridiculous. You can get rock easier than a pint of milk round ere. That's meant a be the best, that's summat I gotta try – rock that is. I've ad milk and I can't be fucking doing. Our Ma says er milk curdled in me mouth.

Black Phil nearly ad a fucken ead fit when e saw I on is doorstep. E's living over ere with is dad, Norris, now. Is Ma've got such a fucking crack abit she've totally lost interest in im: bit like mine I suppose. She lives in some fucking ore ouse over Easton but e don't ave nothing a do with er. I didn't old no grudge against Norris. E's a decent fella. Phil was still going a school over Artcliffe. Bit of a fucking journey if you asks me but e'd turned into a right fucking keener.

'I wants a get a fucken edjucayshun, man. I wanna gev meself opshuhns.'

'You got opshuns, Phel. You can lev en a black shet-ole or a white shet-ole but you stell gotta get yer wedge.'

'Tha's why I wanna pass me GCSEs, man. Then I can do business studies, computurrs –'

'Fuck off, Phel. Thes ehs me yer talken to. Member turnen over that Pakay shop? Twice? Steamen that offay over Bemenster? Fucken dog's, man. We're a team, man, the best. Phel, I'm doehn mobiles now. Et ehs such a fucken piece a pess.'

'I ain't doehn that shet no more, man. I'm on the level.'

'So you won't be wanten a dodgay fag then? Mr Clean eh?' I goes, lighting up. E took one. I always knows ow to make someone look small or stupid or like they're contradicting themselves, look.

'Fuck et man, we were jus fucken over the fuck-ups who ain't got fuck all en the first place. I'm going enta besness, man, then I can fuck over mellions a people at the same time – on the level.'

'On the level? What you fucken chatten about, man? You don't fenk you ain't be-ehn screwed ovurl evray fucken day of yer life?'

'Don't fucken tell me what a do, man. I wants a stay alive, I wants a stay en one piece and I wants a stay out a neck. Fiy dooz jobs wev you, at least one a they free fengs ain't gonnal appen. Few wants a stay ere a couple a nights, you gotta keep yer fucken nose clean, no shet, man. And I means a couple – tha's two, right?'

'Whatever you sez, boss,' I goes, reckoning I could get as long as I fucking fancied cos I could play im like a fiddle.

'And I don't wanna fucken *know* why you gotta get outta Knowle West so bad.'

'You knows I can't lev wev that Cocknay cunt thurr.'

'I knows all yer mates levs on the estate.'

'They ain't me mates. I got one fucken mate I can trust.' Jesus, *me* getting slushy.

'Fuck off, battay boy, you after my black ass or summat?' and we both laughed and we were both embarrassed. This is where they always ugs on telly, like on *Friends* and that but fuck that.

'I ain't that fucken desprurt. I got fucken pork queuen up fer thes slice of white meat, man. Less be honest ere, Phel, no one actually fucken *likes* black puddehn.'

'What, feh's that or a fucken chepolata?'

I swung for im, just messing about like, and e went, 'Wankurr,' when I smacked im on the shoulder and we traded a few blows in a pretend fight until we got too close to each other and we fell on to the bed wrestling. E ad me pinned from behind so I went, 'Ey, battay boy, keep that fucken black pudden away from my skinny white ass,' so e ad to let go cos e was embarrassed and e give me a little shove to make sure I never caught im with a fly one on the break.

'Yer a cunt, Jason,' e goes, and we both giggled like we was kids.

Phil's dad, Norris, was so fucking shocked when e come back from work and seen me there. E went, 'Jeeezas,' when e come in the front door and saw I sat in is chair. I could see e thought I might smack im one or summat but I just said, 'Right Norrehs, dedn't ardly recognize you wev yer cloves on,' but I never smiled or nothing cos I wanted a keep im guessing.

Black Phil gave me the dodgiest look and said, 'Dad, Jaysan's staying a beht, coupla nights, look.' E didn't know which accent to use. Norris couldn't ardly say no, could e?

E muttered summat Jamaican as e walked out the front door and I never saw black ide nor curly air of im after that.

Phil started cooking chicken and rice and I swear, no joke, it was the business. It was the best fucking meal of me life. Last fucking supper as it turns out. I got im a tell me where the nearest offy was and I spent the last of me money on eight cans of Lynx Super and forty Grosvenor. I tell you what, I wasn't gonna be steaming *that* offy in a urry. Fucking rough boys in there, man. I mean, I could take em and that but there ain't no point when there's easier targets.

I ate a shit-load of Phil's amazing food and shared me cans, e only wanted two, look. I woke up next day with me clothes on and Phil long gone. School I suppose. Loser.

Fucking strange, that's for sure. Norris was at work so I ad the place to meself. There was alf a can left next to me bed so I finished it off with me first fag of the day while I got me shit together. I was on Phil's bed cos e'd slept on the settee, look. You really feels Lynx Super when you aves it first thing. It's almost like browns. I ad a few phlegmers, put me ead down and started a feel uman again. It was only ten so I kicked off me trainers and T-shirt and track-suit bottoms, pissed in the sink and went back to the land of nod, with a little elp from me right 'and. Nearly fucking dinner-time by the time I wakes up so I drifts downstairs in me boxers and starts poking around. I chewed on a piece of toast as I looked at their CD player. Nice bit of gear and I could get a tidy wedge for it but you don't rip your mates off.

I knew, I fucking knew that Norris would ave a rum stash and I never even ad to search for it neither cos it was on the sideboard in the front room. Two thirds of a bottle. When I found it.

Norris and Black Phil ain't got Sky so I ad to watch shite on telly: *Neighbours*; *Doctors*; *Bollocks, She Wrote*; *Design Wars* with Lorraine Fucking Kelly for fuck's sake. That rum was in me belly and I couldn't give a shit.

Never ad Woods 100 before (the fucking strength of it, Jesus) but it slips down a fucking treat and warms you from your innards. Fucking ell, I was even enjoying *Ready Steady Cook* – I mean, gobbing at Ainsley Arriott obviously. I loves the way spit on the screen makes the little coloured dots look uge.

I eard car doors slamming outside but I didn't think nothing of it cos you gets so much of that round there. I eard the key go in the door and I figured it ad to be Phil cos it was too early for Norris a be back from working with that cunt Steve, look, so I kept me 'and down the front of me boxers and I kept on rubbing me big toe into the trail of spit that was trying a run down Ainsley's front.

'Phel mate, I gobbed on the black cunt, look.'

'Hello, Jason.'

Posh voice, posh tart. I tucked me knob in, took me 'and out me pants and turned to look at er. Well past it: floppy tits, phoney smile, St Werburgh's get-up. Wish I'd fucking saved me gob for she. She ad two coppers stood behind er. Behind them was My Little Judas, Black Phil, putting is keys in is pocket, looking down at the nasty carpet.

'Jason, my name's Theresa. I'm a social worker attached to Broad Walk . . .'

LISA

blocking out the light

Our Jase ad scarpered by the time I woke up. Big surprise. Mind, e never left no visible marks on me so summat's gotta be getting better.

I was feeling a bit fragile, truth be known, cos after I put Jason a bed I ad a bit of thinking a do, in fact, I ad a lot of fucking thinking a do and God's own drink always elps that. I played, you know, emotional stuff – and it ad to be tapes cos our Jason ad gone and broken the CD player, adn't e? – what let me think: Whitney, Bryan Adams, stuff like that. Stuff what our Shawnie says is 'rubbesh' and our Jason says is 'fucken sad'. What do they know? What does it matter? They ain't fucking ere no more.

'Everything I do, everything . . .' I do it for me. It's true, ain't it? Let's be brutally fucking honest ere, I never done fuck all for our Shawn and our Jase. I can't pretend no different. I only ever thought about where the money's coming from. And the next drink. Same thing really. I'm a waste of space but our Shawn's a diamond. Some'ow. No thanks a me. Jason's a wrong un. No two ways about it. A wrong un, e was born that way. I been fucking kidding meself for ever but e've took a bad turn, no mistake. When e was a babby look, e used a bite me, kick me. When e was three e used a ave paddies, oohh, I couldn't go out, couldn't go past the shops over Melvin cos e'd ave a paddy about they little toys over there; couldn't go past the shops over

Leinster cos e'd ave a paddy about sweets. I couldn't fucking move. What could I do? I stayed in cos I couldn't stand the paddies and I never ad the money a get im stuff every day. I'd nip out for me cans and that when e was asleep, look. That or I'd stick im in front of the cartoons. E was alright with that and it meant I could get a quick one down while I give some time to our Shawnie. Change er nappy an' that. She was a lush babby. Never cried or nothing, well, ardly. She liked rocking backwards and forwards like she was dancing or summat. She done it for hours and never screamed for nothing.

Our Jason was a fucking nightmare, e never stopped. When e was five e started urting imself on purpose: sticking knives into is arm; jumping on broken bottles with no shoes on; burning imself with a lighter, e just never give a monkey's. Nothing changes. Once we got a video player e was so much better, mind. Big, clunky old thing. We ad loads of videos: *Fireman Sam*, *Scooby Doo*, *Power Rangers*; stuff like that. Shut im up for ages and give us a chance to spend a bit of time with our Shawnie. Fuck that, who am I kidding? Shawnie never got a look in. She done er rocking and I done me drinking. Like I always done. Like I dooz now till nothing makes no sense no more. Till nothing matters.

Except it do cos our Jason's a nutter and our Shawnie's just surviving, nothing more. It's never been nothing more than that for she. I knows you can't change the brains and the personality you're born with and that but it's gotta be partly down a me.

Loads a fucking stuff's my fault but I'm gonna change, I'm gonna be a proper Ma, to our Shawn at least. I knows I lost our Jase. I just needs the fucking chance but I can't do fuck all now, can I? They fucking took er, ain't em? I aven't known what our Jase ave been doing for a long fucking time. E don't fucking say nothing a I and e don't fucking listen, do e? It's gotta be ormones and that. Boys aves ormones an' all. And the fact e's a nutter. Never ad a dad. Never ad a Ma really. I mean, I always loved im and that. Always loved the bottle more – and that's the truth. More than our Jason, more than our Shawnie, more than our Tony, more than Steve. It's shit when the turd of truth drops into your lap – means you aven't drunk enough.

I've made eight cans of White Lightning last all day and now I've got me bottle of Red Square next to me flabby right thigh. Me legs are splayed on the bathroom floor. The glass of vodka an' Coke is nestling between me thighs so's I don't spill it. I got me Smiley Face T-shirt on and I'm sweating cos it's still so fucking ot, I mean, when's it ever gonna break? Whatever appened to autumn? Don't need the T-shirt really but I'm sat in front of the bathroom mirror and I'm not sure I wants a look at where me body's to right now. Can't see too straight anyhow. Our Shawn's worse: fucking flab on she. Our Jason's lush, mind: skinny but muscly. E've got muscles on is eyelids. E've got muscles on is fucking muscles. I'm in front of the mirror and I'm looking at cellulite, dimples, rolls, red veins and that, fat ankles, stretch marks when I lifts up me T-shirt. I ain't got a waist no more – I got three rolls: tits, belly, lower belly. Second belly. Extra belly. What was Gazza's mate's name? Shit, me chin's the same. Chins *are* the same. Whatever appened? Good job there's no fucking Eskimos round ere, I'd get arpooned. Right our Poon? I never was funny; Steve says I ain't got a sense of umour. I'm just sad. A sad old slappurr. And I'm getten spots, can you fucking believe I'm getten spots? Fucken acnay. Twenty-nine years old and I'm getten fucken acnay. I looks like condemned fucken meat. I takes me T-shirt off an' et looks like summat what's ben decomposen fra mumf. Urr a lifetime. Least I gets a bet a breeze a dry some of the sweatay patchehs.

Our Ma nevurr got back. I fucken wrote a she but she never got back. When she got away from that evil cunt what called emself Dadday, she lehved ovurr arrs fra a beht, well, Tonay's reallay, I took the chance a move en soon as I got pregnant with our Shawnie, look. Tony nevurr wanted er thurr and they nevurr got on and et wuz reallay awkward, like, cos me and Tonay wanted a, you know, make love a lot and we wurr a bet noisay look and she said evrayone en the ole fucken street could earl and et wuz dirtay and arr Tonay jus turned round an' said e's ehs fuckehn ouse an' e'd do whatevurr the fuck e wantehd. Our Ma said we uz fucken animals. We tried a be quiet. Well, *I* tried a be quiet but our Tonay jus made even morr noise on purpose look and ded fengs like stand reallay close to er and gev er funnay looks and touch bets of er when e brushed past an' that and she said e gev er the wellays. She wuz en a reallay bad state and she went up the docturr's cos she couldn't get no sleep or nuffehn. E gev er pells but she said et weren't pells she needehd. She nevurr took em. She went a lev ovurr Lawrence Weston enstead; lettle granny flat ovurr Long Cross, look, fra lettle grannay uv thirtay-seven.

The Coke's downsturrs so I teps meself a neat vodkal an' et mengles wev the lettle bet a Coke wass left en the bottom of me glass. They sez you can't smell vodka but I smells et sure anuff. Our Steve sez you cun snort et but I ain't a fucken animal. Smells like one, mind. Showurr's thurr but I ain't shurl I can get up an' do the controls and that. I ain't shurl I wants to. Can't be arsed. Fiy stecks the glass next a me nose (easyurr fer me mowfe then, look) then I ain't gotta smell ow bad I mengs.

I needs a pess and I clamburrs up onto the seat and aves one. I manages not a fall off of it or nuffehn and I tries a get old a the baaffroom cabinet, look, but me legs keeps taken me away from thurl and I gottal old onta both sides uv eht a stabilize meself, look. I rests me ead against et and fenks about our Jason an' our Shawnay.

I ain't a Ma. I pulls the sliden doorl uv the murl ovurl an' loses me grep an' crashes back on me fat arse and it's like a slow moshuhn action replay va foul on the telly an' me ead smacks back an' all but lucklay don't et neffehn an' after cryen a bet I pulls me naked ulk up usen the baaff an' the senk. Me lovelay face fucken looms up ento the murl on the cupboard look. I pulls the doorl again and grabs they packets uv pells what ave sat thurr fer yurrs.

Our Ma nevurl ad fuck all but er sesturr, my Auntay Soozay look, got a job wev the *Eevnehn Post* and she ad a carl an' evrayfehn an' I memburrs when she took me an' me sesturrs over Ashton Court an' et uz luush. We walked through the woods an' et must ave behn autumn an' that cos the leaves wurl on the ground and all coulurrs look, an' we made piles of em an' Janay and Cherray burrayd I right undurl an' et uz luush cos they leaves wuz dry an' thurl uz no weight to em an' I couldn't ardlay feel em though they blocked out the light an' evrayfehn. They smelled like nuffehn I smelled before. I could ear me sesturrs gegglehn, but I knew they wouldn't nevurr do nuffehn evehl, look. I felt like I wanted a stay thurr frevurl. I wants a be thurr now. Afturl a beht they piled en on top but et uz alright cos I knew I ad a buray they en a meneht. When I done eht, et wuz like they wuz dead undurl a burial mound, cept they kept gegglehn. I left em thurr for fucken ages and watched the squerrels. Doehn what squerrels dooz.

Et'll be autumn soon; gotta be. Our Steve could drive us up. Et feels like the othurl end of the fucken world but eh's onlay ten menehts. Or our Tonay could do et. I likes they spikay leaves what goes reallay red round the outside.

Tha's jus shet. Steve and Tonay ain't goehn fucken nowhurr. Shawnay an' Jason ur gone. I'm on me own, on the baaffroom floor. Our Ma's washed erl 'ands. Fellas don't come no morr. I'm spredehn ovurr the floor like a used condom. Looken at a load a pells. Clutchen me glass a vodka.

SHAWNIE

a beautiful butterfly

'We're thinking of getting a place in West Cork,' goes Sophie. 'We went for a long weekend and it's just so beautiful there. Every corner you turn, there's another amazing view and as for the people, they are so bloody friendly. I thought our accents might make us unpopular in the pubs but I couldn't have been more wrong.'

'Yeah, they're my sort of people; Brits are so uptight.'

I could ear every word they were saying. That was Mimi. At breakfast Sophie'd said, 'Mimi is *amazing*, she's just mad. She's been my best friend since school.'

'What about the Guinness? Is it true what they say?' goes Mimi's bloke, Adam.

'Ah, no shit, it is just superb,' says Simon, 'it's an entirely different drink. You could drink it for ever but I tell you what, I didn't half get a nasty shock second morning in –'

'Oh God, here we go . . .' goes Sophie.

'I went for my morning shit, yeah?'

'Oh, do tell us more,' goes Mimi.

'And it was black, I mean really, fucking black.'

'Oh, lovely.'

'Thank you for sharing that with the group, Simon.'

'I thought I had some horrible disease or something. I just didn't know Guinness did that.'

I could ear every word.

Sophie ad asked me if I wanted to join them for the meal (little balls of melon, that I cut out, wrapped in posh am followed by duck breasts with blueberry sauce) but I was like, 'No fank yowe,' and I got er a give me a load of nibblies a take up to me room. Pringles and yoghurt raisins. Yoghurt raisins sounds disgusting but they're really nice. I insisted on the Pringles – you can suck they for ever.

'It's like asparagus, isn't it?' goes Simon. 'In fact, this really *is* interesting –'

'Oh great, it'll be piss now,' goes Sophie.

'Yeah, what does *your* piss smell like after you've eaten asparagus?'

Our Ma swears and that all the time but she don't ask questions like that. We don't eat asparagus, mind. I was sat on top of the stairs, carton of cream cheese and chives Pringles in me 'and.

'. . . not everyone can smell it. I mean, everyone's piss smells like corpse juice after eating asparagus . . .'

People talks so loud when they been drinking. I don't like it when Sophie and Simon dooz it.

'. . . but only a quarter of us can smell it. I always thought it only had that effect on some of our piss but it isn't that, it's like tongue curling: some of us can, some of us can't.'

I don't never talk about me wee. I thinks it's dirty.

'Si, if we could get off the subject of bodily excretions for a minute . . .' goes Sophie.

'Have you seen a place you fancy?' goes Mimi.

'There's farmhouses out there for fifty grand,' goes Simon. 'Fifty fucking K! Big bastards, solid as you like, thick stone walls, slate roofs, an acre or more of land. I mean you could grow half the food you need – only trouble is, it never stops bloody raining – but I don't really mind.'

'Si, is this you talking or your mate Charlie?'

'Oh, me and Adam had a quick line while you were fixing the food.'

'Simon, don't you dare let Shawnie see you and don't you dare touch that gram again without me in the room.'

I don't know who Charlie is. I fancied a fag and Sophie says I gotta do that in my room cos she don't want that 'bloody stink all over the house'. I blew me smoke out the window and watched the guinea pigs. They were eating grass, then running round their little utch, then eating grass, running round, doing silly little jumps, eating grass, then running round their little utch some more. I ad alf a packet of Pringles left and I likes a split they down the middle, then suck all the flavour off, rubbing it tasteless with me tongue. I can float away when I dooz things like that. I can still ear stuff look, but it don't bother me – don't get through. I thinks but I don't fuss. I was in another world but I still eard me name. From downstairs, look. I went back to the top of the stairs.

'. . . Shawnie *this* time. I asked her if she wanted to join us tonight but I think maybe it's too soon. It's a lot to ask for someone who's been through what she's been through,' goes Sophie. 'She'll get there, I've got faith in Shawnie.'

'She's a brilliant kid,' goes Simon, 'she's just never had a chance.'

A brilliant kid? Well, I ain't, but it's nice to ear someone say it about you. That's another thing what's never appened before.

'They didn't tell us all of the details – just what we needed to know,' goes Sophie, 'but we *do* know she's suffered severe sexual, physical and emotional abuse. Drink and drug problems in the family. Poverty, crime, mental illness; she has learning difficulties –'

'Well that's Knowle West, isn't it?' goes Adam. 'All that stuff's pretty much compulsory around there.'

Mimi said, 'Our first nanny for Josh – Tina – she was

from Knowle West. Lovely girl; could barely construct a coherent sentence but a lovely girl, salt of the earth. But you do worry about your child's language development. So bloody fat as well – we had to let her go, not because she was fat but just –'

'They plead poverty, Knowle Westers,' goes Adam, 'but they can all eat themselves into the shape of a bloody blimp. And any spare they've got goes on booze and drugs.'

'And you wouldn't do anything like that . . .' goes Sophie.

'Perish the thought,' goes Adam. 'Hey Si, let's get that gram out again.'

'We've got a bottle of Laphroaig too – goes beautifully.'

'Wait a minute, Simon, sorry,' goes Mimi. 'Sophie, what about Shawnie's brother? Jacob?'

'Let's not put a total downer on the evening, eh?' goes Simon. 'We'll save the subject of "Arr Jasuun" for when you've got a bit of Colombian Courage inside you.'

That was meant to be me but I don't talk like that.

'For fuck's sake, keep your voice down, Simon, they can hear you in Henleaze,' says Sophie.

'Hey, do you remember they used to talk about the drugs menace?' goes Simon. 'Well, that was Adam . . .'

'Oh, I remember,' goes Mimi, 'but we always called him the sad prick who can't get it up.'

'Got it up you often enough,' goes Adam.

'Do you think so, darling? Do you know how often I've brought myself off, while you're snoring beside me?' goes Mimi.

Ow can they talk like this?

'Who fancies a Laphroaig?' goes Simon.

'Ahh, proper job, my friend, mine's a large one,' goes Adam and they all starts laughing.

'Mine's a stiff one,' goes Simon and they laughed till I ad to go away. I couldn't stand a listen a no more.

I went in the bathroom and started running the bath. When I don't know what else to do, that's what I dooz, I aves a bath cos the bath ere's lush. It fills up in no time and I can ave one every day. Whether I needs it or no. Sophie've got all these bubblies and aromatic oils and bath bombs and aqua-salts and that. I likes the ginseng and tea-tree bathing pearls best. They smells lush. Sometimes I mixes two or three things together.

There's even a lock on the door. We never ad a lock over me old place cos our Jason broke it, and Steve always ad a do summat in the bathroom when I was in there. I started aving showers instead cos at least you can get they over with in a minute or two. I aves baths ere what goes on for hours. They got a radio what looks like a fish – Nemo yeah? – and it's stuck on the tiles with suckers and that and I listens a GWR. Sometimes I even sneaks a Snickers in there cos the water don't spoil they.

I thinks about life over Lurgan loads and it's funny cos it don't seem real now: it's like someone else's life. I always thought it was normal and that, what everyone dooz, but it ain't. Everyone don't drink themselves into a coma every night; everyone don't suck ten willies a day; everyone don't do stuff, all of that stuff, with their own dad and that. Sophie's taught us that, Sophie's taught us loads. Sophie's taught us I ain't normal, wasn't normal. I'm so blooming glad I'm normal now. Normal's boring, normal's good, gimme blooming normal any day. Means you ain't gotta do orrible stuff. I can just ang about looking after me Barbies and eating sweeties and listening a Ms Dynamite and straightening me air – Sophie's got they ceramic straighteners what they uses in salons and they're just amazing.

Police ave got Steve now. And our Dad. Our Ma says they ain't coming out for years, long as I tells everyone what appened. I thought I ad told everyone, I mean, I thought the ole world knew by now. I been questioned and poked and prodded and God knows what by God knows who, pardon me French. Sophie says it's alright and they're only trying to elp and I just gotta tell the truth. That's what I'm gonna do then.

My room's lush, my room's got what Simon calls 'underfloor heating' and it's so cool. I can just wear me Krazy Kat T-shirt and *nothing* else, nothing, and it's alright cos no one's gonna come in. I could be stark naked and there'd be nothing a worry about, nothing a be scared of.

Sophie come in and sat on the edge of me bath once cos I never locked the door and it was alright. I was *starkers* and she never stared or nothing. She just chatted about conditioners and that look, and it was OK. First off, I folded me arms and sort of crossed me legs a bit but you ain't gotta do that cos Sophie don't give a monkey's. I seen er with nothing on loads of times. She don't care and after a bit I didn't neither and I just lay there, normal like, and got on with washing meself. Simon always goes in their bathroom when Sophie's in the bath but e never comes near me in here. I don't ave a lot to do with e look, just cos e's a fella really, but e's nice. Really.

I got this beautiful bath-robe; Sophie gave it to me. It's white and made out of really cuddly material. I wrapped it round meself, unlocked the bathroom door and started walking back to me room. I could ear Jason's music playing from behind is door. The blokes downstairs were laughing like they'd just eard the funniest joke in the world and I eard Mimi say, 'Soph, let's go to the kitchen, babe, I can't be arsed with all this. There's loads I need to talk to you about.'

'You're missing out, girrls; but hey, it's more for us, eh Si?'

'Hey Ad, *PlayStayshuuuhhn*.'

‘Yeahhh.’

I eard Simon and Adam starting towards the stairs and I just blooming scarpered back to me room. They burst into Simon’s work-room like a couple of kiddies. I squirmed right under the duvet at the wrong end where your feet are meant a go, look. It’s lush under the duvet: I feels like the Very Ungry Caterpillar in is little cocoon. One day I’m gonna wriggle out and I’ll be a beautiful butterfly. I can’t be so bad, I mean, loads of fellas fancies me. I’ve ad more fellas squirt in me ’ands and me mouth than . . . well, loads. More than *I* could ever work out. Once, Sophie ad a bottle of wine inside er – I means the wine, not the actual bottle – and she said, ‘After a few pints, most blokes’ll shag anything. It’s no bloody compliment, it just means you’ve got tits and a pulse.’

That’s true enough I suppose but most of Jason’s mates never ad no booze in em and they still couldn’t get enough a me. I mean, I got sick of it and that but I sort of misses it an’ all. I aven’t told Sophie about Jason and is mates. I aven’t told no one. I don’t want a get im into trouble. Or me.

Sophie and Simon lets me ave five pounds a week. I been ere six weeks now so that’s loads. Don’t ave to do nothing for it.

Once Simon and Adam’d switched the computer on, I went back to the top step and sucked on a ole Pringle trying to see ow long I could keep it in one piece while they played some football game. Sophie and Mimi were putting the world to rights (our Nan always said that) down in the kitchen.

‘We don’t know the exact ins and outs of what happened, but it was sexual abuse and it was bad – seriously bad, there’s two court cases coming up,’ goes Sophie from downstairs.

'Jesus. Can they ever be normal? I mean after all that vile stuff?'

'We've seen a big difference already, especially in Shawnie. I think Jason's going to be a tougher nut to crack.'

'What's he like?'

'To be honest Mimi, he scares the living crap out of me. I won't be alone in the house with him . . .'

The first day over Sophie and Simon's I was a right misery and I felt like such a cow cos they were being so kind and that but it was alright soon cos they only went and found our Jason! E was stopping over Black Phil's, look. They've bought im over ere and e've got is own room an' all (it is *such* a big ouse). I was like, '*JASE!*' when e turned up with Theresa and I give im a great big ug but e just turned round and e was like, 'Sehs,' and finished ugging me as quick as e could and walked straight past with is bag. Sophie and Simon are so nice to im but e's like, really rude, tell the truth. It's lush to be with im again, mind. E ain't rude a me.

Sophie drives me and Jason a school every morning. I still goes up Florrie. She drops me off first, then takes Jason over Artcliffe. Theresa says she gotta make certain we gets a school. We gets the bus back, 75 takes us all the way. Sophie drives our Jase there but I don't reckon e goes in. E just angs round with is mates all day. It's only fifteen minutes' walk from Artcliffe a Knowle West. Is mates are so dodgy: druggies an' that.

We ain't allowed a see our Ma or go back over Lurgan by ourselves but Jason says no one's gonna know and I could start earning meself free fags again after school, especially if I bunked off the last lesson. I don't wanna do that no more but e keeps on going on. I ain't gonna do it. Sophie says I don't ave to do nothing I don't wanna. Sophie's right. Sophie's funny, she uses loads of funny words and loads I don't understand an' all. She says things like 'snug as a bug in a rug' and 'serendipity' and 'yeah, in a dead dog's arse'.

Our Ma ad a go a ospital after . . . you know. She's alright now and I sees er on Saturday mornings. Simon drives us over. She's normally sober and we just eats chocolate and smokes and that – it's nice. She says we'll be a family again soon and I'm like, 'Yeahl, alright Ma.' Theresa's always there. Our Jason don't come.

When our Ma was in ospital, Simon and Theresa took me back over Lurgan a get me clothes and that. I bought me Barbies and all me fags an' all. I counted the fags when I got back. One undred and three packets.

I done all the cooking over Lurgan, look, but it was only ever stuff for the frying pan or the microwave. Now Sophie's teaching me to cook properly! Not just burgers and microchips mind, but posh stuff. We talks a lot when we dooz it cos it's easier when you can look at the food and that and you ain't got someone staring into your eyes. We made scones yesterday. We ad em with chocolate spread and real cream; clotted cream, look. They was beautiful. I was sifting the flour – that's what you calls it when you shakes it through a sieve – and Sophie said, 'Shawnie, I really admire you, hun, seriously. You've been through so much, darling, and you're still smiling and having fun. *And* you're great fun to be with.'

I never knew what to say, did I? I mean, I couldn't believe she said it, and I couldn't believe she really meant it. Loads of blokes ave told me I'm good at blow-jobs and that and I reckons it's true cos they always comes back for more and some of them's just dirty but some of them says lush stuff to me when they squirts and that but I never done nothing for Sophie. I felt a tear in me eye but I never said nothing cos I never knew what a say.

'You know you can tell me anything, Shawnie, anything at all and if you don't want to talk, that's fine. If you do, that's fine too. I'll always listen and I'll never breathe a word to another living soul, not even Simon.'

I felt like I ad a say summat then and I felt like I ad a say summat about sex cos that's all anyone ever wants me a talk about, dirty stuff an' that.

I said, 'Do you like eht, you know, when Simon aves . . . you know, when e dooz eht t'yowe?'

It went quiet for a bit before Sophie said, 'Shawnie, Simon loves me. When we have sex, it's not Simon doing something to me just because he wants to or because he can. It's a way of Simon and I saying that we love each other; saying it without words.'

Sometimes I just can't elp saying things I really don't want to. 'Do that mean our Dad loves may?'

'Is that what happened, Shawnie?' She looked at me and started a fill up. 'I don't know your Dad, darling –'

'Cos e've never said nuffen, in words look, cept when e's phoned up from neck and that an' that uz jus dirtay stuff.'

'Shawnie, people express their emotions in different ways. Sometimes they choose the wrong way, like when they're violent or . . . or as you know, when they have sex with someone that they shouldn't have sex with.'

'Eht nevurr felt like love, not like our Jase loves may.'

'But Jason doesn't do . . . doesn't do what your Dad –'

'No, but I knows e loves may.' Well e don't do *that*, do e?

'I've got a big brother,' goes Sophie, 'and he still treats me like I'm some sort of annoying little toddler, pulling his willy when he takes his T-shirt off.'

'What, you dooz at?'

'Oh, once when I was two apparently. He was four. Mum says he was outraged. Didn't you ever do that? The thing is, even though he's a stroppy sod, I know he loves me, but it's a different sort of love, Shawnie. You understand that, don't you?' and she looked at me and I just looked down at her bare feet (and er toe-ring) and I never said nothing but after a bit when she never said nothing neither, I nodded and Sophie put er arms around me and said, 'Shawnie Shawnie Shawnie Shawnie Shawnie,' and we stayed ugging like that in the kitchen for ages till she put er 'ands on me shoulders and said, 'Shawnie, just remember, you don't ever, ever have to do anything you don't want to do . . . except mixing that bloody flour into the butter – scones don't make themselves, you know. Put a little pinch of salt in there as well; you won't taste it but it lifts the whole flavour.'

Simon and Adam were talking about Jason an' all.

'Tell the truth,' goes Simon, 'tell the truth, mate, Jason's a nasty piece of work. Shawnie, I mean, Shawnie's damaged goods but she's a sweet girl. Jason, fuck: I don't wanna share a world with him, let alone my house. Shawnie bloody worships him . . .'

I oped our Jason couldn't ear.

We done flapjacks, bluebray muffens. We done cornflake crunchays an' all and I knows we done they at school loadsa times but these uns wuz luush cos way used real butturr and golden serrup an' that. I'm makehn me own nibblays. En't that mazehn? *An'* I'm losen weight. I done a Sunday roast last week. Well, Sophay elped an' that but I done loads and it was luush: roast checken and tatoes, propurr gravay and evrayfehn. Wev wine, mind. Sophay puts mustard and roastehd garlec en et an' all so ehs like, forehn. Posh. Luush.

I loves et ere.

JASON

bonurr pointen at the starrs

Muffins, fucking muffins for supper, she says. 'No I do not want fucken muffehns.'

You can stick your fucking muffins up your fucking ass, Sophie darlehn, along with your onion marmalade; your 4 by 4; your rocket salad; your olive oil; your raspberry vinegar; your mineral water; your cat called Che; your guinea pigs called Dusty and Sandy; your pink, see-through computer; your Ecuadorian kitchen tiles; your Dizzee Rascal CD; your ironic seventies football calendar; your black bamboo; your ome-grown vegetables; your Fair Trade coffee; your Egyptian cotton towel set; your 'empathy'; your sad twat of a 'partner' and your Mona fucking Lisa fridge magnet. You'll ave to take your ead out first mind, and leave plenty of room for some good fat Knowle West cock.

Sophie and Simon, Simon and Sophie. They makes me want a fucking die, I swear. They dooz my fucking ead in. I ain't gotta stay ere, I can do whatever the fuck I fancies. It's our Shawnie, ain't it? That kid's ad too much shit in er life, too many people letting er down. I'm all she got fucking left. I can't walk out on er.

Sophie takes er to see our Ma (in er 4 by fucking 4, all-terrain vehicle) every Saturday morning. Always asks me if I wants a go: 'Are you ready to start building bridges with your mother yet, Jason?' and I always says, 'Fuck off.' What else am I gonna say? Why would I wanna see that fucking slapper? Shawnie's just a kid, ain't she? You can understand it, wanting a see er Ma and that but I ain't fucking going unless there's summat in it for me and that drunken waste of space ain't got fuck all left. I blags a lift down with them far as Lurgan, then fucks off over Padstow, do some gear with Jez and the lads.

I goes over most weekdays an' all cos Sophie gives us a lift over school. Yeah right, and I just waves bye bye and dooz whatever the fuck I fancies. Alf the time I goes over Padstow, alf the time I goes up Millmead Ouse over Artcliffe cos Lee and Lola ave got a flat there what's more like a fucking fort or summat: metal shutters, metal doors, the fucking works. They're alright even though they're Artcliffe. Tell you what, we've got a plan, we ave got a fucking *scheme*. They're getting a shit-load of browns yeah, and I'm buying in and I'm gonna set up business over Redland, yeah? I'm gonna make a fucking killing, man: there are fucking, I don't know, undreds, thousands of nice middle-class boys and girls round there (we're not just talking Redland, we're talking Cotham, Enleaze, Bishopston, Westbury, Stoke Bishop) who wants a walk on the wild side but they're too fucking shit-scared a come over Knowle West to get their gear. They ain't gonna ask Daddy to jump in is Volvo and give them a lift over St Pauls or Southmead, are they? But if it's on their doorstep. If they got their own tame rough boy: 'Yeah, my man's cool, yeah? He's a face, he's a goddamn fucking Knowle West gangster right, but he cuts me a special deal. I can get you skag if you want it.' Sweet. I'll fucking keep alf of it for meself, cut the rest with bicarb of soda or fucking rat poison or fuck knows what. They won't know no fucking better. Even if they do, they gonna complain to the fucking Trading Standards Authority? I got a fucking goldmine ere.

I'm working on Shawnie an' all. That cunt Steve only ad er turning tricks for im, didn't e? We're talking proper money ere. Shawnie says she ain't doing that stuff no more but when I shows er what she can be earning . . . she'll do what I says, whatever. There's so many sad cunts what've gotta pay for their pork, I ain't missing out on this.

Ere's a little tip Sophie darling, or should I say 'babe' like that ridiculous fucking posh slapper, Mimi. Just because someone's door is closed and there's music playing inside, it don't necessarily follow that e's behind the door. You might like to consider, Sophie babe, just consider the possibility that that someone is sitting outside your wide-open kitchen door, swigging the 'rather special' bottle of wine that wanker Adam brought and listening to every sad, stupid, smug fucking word that dribbles out of your mouth.

Outwitted again, Sophie babe, outwitted again.

Life's about learning and I don't mean the shit you dooz at school. With one little scam I learnt about property prices in Ireland, what Guinness and asparagus dooz to your insides and that Simon's an even sadder fucking twat than I'd realized. I learnt that the wonderful Sophie and Simon ave got a nice little coke abit going: well worth saving that one up for future reference. Now, there was one other thing . . . oh yes, I learnt ow I 'scare the living crap' out of Sophie. I bet you don't even know what exactly you're scared of, Sophie. A proper fucking seeing to, perhaps. All in good time, babe, all in good time.

Sophie and Mimi went out of the kitchen and I nearly fucking laughed out loud as I put the empty bottle down, grabbed a new one and slipped upstairs.

Sophie's too scared to be alone in the ouse with me, apparently. Well, we'll ave to work on that fear, Sophie babe, you gotta work on your fears.

That's another good thing about this neck of the woods – all the fucking posh slags. They goes weak at the knees for a rogue like me.

I reckons I gets the best of both worlds; I just gotta put up with Sophie 'understanding my anger'. Yeah, right. What you don't understand Sophie darlehn, is ow much cash and booze I'm nicking off of you. Always one step ahead.

They got Steve and Tony. They two's fucked; stupid cunts. Me, I've always got a plan for tomorrow but they two's divvies and we ain't seeing they for a long time and we ain't gonna miss em neither. I was gonna sort Steve out meself but fuck it. Let the wheels of British justice mash im up.

I got me comfay bed, me scams, sex and drugs: oppertunetays, tha's what I got. And I got Shawnay, yeah, cuddlehn up. I'm lyehn on me back, two bottles a wine enside may, bonurr pointen at the starrs, smile on me face. Beggurr smile than you, pal, beggurr fucken bonurr an' all, I'm tellen yuh. Tellen yuh straight, cunt.